WHAT WILL IT TAKE TO REPAIR A ONCE UNBREAKABLE BOND?

"Can we talk for a bit?"

The moon outside the window lit up the room enough that Ally could see Beth's eyes focus on her, but she couldn't make out their expression. Trepidation or impatience?

"Sure," Beth said, sounding more alert. "What's going on?"

"I just—where did you go?"

Beth was silent, so Ally forced a laugh as she continued. "I mean, obviously I know you were in Haiti and you were busy. But I sent you so many e-mails, and you barely wrote me back. Nothing, from December to the end of April."

Still, silence. Ally plowed on. "I just really needed my best friend to be there for me, especially with all the awful shit going on in my life. It felt like I was sending the most vulnerable parts of myself into a void, this blankness, where there used to be so much love and support. I was having a really terrible time, and you weren't there."

She waited, tensed and bare, goose-pimpled, feeling like she'd just cut herself open and proffered her insides in the most haphazard way. Though she'd spent months thinking about this conversation, she still didn't have any clue how it was supposed to go.

THE
SUMMERTIME
GIRLS

LAURA HANKIN

BERKLEY BOOKS | NEW YORK

BERKLEY

An imprint of Penguin Random House LLC
375 Hudson Street, New York, New York 10014

THE SUMMERTIME GIRLS

This book is an original publication of The Berkley Publishing Group.

Library of Congress Cataloging-in-Publication Data

Hankin, Laura.
The summertime girls / Laura Hankin.
pages cm
ISBN 978-0-425-27963-2 (paperback)
1. Female friendship—Fiction. I. Title.
PS3608.A71483S86 2015
813'.6—dc23
2015003049

PUBLISHING HISTORY
Berkley trade paperback edition / August 2015

PRINTED IN THE UNITED STATES OF AMERICA

10 9 8 7 6 5 4 3 2 1

Cover design by Lesley Worrell.
Cover photo: *Women on Beach* © Masterfile.
Interior text design by Kelly Lipovich.

Penguin
Random
House

PROLOGUE

Elizabeth Abbott and Allison Morris decided they'd be best friends forever on the day they met.

When Ally walked into her fifth-grade classroom, one week late for the start of school, she wondered if her classmates could see the anger rolling off her, the steam escaping her pores. In the wake of her parents' divorce, she'd fought desperately against her mother's decision to move from Baltimore to Wilmington. Upon losing that battle, she'd launched a new offensive: to get settled in time to start school with everyone else. When that too inevitably failed, she'd told herself that at least she'd get to school five minutes early on her first day. Naturally, her mother dropped her off five minutes late, spouting apologies and kissing the air centimeters away from her cheek.

Ally didn't want to be the new kid. She'd seen transfer students at her old school, those midyear immigrants, panicky as they submitted to inspections that even the Ellis Island authorities would have considered too thorough. Sometimes, she hadn't been able to stop herself from laughing at the desperate need for approval written all over their faces. So now, she kept her eyes fixed on the hangnail pestering her thumb while the principal introduced her and asked for a volunteer to be her "special buddy."

"Elizabeth A.?" The principal sounded unsurprised. "Thank you for volunteering, sweetheart!"

And that was when Ally brought her head up, and she and Beth looked at each other for the first time. Ally thought she'd never seen a person her age who looked so serene or—what was the word she'd just learned?—benevolent. This girl was pale, with hair the color of roasted pumpkin that fell, unbroken as a bolt of fabric, down her back. While the other kids fidgeted and passed notes, she sat with her hands on her desk, two sharp pencils laid out parallel in front of her. She smiled at Ally, revealing gappy teeth that braces would soon force together, and Ally thought, *Elizabeth A. is my angel.*

WHEN the recess bell rang, Elizabeth A. led the new girl to a patch of grass at the edge of the schoolyard, looking over her shoulder to make sure she didn't lose her way. As they settled themselves on the ground, Ally said, "You should tell people to call you Beth."

"What?" Elizabeth A. asked

"Have you ever read *Little Women*?"

Elizabeth A. had devoured it in two days that summer. "Oh my gosh, I love that book!" she said.

"Me too!" Ally said. They impulsively grabbed hands. "You're totally Beth March," she said. "She's so good and nice."

Elizabeth A. raised one eyebrow. She thought Beth from *Little Women* was kind of boring. Jo got to be the one with adventures, with the fire inside her. "Yeah, but then she dies," she said.

Ally pondered this, then nodded vigorously, stray strands of fine brown hair escaping from her ponytail. "Okay, so you're Beth minus the early sad death part. Ooh, plus if people called you Beth, then you wouldn't have to be one of four Elizabeths anymore." They looked over to where Elizabeth W. and Elizabeth K. were playing an ear-piercing game of capture the flag, then to where Elizabeth L.D. sat alone in the dirt, methodically ripping the legs off a daddy longlegs. Put that way, the prospect of a nickname had a certain appeal.

"Which March sister would you want to be?" Elizabeth A. asked.

"Meg, definitely. She's the prettiest," Ally said. "What about you? Beth, right?"

Ally smiled then, a smile far more radiant than any other smile Elizabeth A. had previously seen. It dimpled her round cheeks and lit up her dark brown eyes. It was a magic smile, a smile of confident, long-awaited recognition, and Elizabeth A. didn't want to disappoint it.

"Um, I think you're right. I'm a Beth," she said. "I'm definitely gonna ask Ms. Applebaum to call me that from now on."

Newly christened, Beth talked to Ally nonstop for the rest of that blissful recess, ignoring the chaos around them. They sat cross-legged facing each other in the September sun, squealing whenever they discovered their similarities—they were both only children, cruelly denied puppies because of parental allergies! Neither one of them understood the fuss their female classmates made over the color pink! And, sure, perhaps outwardly, they didn't seem a perfect match, with Beth's ironed jumper standing in stark contrast to the missing button on Ally's sweater. But Beth sensed that somehow they finished each other. She imagined the two of them balancing on a seesaw. Together, one on either end, they could maintain a perfect equilibrium, a straight line parallel to the ground.

"Ugh, the lunch bell," Beth said when it rang. "I don't want to stop talking and go inside."

"I know," Ally said. "Can we just be friends forever?"

Beth could feel her cheeks reddening in pleasure. "That sounds good to me," she said.

ONE

⟡

"heck, check. Hi, I'm Ally Morris." Ally breathed the words into the microphone and listened to them reverberate. They wended their way through the air of Looseleaf Music Hall, off the little stage on which she sat, bouncing against the exposed brick walls. Then they poured into the ears of her audience, whose members, she counted quickly in her head, numbered a grand total of six.

"Wooo, Ally!" cheered her roommate, Gabby. Her friend Lucy, from college, wolf-whistled, and Scott, who played drums in this terrible cover band she used to sing with, clapped politely. He'd been trying, in his Nice Guy way, to sleep with her ever since her breakup with Tom, but she couldn't get past his tendency to shout when he talked, as if drumming so frequently had destroyed his ability to speak at a normal volume. She pictured him trying to whisper sweet nothings to her and accidentally bursting her eardrum. The two bartenders and the sound guy constituted the rest of her listeners.

She readjusted the microphone, which had been slightly too high for her five-foot-one frame, and began to pluck absentmindedly at her guitar strings. "Thanks for coming out tonight, guys," she said, staring at the door, willing passersby to enter. All the people outside power-walked right by, bending into the late April rain drenching New York City's Lower East Side. "Let's give the latecomers a few more minutes to get here."

The sound guy leaned out from his booth and said, "It's 6:03. You should probably get started if you want your full set time."

"Okay then!" She hoped her tone was bright enough to disguise the dismay she felt. "Lucky you all, you get an intimate concert experience." She cleared her throat, strummed a C chord on her dark red acoustic Fender, and leaned toward the microphone.

I want a snowy day to come
I won't settle for the sun.
I just want to stay with you in my bed.

The tune she sang was bouncy and sweet, like ersatz Ingrid Michaelson.

We'll watch it pile up outside,
It's a great excuse to hide,
And we'll order in delivery instead.

She'd sung this song so many times before that the lyrics came out of her mouth automatically. She didn't need to think about them—didn't want to think about them, actually, given that she'd written them about Tom back when they'd been the kind of couple that did sometimes stay in bed all day, instead of not a couple at all. She sang mindlessly, but her mind kept busy. It detached itself from her body and leaned against the back wall, watching her. It said, *Stop trying to wear sundresses all the time. It doesn't make you look winsome, it makes you look like an idiot. It's fifty degrees and pouring.*

When the booking agent at Looseleaf had called to ask her if she wanted a last-minute concert slot, she'd very calmly accepted. Then she'd hung up the phone and shrieked, and danced around her Queens apartment in her flannel pajama pants. She'd twirled and shimmied and jumped until she ran out of breath. Looseleaf was a big deal. Okay sure, it was no Madison Square Garden, but occasionally when she walked by and looked at the list of upcoming concerts, she actually recognized the names of some of the singer-songwriters. She'd been sending Looseleaf her demo far more often than was proper ever since she'd moved to New York nine months prior, and she'd been on the verge of giving up on ever playing there when the phone call came.

After her impromptu solo dance party, she'd immediately taken to Facebook and written promotional statuses every day for the week leading up to the concert. She'd sent personalized e-mails to potential managers and harangued her friends until they told her they'd try to make it. Normally, she felt guilty inviting them to the tiny solo gigs she played, because the venues so clearly meant nothing. When she sent out those invitations, she always couched them in apologies or offers. *It's not going to be big, but you should come hang out with me. Listen to some music!* she'd write. *I'll buy you a beer and be eternally grateful.* Looseleaf's smaller concert room, though, where she was playing, could fit up to seventy-five people, and regularly did. She'd been there before, at crowded shows, where people swayed and cheered, and she'd watched the performers with an envy so strong she nearly choked on it. This concert, she'd told herself, would be a turning point for her.

Except it wasn't. Barely anyone had shown up. She played her whole forty-five-minute set feeling like a total fool, a smile affixed to her face. Her friends danced along in their seats, laughing at her banter. *They pity me,* she thought. A couple more friends trickled in as time went on, but the audience didn't even break ten. Although the box of CDs she'd brought to sell after the show burned a hole in the bag at her feet, she left them unmentioned, and they remained zipped away, out of sight. Shame prevented her from shilling.

When she finished her last song and hopped off the stage, Gabby was waiting for her with a hug and a beer. "That was so fun!" she said, handing her the bottle. "This rain is insanity. It's like absolutely biblical proportions. I bet that's why more people didn't come, 'cause everyone just wants to stay in bed when it's like this."

"Yeah, probably." Ally put the beer bottle to her mouth and didn't pull it away until the liquid inside was half gone.

"So, you want to head home?" Gabby asked. "Drink wine and watch a movie?"

"I think I'm going to hang out a bit and watch the next set. Be home soon." She hugged Gabby and the rest of her friends as they headed out, thanking them for coming, committing to coffee dates the following week with a chipper smile. She turned down

Scott's deafening offer to buy her another drink as nicely as she could. Then she went and sat at the bar, watching the band with the seven o'clock slot start to set up. She didn't normally act like a masochist but, she thought bitterly, tonight was different.

One of the bartenders, a skinny guy with a shaved head and long fingers, took her empty beer bottle away. "Cute set," he said. "You sounded like a songbird."

"Thank you," she said.

"Can I get you something else?"

"How about just an endless amount of whiskey?"

He laughed. "Ice?"

"Sure, thanks."

On the stage, a guy in suspenders pulled out a mandolin, while another with a bow tie picked on a banjo. The bartender brought her over a double. She tried to pay him, but he insisted that it was on the house.

"Tough luck, with the weather," he said. "Otherwise I'm sure you would've had a better crowd." Even as he said it, though, the door opened and a group of people poured in. Mr. Mandolin Suspenders waved at them casually.

She hated them all.

Whiskey, though, that was something she loved. She adored its charred flavor, its smoothness as it raced down her throat, its amber color in the glass. Most of all, she loved how effectively it dulled everything, so as the room continued to fill up, she drank it faster and faster. The two guys onstage started to sing a plaintive song with so many confusing metaphors, it made her head hurt.

When she'd drained the glass, the bartender brought her over another. He had knobby wrists, like Tom.

"What do you think of these guys?" she asked. She'd been too nervous to eat anything since breakfast, and the whiskey was hitting her faster than normal. She fought valiantly to keep the slur out of her words.

"Eh," he said. "Derivative hipster crap. I liked your stuff better."

"Compliments *and* free whiskey? I'm going to nominate you for bartender of the year."

"I'll accept your nomination if I can be president of your fan club," he said.

"Deal." She took another big sip of her drink and then said, "Hey, you wanna make out with me in the bathroom?"

He blinked, taken aback, and then the corners of his mouth tugged upward. "Uh, yeah. Let me just get Jack to cover for me." She slipped off the bar stool while he said something to the other bartender, who shot an appraising glance her way. Then he came around the bar and led her through the crush of people to a black door with a handicapped sign on it.

As soon as the door swung shut behind them, he pushed her up against the wall. She twined her arms around him, and he stuck his tongue, with its leftover cigarette taste, in her mouth. The music from outside thumped gently through the door and the light above the cracked mirror cast an ineffectual glow on the ground. She floated in a whiskey bubble that separated her from the rest of the world, even as she pressed against the bartender's body.

He ran his hand up her leg and under her dress, pushing her underwear to the side. She looked over his shoulder at the graffiti-covered walls, as he stuck his finger inside her. *Fuck this misogynistic bullshit*, someone had scribbled with a black Sharpie.

Constipation happens, someone else had written in a loopy cursive. She could tell, as he moved his finger roughly, that whatever he was doing wasn't going to work—none of the guys she'd drunkenly hooked up with since Tom had been able to make her come, and this bathroom didn't particularly lend itself to romance. He kept going, dogged, although she was ready for him to stop, so she pulled away, dropped to her knees, and unzipped his pants instead.

On her subway ride home, she chewed two pieces of gum and tried not to fall asleep. She hated missing her stop and waking up at the end of the line in Flushing, but it had happened more than once recently when she'd taken the subway drunk. She balanced her guitar, in its soft dark case, against her knees.

When she'd daydreamed about her first year out of college, she'd pictured instant stardom, a Grammy nomination for Best New Artist, a profile in the *New York Times* that began, "Ally Morris, radiant in jeans and no makeup . . ." Even when she'd tried to tether herself to reality, she'd still believed she would stand out. She knew that she didn't necessarily have the best voice of anyone in the world, and she didn't write the most deeply felt songs—but still, she thought she had something special, some extra sweetness in her smile that would make people want to smile back at her, some quality that she could diffuse into the atmosphere just by sitting on a stage and singing, until it affected all those watching.

So far, though, New York had crushed her soul with a con-centrated glee. At first, when she didn't hear back from any of the clubs or managers to whom she'd sent her demo, she told herself that maybe she'd accidentally given them the wrong con-tact information. She double-checked the way she'd written her phone number and her e-mail address, searching in vain for a misplaced digit or letter.

She'd auditioned for bands, for concert spots, for everything she could, and each time she'd spent entire weeks afterward with a constricted throat whenever an unknown number called her cell phone (it always turned out to be the pharmacy, reminding her to pick up her birth control, or someone asking her to babysit), and a shaky hand whenever she checked her e-mail. Finally a mutual friend introduced her to Scott, who paved the way for her to sing with Projected Trajectory. They performed in the corner of a different dingy bar every Saturday night for pitiful tips while twentysomethings screamed conversations above the music. She could tell as she sang her No Doubt and Journey covers that her audience would rather be dancing to a DJ.

No one in Projected Trajectory had seemed happy with what they were doing, with the possible exception of Stephen, the lead guitarist who'd started it all. He claimed a total monopoly on writing the band's few original songs, which all seemed to be about how much he wanted to cheat on his girlfriend.

(The chorus to the song of which he was most proud:

Hey you! Wearing that white
Dress so tight—
Come on over tonight.
Nobody needs to know.
Whoa-oh!)

Everything got worse after she and Tom broke up and Beth, without explanation, stopped responding to her e-mails. Beth had always been supportive, engaged, the definitive example of what a best friend should be. Her sudden disappearance from Ally's life was the last thing Ally had expected, and it threw her even further off-kilter. Those Saturday night bar gigs began to seem insurmountably depressing. So Ally quit. She tried to be as diplomatic as possible, even writing out a little speech and practicing it beforehand. "I just need to focus on my solo career right now. I'm so sorry," she said to Stephen, under the fluorescent lights of their sixty-four-square-foot practice space. But he called her a flake and a deserter anyway. Then he'd said the thing that wormed its way into her mind and wouldn't leave. "Whatever. We'll find someone better than you." Of the three insults he'd hurled at her, that one stuck because she was starting to believe it was true.

Most nights, self-loathing crawled into bed alongside her. It burrowed under the covers and wrapped itself around her body. It pried apart her eyelids and pinched the fat on her arms. *You're not pretty enough for this*, it hissed into her defenseless ear. *You're delusional if you think your voice is exceptional.*

Now she leaned her head against the subway seat, letting the train rattle her around. As she jolted, woozy, she thought, *I don't have to do this. Maybe I should just give up.* The idea held such a strange fascination for her that she didn't realize she'd reached her stop until the doors slid open. Quickly, she slung her guitar case over one shoulder and bolted up from her seat, power-walking toward the doors. She stepped out right before they shut with their *bing-bing* bell sound, and they closed on her guitar, grasping the neck of it in their dull silver grip.

"Shit," she said. She wrenched the instrument free, and it came unstuck with a loud crack, a jangling of strings. "No, no, no!" She knelt on the platform and unzipped her case to assess the damage. The neck of the guitar had snapped in half. The top part of it bent jaggedly away from the bottom, and the strings poked up in a random tangle. "Fuck!" she exhaled, trying in vain to fit the parts of her instrument back together as late commuters walked around her, giving her a wide berth like she was a crazy person.

When she got back to her apartment, Gabby was sprawled on the couch, watching some reality show about wedding dresses, her hand in a bag of pita chips.

"How was the rest of your night?" she called.

"Well, I went down on the bartender in the handicapped bathroom, and I broke my guitar on the subway," Ally said, and then immediately burst into tears. "I give up. I quit music." She dropped her useless guitar on the ground, not even bothering to be gentle, and slid down next to it.

Gabby turned off the TV and knelt down beside her, wrapping her into a hug. "Ice cream?" she asked.

"Yeah," Ally said, wiping an icicle of snot away from her nose with the back of her hand. "Ice cream."

THEY ate an entire pint of Phish Food. Ally devoured most of it, dragging her spoon along the bottom to get every last bit of the melted chocolate. Then, hyped up on the sugar and starting to sober up, she ran into her bedroom. She pushed her mangled guitar under her bed, way back behind her winter boots, and grabbed her laptop. She plopped it down on the Ikea kitchen table, which wobbled a bit. (When she and Gabby had put it together, they must have forgotten some screw, or skipped some step in the instruction booklet, and they'd never bothered to fix it. Someday, in the middle of a dinner party, it would probably collapse completely, spilling Three-Buck Chuck all over the floor.)

"I'm going to edit my résumé," she announced to Gabby, who'd turned the TV back on to a show about cats from hell. "And see what the fuck else I'm qualified to do, besides babysitting."

She pulled up the neglected Word document and tried to make herself sound more impressive than she was. She changed *Filed papers* to *Facilitated documentation organizational system.* It barely made sense, even to her, and she couldn't keep her mind on it. Every few minutes, her eyes flickered involuntarily toward the tab that told her if any new e-mails had reached her inbox.

She nurtured a tiny hope that, someday, she'd get an e-mail that would make everything clear and easy. On that glorious day, she would log in to Gmail and have a miraculous, unsolicited record deal or, she told herself now, a job offer for the career she was meant to pursue, instead of another advertisement from a store she didn't shop at. As she deleted a swath of text about her music credentials, she saw the little *Inbox (1)* pop up, and clicked over to it. She warned herself, as always, that it was probably nothing exciting. But then she saw Beth's name in her inbox, next to an e-mail titled Hey There!

"Oh my God," she said aloud.

"What?" Gabby asked.

"Beth just e-mailed me."

"What?" Gabby sat up and peered over the couch, primed for something juicy. "What did she say? Is she e-mailing to explain that every single Internet café in Haiti burned down, and that's why she hasn't responded to you in months?"

"Um, I don't know. Hold on." Ally opened the e-mail. There they were, words that Beth had written, and suddenly she felt that she needed to be alone to read them. "I'm actually going to go into my room. I'll be right back."

"Oh. Okay," Gabby said, her eyes puzzled and a little hurt. She turned back to the TV, where a tabby cat was mauling its owner. Ally took her laptop and closed the door behind her, turning the television noise into a soft murmur. Then she got onto her bed and started to read.

Hey, Ally,

How's your life going? I'm sure you are just taking the city by storm. Has the mayor started sending you flowers yet, thanking you for bringing new light and joy to New York's music scene? Sorry I've been a bit MIA—so much to do here. Sorry, too, to hear about Tom. You deserve better.

Anyways, Grandma Stella has decided to sell the house and move into a retirement community. I'm really sad to see the house go, but it's the best thing for her now. She's still herself—aka super-sharp and amazing—but an entire house is a lot for an 84-year-old to handle. Plus, last week she had a scary incident where she fell out in her yard gardening, and had trouble getting back up. Luckily one of her friends came by for, according to Grandma Stella, a "gossip session" (of course!), and found her just about 10-15 minutes after it happened. She drove her to the hospital, and they bandaged her up, and she's okay, but everyone in my family is freaked out that it might happen again when no one's nearby.

I offered to help her pack up all her stuff and get everything in order before the move. I'll be going up to Maine pretty soon after I get back to Wilmington next month, for a week and a half around Memorial Day, and was wondering if you wanted to come with me? Grandma Stella really wants to see you. Plus it could be nice to have one last Britton Hills hurrah, a chance to say good-bye to the town. Let me know if you're available. I completely understand though if you've got too many things going on and can't make it. Seriously. No pressure at all.

This Internet café smells like damp goats,

Beth

When Ally finished reading the e-mail, her eyes were watering dangerously. She'd known that Beth's grandma was getting into her mideighties, but still, she always thought of her as a constant, forever lording over her cozy home, waiting to welcome Ally inside.

The first time she met Grandma Stella, she was with Beth's family, who had invited her on their annual weeklong summer trip to Maine after fifth grade ended. As they lugged suitcases toward a cream-colored bungalow, its window boxes filled with flowers, Beth ran ahead. She clambered up the three steps to the porch and rang the bell. After a minute, the fire-engine-red door swung open to reveal a tiny lady with a smile as wide as her head, practically about to combust with excitement and love.

"Hello, hello, hello!" she shouted, doing a remarkably spry little jig. Beth plowed straight into her arms, and Ally felt a sharp jab of jealousy. But then Grandma Stella turned to her.

"You must be Ally," she said, and immediately smothered her in a hug. She smelled like lavender. "Oh, I have been waiting all year to meet you!"

That first vacation with the Abbotts had seemed to Ally like it took place in some parallel universe, where families cared about each other openly and consistently. She saw no shortage of affection, no rationing of love. After that first moment in Grandma Stella's arms, Ally didn't feel like an outsider at all. She'd been invited back every summer since, and for the occasional Christmas trip too. As the years wore on, she and Beth started staying in Britton Hills after Beth's parents had used up their allotted vacation days and gone back to work. Once, they stayed there for two whole months and got summer jobs together in the town's ice cream shop. Stella treated Ally like a surrogate granddaughter and, even now, although their monthly phone calls had started leaning toward the biannual, Ally knew to expect a package of cookies and a twenty-dollar bill from Britton Hills on her birthday.

This e-mail contained no real apologies from Beth. No explanations for her disappearance that actually made sense. Sitting on her bed in a cramped, windowless room that felt worlds away from small-town Maine, Ally thought about taking some time to make the decision. To go away for a week and a half and still be able to pay rent? She'd have to babysit like mad over the next month. But more than that, surely it was crazy to go on vacation with the girl who'd abandoned her when she'd needed her most, and whose halfhearted apology for it was almost more insulting than no apology at all.

Yet Ally's fingers weren't listening to her brain. They were already typing out a message and hitting send:

Beth,

Yes. Definitely.

Ally

TWO

Beth stood in the train station, car keys in hand, shifting her weight from one foot to the other and waiting for Ally. The car keys jingled, hitting each other with a delicate *clink*, and she realized that her hand was shaking. Just a tiny tremble, but still. She clenched the keys tight in her palm, and the noise stopped.

They'd decided, via e-mail, that Ally would take the train from New York to Secaucus, right outside the city. She'd arrive at 11:35, Beth would pick her up, and from there they'd head north to Maine. So Beth waited as the train station loomed around her, all high windows and shiny floors, fancy ticket machines, and an odd titanium sculpture of a massive cattail that glowed the colors of the New Jersey Transit logo—purple, blue, and orange. She stared at the cattail, trying to get used to it. Since she'd gotten back to the States a week before, she felt like she'd been trying to get used to everything all over again. Open Arms, the mission clinic in Haiti where she'd spent the last year working, seemed to exist not only in an entirely different part of the world, but in an entirely different universe—light-years away from a place where people spent money commissioning sculptures of giant wetland plants.

At 11:35 on the dot, people started trickling up the escalator leading from the train platform. Beth scanned them as they appeared—a few men, a teenage couple stopping every few feet to smash their faces together, a visibly overwhelmed mom who cradled a baby in one arm and used her other hand to hold the end of her toddler's leash. Trailing the others, a young woman came up the escalator, looking down at the phone in her hand. She seemed about the right height, and Beth started to smile, nervous, as she approached. As she got closer, though, Beth realized the woman's face wasn't Ally's at all. She was surprised at the strength of the relief that washed through her.

The people stopped coming and Beth waited, looking through the passengers again to double-check. The overwhelmed mom sat on a bench, taking out a snack pack for her toddler and a bottle for her baby. The teenage couple continued on their merry, hormonal way. Finally Beth thought to check her phone. Having just spent a year without it, she kept accidentally leaving it on silent and forgetting about its existence. A text from Ally waited for her: Gahhhh missed the 11:35 but I'll be on the 12:02. I'm really sorry! Of course. Ally was incapable of punctuality.

Maybe it had been a mistake inviting her. Everything would have been easier if Beth could've just gone up to Maine alone. But, no, Beth thought, Grandma Stella's excitement over seeing the two girls together again trumped all else. For her grand-mother's sake, she could make nice for a week and a half. So she swallowed her frustration, typed back No worries, and put her phone away.

As she slipped it back into the pocket of her shorts, a yell pierced the air. She looked up, confused, her heart punching the walls of her chest, as the mother on the bench struggled to her feet.

"Grab him!" the mother screamed at no one in particular. Then, her eyes locked with Beth, and she directed the words toward her. Beth understood on some level that the toddler had wrenched his leash free, and that he was tottering wildly away, past her, headed for the escalators, where any number of terrible things could happen to injure him. She turned around, reaching out a slender arm that did nothing as it moved through air as dense as Jell-O, failing once again, and the toddler kept toddling until a security guard scooped him up, laughing.

"Whoa there, little guy," the security guard said, and depos-ited him back with his mother. Everything went back to normal— the passengers who had stopped to watch, or who had made some cursory moves toward the boy, turned around and went on read-ing their papers and sipping their coffees. But Beth's hands were so slick with sweat that she dropped the keys she'd been clenching. She picked them back up again and hooked her finger through the key ring, then leaned her head against the station's cool wall, breathing from her belly until her heart rate slowed back down to normal. She tried to fit her guilt back into the compartment where she normally kept it, but it wasn't working so well.

She decided she needed to move. She stepped out to the parking lot and double-checked that she'd locked the car, made herself go to the bathroom one extra time in anticipation of the hours ahead on the road and, with fifteen minutes still left to kill, sat down and attempted to read her book. She pulled it out of her bag, the copy of *Mountains Beyond Mountains* that Deirdre, the founder of the Open Arms Mission Clinic, had given her, but her normal focus and concentration eluded her. She ended up just staring at the Arrivals and Departures board until the clock turned to 12:02.

This time, Ally burst up the escalator ahead of the rest of the pack, trailing a big rolling suitcase and breathing heavily. Her round brown eyes darted around the large waiting area until they landed on Beth.

"Oh my God, I am so sorry!" she called as she got closer. "The subway is the worst ever. It kept doing this thing where it would jerk along for ten feet and then sit without moving for five minutes, so I ran into Penn Station just as the 11:35 was leaving." She stopped in front of Beth and let go of her bag, which skidded to a halt next to her. "I swear the MTA gets off on making people late for their commitments. Anyways, hello." Though her words were typical Ally, bright and fun, the smile she gave Beth was wary. Her dimples were nowhere in sight. She seemed somehow a little duller, less shiny than the girl Beth had hugged good-bye at the airport a year ago, before flying off to Haiti.

"Hi," Beth said. "How are you?"

"Good," Ally said, nodding. "I'm good. Well, a little hungover, but good. How are you?"

"Good." Beth's whole body felt uncertain. She didn't know where to put her eyes, how to hold her hands. She folded her arms across her chest.

"You look nice," Ally said. She tugged her sundress down from where it had ridden up. "Very . . . thin."

"Thanks. You look nice too. Your hair's different."

"Oh yeah," Ally said, moving her hand up to the side of her head. "I grew out my bangs."

"It's pretty." They stared at each other while somehow, impressively, avoiding sustained eye contact. Beth tried to figure out whether she should move forward for a hug, and wondered if Ally was debating the same thing. Neither one of them held out their arms. "Thanks for taking the train out here," Beth continued, to break the silence. "I just figured that you never know with New York traffic."

"No, please, of course. If I can make it through my whole life without ever having to drive in New York, I will die happy."

Beth tried to picture Ally, who was terrified of driving, lurching through NYC traffic. It was not a good image. "Yeah, totally." She paused, awkwardly. "Anyway, ready to head out?" She grabbed Ally's suitcase, despite Ally's protestations that she'd happily carry it herself, and rolled it out into the sunlight. They climbed into the car, and Beth put the key in the ignition, checking her rearview mirror.

"All set?" she asked.

"Yup," Ally answered.

"All right then. GPS says seven and a half hours to Grandma Stella's house. Let's go." Beth turned the key and the car started up.

"Wow, I haven't seen your grandma in forever," Ally said.

"I know. It's been, what, three years since we went to Maine together?"

But Beth knew exactly how long it had been. Last year, she'd flown off to Haiti just days after arcing her graduation cap into the sky. The year before, Ally had chosen to spend her free summer time with Tom instead. "She's very excited that you're coming with me," she continued, in the understatement of the year. When Beth had made a rare long-distance call from Haiti to offer her help in packing up the house before the big move, Grandma Stella had erupted in the declarations of love and gratitude that accompanied every conversation they had.

"You are the sweetest girl! You know, I ask God every night why he didn't give me more grandchildren. But I did get the best only-grandchild in the world." Beth smiled at the familiar gushing. Then Grandma Stella had gotten right down to business. "And Ally will be coming with you, of course."

"Oh, well, I don't know. She's probably very busy," Beth had hedged.

"Oh, for crying out loud, darling. I love you, but did you pour bleach all over your brain? Ally *has* to come with you. This house is almost as special to the two of you as it is to me, and I've lived here for fifty-three years. Plus, I'd like to see my surrogate granddaughter at least once more before I croak. So, you'll ask her and she'll say yes, and I'll see the two of you at the end of May." Beth had reminded herself that the purpose of her trip was to help Grandma Stella, in any way possible. Then she'd broken the months of radio silence and sent Ally an e-mail.

Interrupting Beth's reverie, Ally suddenly ventured, "Hey, do you think your grandma would mind if I interviewed her?"

"Interviewed her? For what?"

Ally looked sheepish. "I'm not sure exactly, yet. I've just been thinking a lot about your grandma's town, and part of me thought it could be really interesting to talk to some people about how it's been changing. It would be a good subject for a documentary about"—here, without fully seeming to realize it, she put on a newscaster's smooth voice—"the homogenization of small-town America, or one town's struggle to resist suburban sprawl, or something like that. You know?"

Beth did know. The town toward which they were steadily heading, Britton Hills, was quintessentially New England, with a population squeaking in at barely five thousand. Whenever Beth thought about Britton Hills, she felt an uncontrollable longing to dig up clams and attend services at a white clapboard church. In trying to describe it to new acquaintances, words like *quaint* and *sleepy* kept spilling out of her mouth as if she had Tourette's.

Britton Hills had once sustained itself almost entirely through the fishing industry. But after years of overharvesting, most people couldn't count on the fishing trade anymore. Now most residents either commuted nearly an hour to Bangor, the closest city, or floated from one temporary job to another with long periods of unemployment in between. Five years ago, a Walmart opened up a twenty-minute drive away, and it seemed like every time Beth visited, she saw another mom-and-pop store boarded up along the town's main street. It wasn't a big story, the way the town's economy was dwindling, and its character slowly and irrevocably shifting, but the change seemed to live in the bones of all the town's inhabitants.

"Anyway," Ally continued, "I brought a camera, 'cause I thought it could be useful to have some interview footage, and some footage of the town in general, for when I apply to production companies."

Beth could almost hear the rewind sound in her head. "Wait,

wait, wait. Production companies? Are you not doing singing and songwriting anymore?"

Ally's face snapped shut. "Um, yeah. I don't know. It's just—it's really hard." She looked down at her hands, picking at her fingernails. "Like, there's no certainty to it at all. Not that film is that much better, but with the singer-songwriter stuff I was doing, you never know where your next gig is going to be, or if you'll get paid anything for it, or whether anyone actually likes what you do."

"I'm sure people like what you do. And you've only been doing it for a year. It takes time, doesn't it?"

"Yeah, but it doesn't really get better. It's not like there's this goal you have to reach, and then you're set. You never get any measure of stability unless you become a big star, which, let's be realistic, what are the odds of that happening for me?"

"Oh come on, you're really good!" Beth protested, even as she thought to herself that her words were only half true. Ally's voice was like a little pot of honey, steeped in sweetness to its core. But sometimes Beth felt that she could eat up Ally's voice in a couple of sittings, and then there would be nothing left. The songs Ally wrote were also cute and sweet and fun, just like Ally herself seemed to be if you didn't know her too well. Beth used to smile along to Ally's songs, but they never made her cry. They lacked pathos, or maybe it was just weirdness, *something* that could make them memorable. Still, whenever Beth tried to picture her doing anything else, the most she could see was a business suit and Ally's brown hair. The face it framed was a hazy Picasso of nose, eyes, and mouth.

"Well, thanks. That's sweet of you to say," Ally said. "I think I just picked the hardest career out there."

A laugh slipped out of Beth before she could stop it. Ally looked over at her, and Beth tried to turn the laugh into a cough. It came out stilted, like an imitation of a cough from someone who'd never been sick before.

"Did you just laugh?" Ally asked, a disbelieving edge to her voice.

"No, sorry. I didn't mean to." Ally stared at her unblinking, so she said lightly, "It does sound really hard."

"So why did you laugh?"

"I just—because, well, it's not actually the hardest, right?"

"Okay then, enlighten me. What is?" Ally's face had turned frosty, her little bow of a mouth tightening.

"Well," Beth said carefully, "not that medicine is definitively number one, but I have a bunch of friends who applied to med school this year. They were top of their class at college and got pretty good MCAT scores. Still, though, they didn't get in anywhere, so now what do they do? And it's making me really nervous, having picked that for myself."

Beth had told Ally of her decision to become a doctor in a recent e-mail, one of the few perfunctory messages they'd sent back and forth over the course of trip planning. She'd tossed the news in casually, among some pleasantries. No mention of the real reason for her decision, of the little boy in her lap and the constellation of blood on her leg.

"Yeah," Ally said, "but with being a doctor, once you do get into med school, at least you know where you go from there. You have the life path laid out ahead of you and maybe it sucks and you have to push yourself super hard and somehow make life-or-death decisions on two hours of sleep a night, but there's a clear ladder to climb. A ladder is important. With me, it's just like—people say, 'Follow your dream, no matter what, and eventually people will recognize your brilliance!' But what if you're not actually brilliant? What if the people who ignore you are right? I don't know. I'm starting to think that 'Follow your dream' is code for 'Wake up in ten years having accomplished nothing.'"

"That's scary," Beth said, trying to rustle up some sympathy.

"Yeah. Believe it or not, it is," Ally said, and turned her face away. She hunched her body toward the door like she was trying to disappear into her side of the car.

A silence hung between them. Beth felt her hands squeezing the steering wheel too tightly, and loosened them. She sneaked a glance out the window. The suburbs stretched endlessly, houses turning into more houses, fast-food restaurants repeating themselves. Ally rested her head on the other window and they drove like that, not speaking, until Beth's eyelids grew heavy, and the only thing she could think was the word *coffee*, over and over again.

She looked over to ask Ally if they could stop. Ally was squinting down at her phone, her bottom lip caught between her teeth, shock written all over her face.

Suddenly, Beth felt awake. "Everything okay?" she asked.

"Huh?" Ally's eyes, when she turned them to Beth, were a million miles away.

Beth indicated the phone. "Seems like something serious."

"Oh," Ally said, shaking her head, her eyes unclouding. "No. Just a babysitting thing." She waved her hand through the air dismissively.

"Okay. Well, I was going to stop for coffee, if you want anything. Now would be the time for food."

"McDonald's?" Ally yelped, jerking back in her seat and bonking her head against the headrest.

Beth laughed in sheer delight, slapping her hand against the top of the steering wheel. "I'd forgotten about your all-consuming lust for Big Macs!"

"Oh God, I want one," Ally said. "I *need* one. I never go in Queens, because there's too much delicious ethnic food that I have to eat or I'll feel guilty. But now? I think it's fate."

"It was an unlikely match," Beth intoned.

Ally smiled. "A girl who ate a lot of kale. A patty of low-quality meat."

"No one expected them to fall for each other. And yet, sometimes, love surprises us all."

"But seriously," Ally said, "let's go."

AS Beth watched Ally wolfing down her burger with near-orgasmic joy, her feet kicked up onto the dashboard, puzzle pieces started fitting together into a person that Beth recognized. Ally's delight in her Big Mac linked with Ally's vanilla scent ("Yes, I *would* like my armpits to smell like cookies," Beth remembered Ally saying when they'd wandered the deodorant aisle at CVS together after school one day), which in turn fit into the stubble around Ally's kneecaps.

Those telltale hairs sent Beth hurtling right back to seventh grade, when both girls had started shaving their legs. If it had been up to Beth's parents, she would've gone to college looking like a yeti. But, thankfully, Ally's mom, Marsha, had prevented that scenario, bursting into Ally's room one day and announcing, with an overblown sense of import, that *it was time*.

When Ally had told Beth about her mother's latest interest in her, she'd dropped her high seventh-grader's voice to a sexy, smoky rasp and widened her eyes in sincerity, imitating Marsha in an impression that Beth had to admit was uncanny. "It's time to take your first steps toward becoming a woman," she'd intoned, and then, dropping into her normal voice, joked, "No, I'd rather take my first steps toward becoming a man." But the next day, when Beth was breaking in her new set of highlighters, marveling at how seamlessly they transformed her history notes into rainbows, the phone rang and her father bellowed the familiar words up the stairs: "Pumpkin, it's Ally!"

"I did it," Ally said, when Beth picked up the phone. "I shaved my legs." The news of Ally's newfound maturity came tumbling out of her so quickly that her breathing hit Beth's ear in rapid, random bursts. In a moment of confusion, Beth wondered if Ally was jogging in place.

That Monday, Beth and Ally went to the drugstore after school, and together they picked out a razor for Beth, since Ally had proclaimed herself an expert on what kind would be best. Beth knew that her parents were hesitant about the issue. They thought she might cut herself, but that was silly of them. She showed them her perfectly smooth legs afterward and said, "See? You didn't need to be worried." But Beth's father started blinking rapidly, and her mother gave her a hug that lasted too long, although, of course, she stayed in it anyway.

Beth put the blade to her skin methodically. Ally was the one who rushed, who either wanted to be out of the shower doing other things or, she confessed to Beth, daydreamed so much that she used body wash as shampoo. She was the one with the tiny cuts on her legs and the patches of hair she didn't notice she'd missed. As time went on and she mastered the task, the cuts disappeared. But the stubble from nooks on her kneecap remained. And now that stubble was sending up flares of familiarity to Beth.

Ally crumpled up her hamburger wrapper and let out a satisfied sigh. Then she turned to Beth. "I made a road trip playlist," she said. "Want me to put it on?"

"Yeah, that would be great."

After a few moments, familiar boy band sounds filled the car. "Ah! 'Backstreet's Back'? Oh, this is perfect," Beth said, looking over at Ally, who grinned back at her.

"I thought you'd be happy about it." At their first playdate, thirteen years ago, Ally had knocked on Beth's door carrying this CD. The two of them had spent three hours listening to the whole thing twice, debating which of the Backstreet Boys was the cutest (Brian for Beth, Nick for Ally, although each could see the merits of the other's position), but this song was the one they played on repeat, ten times in a row. They worked out an elaborate, literal choreography to it, nodding their heads seriously to every "Yeaaaaaah" and holding up their index fingers each time the singers sang the word *one*.

Now, in the car, they did the dance again, straining against their seat belts. Beth was surprised at how easily it all came back, and how she didn't feel silly at all doing it.

THREE

Hey Al,

How are you? Hope everything is good on your end. Kind of crazy news: I have a final-round job interview in New York next week. I know, I know, stay in a job for longer than six months already. I swear I didn't apply to this one—some headhunter found me on LinkedIn. (I told you it was worthwhile to make a profile!) Anyways, it's all happening pretty fast, but I think I'm going to take advantage of Memorial Day weekend and make a trip of it. I'll be in NYC from next Friday to the Wednesday after that. We should grab coffee or something. I'd love to hear how your life is going.

Best,
Tom

P.S. Saw this really cool documentary the other night that made me think of you, called Phantom Strings. It's about this guitarist who loses his arm in a car accident, and how he reinvents himself as a musician. If you end up checking it out, I want to hear what you think.

Ally reread Tom's e-mail surreptitiously, pretending she was still asleep, her head against the car window. Next to her, Beth sang quietly to herself as she drove. Apparently, "I'm Not a Girl, Not Yet a Woman" had gotten stuck in Beth's head from their earlier dance party. Her rendition of it was hushed, enthusiastic, and gloriously tone-deaf. Beth was so supremely competent, so smart, so graceful, that normally Ally derived an inordinate amount of joy from the fact that she couldn't sing for shit.

But this e-mail from Tom took things out of the realm of "normal." The second time through, it was no less confusing. It left her feeling infuriated (*Really, Tom?* she wanted to yell, *Really? You fuck everything up by moving to Portland, and then decide to come back six months later?*), but also raw with desire. God, she wanted to see him. She wanted to touch him.

"*All I need is time*," Beth warbled. Ally worked out dates in her head. If Tom was flying in from Portland on Friday and leaving on Wednesday, they'd overlap for two days once she returned from Britton Hills. That was enough time for coffee, and then if that went well and he slept over, they could have a full day together before he left. She toyed with responses to the e-mail, coming up with sentences that seemed witty and casual in her head, but they all turned completely mundane as soon as she started to type them out. Eventually, she just wrote, Hey you. That would be great! I'm in Britton Hills now, probably getting back late late

Sunday night. Let's figure something out. Then she forwarded it to Gabby (Subject line: WHAT DOES THIS MEAN?!?!?) and, mentally and physically exhausted, fell asleep.

When she woke up, disoriented, her neck stiff from the way her head had lolled, she looked out the window into the dark. The anonymous highway she'd watched roll by all afternoon long had changed into a familiar Britton Hills road. She recognized the houses, the particular clusters of trees, and she rolled down her window to let in the air's saltwater smell. There was the street sign for Elm Drive. There was the big green mailbox with *Abbott* painted on it in white.

"Hey," she said to Beth, as they turned into Grandma Stella's winding driveway, "I'm totally happy to do some of the driving next time. I mean, I know I'm kind of horrendous at it, but I would do my very best not to kill us."

"Oh, it's okay. I like it," Beth said, a smile obscuring her face like a mask. Beth's assurance did nothing to alleviate the guilt coursing through Ally's body, though she knew she was probably overreacting. After all, she reminded herself, Beth seemed to enjoy driving. She'd always carted the two of them around in high school. It happened that way somewhat out of necessity—Ally didn't get her license until midway through senior year.

Beth's parents had taken her down to the DMV on her sixteenth birthday, a Saturday that year, after surprising her with breakfast in bed. When Ally heard that Beth had spent two hours waiting in line and filling out forms, she'd been incredulous. "That sucks! You had to take a test about different traffic sign shapes on your birthday?" She'd shuddered. "I'm sorry your parents made you do that."

"No, no, I wanted to. I want to get my license as soon as I can.

It's such a pain in the butt for my parents, that they have to drive me everywhere."

So Beth earned her license right on schedule, getting a perfect score on both her written test and the driving itself. (And, Beth's dad had bragged to Ally, holding Beth's mom's hand at the unofficial celebratory "Beth Can Drive" dinner the four of them had shared post-test, she had 20/20 vision too! Beth was smiling down at her plate while her father talked, a blush creeping up her neck. When she saw Ally looking, she rolled her eyes in the most pleasant way possible, as if to say, *My dad is so embarrassing. But yes, I know I'm lucky to have him around.*)

Ally had waited to learn because her mom kept promising to take her out. "We'll go to the big parking lot behind the middle school. That's a good place to start," Marsha said verbatim on multiple occasions. But somehow, she never got around to giving lessons. Besides, Ally and Beth had normally been going to the same place anyway, and Beth had always been willing to go five minutes out of her way to pick Ally up.

One day, though, when they had been driving aimlessly with the radio on, trying to figure out what to do with a free weekend afternoon, Ally had suddenly felt the need to apologize.

"Hey, I'm really sorry I haven't gotten my license yet. My mom is such a bitch sometimes." Here, she'd paused and waited to see if Beth would agree. She often thought that she wanted Beth to join in on the Marsha-bashing. Yet on the rare occasions Beth actually did say something disparaging about Marsha, Ally always had to restrain herself from screaming.

Like that one time, a year before, when Ally had been telling Beth what she and her mother had done that weekend (they'd taken a day trip to a nearby mountain and climbed to the top without stopping to rest, then gone to the movies together, with Marsha keeping up a running, whispered commentary in Ally's ear), and Beth had said absently, "It's like she's a cat."

"What?"

"You know, like you're a ball of yarn, and she wants to play with you until she gets her fill, and then she wants to go away."

Ally hadn't spoken to Beth for three days, and evidently, Beth had learned her lesson. At Ally's latest baiting, she stayed silent.

"Anyway, I think I'm just going to sign up for driver's ed or something," Ally finished. She expected Beth to accept the apology right away, or affirm her new plan of action, so she was startled by a moment of silence that felt interminable. She finally looked over at her friend, who seemed to be working something out in her mind.

"I think," Beth said, "I know what we can do with our afternoon."

Eight minutes later, they pulled into the parking lot behind the middle school. "This is where my parents taught me," Beth said. "It was sort of a nightmare. My mom was whimpering in the backseat, and my dad kept pushing down on an invisible brake on the passenger side. And I was only going ten miles an hour. Okay. Let's switch sides."

Ally settled into the driver's seat, pulling it up toward the steering wheel. She didn't have long, beautiful legs like Beth's. On her good days, she told herself that her legs were athletic, that her shorter stature was cute. On bad days, she couldn't get past the word *stumpy*. She looked at her legs now, tan against the worn brown carpet of the car floor. She realized with a burst of frustration that she'd forgotten to shave her kneecap again. But mostly, she liked the way her legs looked on the driver's side of the car. She decided this was a good day.

LAURA HANKIN

"Wait," Beth said. "I just realized—is this legal? I think you might have to be eighteen to teach someone to drive."

"I'm not sure," Ally answered, hesitantly. She knew Beth scrupulously stayed on the right side of the law. Beth hardly even drank at parties, on the somewhat rare occasions they decided to go to them, usually using Ally as her excuse. "Designated driver!" she'd say brightly, clenching her mouth into a smile at whoever was holding out the beer. With that clenched smile, Beth appeared so far away and far above everyone else that "Beth Superior" became Ally's secret nickname for her. Now, sitting in the car behind the steering wheel, Ally felt an almost painful itch to learn to drive. It threatened to override the concern she felt for her friend, threatened even her resolve never to incur the "Beth Superior" look. She turned her big brown eyes on Beth. "Do you want to go home?"

Beth took a deep breath. "Just try not to wreck my car? And please don't run over any children."

"Betharoo!" Ally shrieked, heaving her body awkwardly over the gearshift to hug her friend, "I love you, I love you, I love you! You are a teaching goddess, a magical fairy of knowledge transmission! I will name the first car I buy after you! And it will be a bright red Ferrari in honor of your hair, and it will be beautiful, but never as beautiful as you!"

Beth laughed, relaxing, her smile natural. "Okay," she said. "I'm holding you to that."

Of course, Beth was a good teacher, filled with patience and lacking any of her parents' nervous tics. Ally ended up passing her test. Still, she could never escape the feeling afterward that Beth was the adult in the car. Beth remained the default driver, the expert, the one you'd want behind the wheel when navigating a city or pushing

- 40 -

through a snowstorm. Reconnecting for the trip to Grandma Stella's, both of them had known immediately who'd take the wheel.

Now, motoring over the last few feet of gravel in Grandma Stella's driveway, Ally tried to swallow away the mingled tastes of sleep and old meat that had taken up residence in her mouth. Her gleefully devoured Big Mac sat like a stone in her stomach. She told her guilt to go away and her excitement to arrive but her emotions didn't want to listen.

"Look at the window!" Beth said. And when Ally did, the excitement kicked in at last. Because at the window, Ally saw a skinny arm pushing aside a lace curtain, and then Grandma Stella's face emerged, topped with a carefully curled mop of bottle-blond hair. Her lipsticked mouth moved frantically, shouting greetings that the girls couldn't hear through the glass. The enthusiasm with which she smiled, combined with her wrinkles, practically caused her eyes to disappear in the folds of her face. She knocked on the inside of the window and pointed in the direction of the door, then gave them a thumbs-up and disappeared.

"I think she's happy to see us," Beth said.

"I think you're right," Ally replied. "Wow, she has not changed a bit."

The front door of the house swung open violently, and Grandma Stella stood there in her full four feet and ten inches of glory. "Gorgeous girls!" she hollered, her legs in a wide stance like a cowboy preparing for a gunfight, her arms flung out into wings. "Get out of that car right now and give me hugs before I explode!"

Giddy, the girls climbed out of the car and obeyed. Grandma Stella had many talents, Ally knew, but foremost among them was her ability to give a hug that conjured up the same sense of wholesome well-being as sitting in front of a lit fireplace on a winter night. Pressing her body into Grandma Stella's after such a long absence felt right.

"Oh my goodness, pumpkin, you have gotten so skinny!" she heard Grandma Stella say to Beth, who had melted into a hug of her own once Ally vacated Stella's arms. "You know, gentlemen like a little curve in your figure. If I don't manage to fatten you up in the next week and a half, you can fire me."

While Stella fussed over Beth, Ally looked around the wainscoted kitchen, which she immediately saw had been stocked with all the Britton Hills treats the girls loved: big, squashy, dark chocolate chunk cookies from the little grocery store on the town's main street, practically more chocolate chunks than dough; downy peaches and plump blueberries from a farm stand down the road; and Ally's personal favorite, the hearty wheat bread Grandma Stella baked herself, encrusted on the top with seeds and nuts, studded with raisins and figs in the middle.

Out the window, Grandma Stella's front yard stretched out for over an acre. The towering leafy trees scattered around the property, under which Ally and Beth had spent many a summer day reading aloud to each other in the grass, looked as healthy and full as ever against the darkening sky, but the flowers the older woman planted and tended so carefully seemed less numerous this year. Ally looked away after noticing a patch of pansies that seemed particularly scraggly. She moved over to the cookies, tore a chocolate-chunk-laden bite off one, and popped it into her mouth.

"So you two get to help me memorialize this old house, before I give it all up for the luxuries of Sunny Acres: Retirement Home of Your Dreams," Grandma Stella said. "I was thinking we could have a party right before I get out of here."

"Wait, retirement home of your dreams?" Ally snorted. Finishing up her first cookie, she helped herself to a second. "Is that its official motto?"

"Nope." Grandma Stella smiled. "But when I say it, I can temporarily convince myself that I'll like living in a place that smells like canned peas. At Sunny Acres, playing bridge is a hot Saturday night. Although, to be fair, they do have some nice-looking men living there. I kept my eyes open for that on the tour."

"Of course you did," Beth said, laughing. "A party sounds nice. We can most definitely help you plan something. I'll grab my highlighters!" She reached into the backpack at her feet and pulled out two highlighters, blue and yellow, along with a Moleskine notebook so well preserved that it looked brand-new, even though, as she flipped to an empty page, it became clear that she'd already filled up half of it.

"You are such a highlighter whore," Ally said.

"Excuse me, no," Beth replied. She uncapped the yellow one. "My highlighters and I are in a very loving, stable marriage."

They chatted about the party, deciding on the date (next Friday night, two days before moving day), the number of people to invite ("As many as possible!" said Grandma Stella, who wanted to put up flyers all over downtown), and what they'd need to buy.

"Booze," said Grandma Stella.

"Yes," said Ally, seriously. "And also booze."

"Good point," said Grandma Stella. "And can we make sure we have enough alcohol?"

When party planning wound down, Grandma Stella switched to

life planning, a favorite topic, Ally had found, of nearly everyone she talked to. Ally reiterated her desire to make a documentary, mentioning her idea about Britton Hills, and Grandma Stella oohed and aahed, fluffing up her hair and saying that she'd always thought she could be an excellent movie star. Then she lasered her focus on Beth.

"So your parents mentioned medical school? How exciting! No family is complete without a doctor, I think. Oh, you know, Harvard has an excellent medical school, and then you'd be so nice and close!"

"Well, Grandma, Harvard is pretty difficult to get into."

"But you're brilliant. They'd have to be idiots not to take you."

Beth laughed, not the genuine laugh of hers that she'd been laughing just a few minutes ago, but a polite one. "Well, we'll see. I still have to apply, and take some science classes I never took in college."

"And what will you do in the meantime?"

"Oh, I guess I'll live at home and catch up on prerequisites."

"Well, that's very practical of you." Grandma Stella beamed at Beth. "You're so sensible." She put one of her hands on Beth's shoulder and the other on Ally's, looking back and forth between them. "I can't believe you're actually here!"

"I thought you would share the back bedroom, like always," Grandma Stella said later in the evening, looking over her shoulder as she led them down the hardwood floors of her hallway. The house had three bedrooms. Grandma Stella slept in the first, which she'd carpeted with Persian rugs, wallpapered in paisley, and hung with heavy flowered curtains, as if daring the conflicting patterns to fight it out for her attention. The second bedroom, the one

Beth's parents always used, had a queen bed, rosy walls, and an intricately carved secretary desk with a computer still running Microsoft Word 2000 and dial-up Internet, where Beth and Ally had taken turns writing up their summer book reports.

But as far as Ally was concerned, the third bedroom blew the others out of the water. Farthest from the front door, it had a big bay window with a pillowed window seat, the perfect size to sit and watch the sun rise over the forest that bordered the back of the house. Ally always tried to wake up at dawn at least once over the course of her time in Britton Hills to see that sunrise. As the sun appeared in the sky, it toasted the room's pale yellow walls until they turned the color of sunflowers. Ally couldn't quite notice it as it was happening, how the pale walls turned sunny. Just all of a sudden, she'd realize that the change had occurred, even though she could never pinpoint the exact moment it flipped.

Grandma Stella had inherited the third bedroom's bed from her mother—delicately wrought brass and iron, a color halfway between silver and copper. She'd added to the already beautiful frame the softest down comforter Ally had ever encountered in her twenty-three years on Earth, along with endless pillows cased in cerulean and white.

The first summer Beth and Ally had stayed in Britton Hills after Beth's parents left, Grandma Stella had asked if they'd wanted to spread out more. So they'd toyed with the idea of splitting up, of one of them moving into the second bedroom. But ultimately, the lure of space hadn't been able to outweigh the charms of the bedroom. Plus, they'd actually reveled in sharing a bed, so that after they'd turned out the lights, they could cuddle and talk until their sentences trailed off into sleep. Tradition had reigned in the intervening years and apparently for Grandma Stella, it reigned still. She opened the door to the bedroom and beamed, and only the slightest pause elapsed before the girls chorused their delight with the sleeping arrangements.

Later, in the bathroom, Beth sat on the side of the claw-foot bathtub and brushed her teeth as Ally washed her face. Rubbing soap into her skin, Ally whispered, "She looks good."

"Grandma Stella?" Beth said through a mouthful of toothpaste.

"Yeah. I mean, she looks older, obviously. But not frail, like I thought maybe she would."

Beth moved to the sink and spat her foam out as Ally toweled off her face. "Really? I think there's a bigger change in her from last year to this year than I've ever seen before. And did you notice the garden? Compared to what it used to be, it's . . . nothing."

"Yeah, I saw. Maybe she didn't want to plant as much 'cause she knew she'd only be here for part of the summer?"

"Maybe," Beth said quietly.

Ally put her hand on Beth's back and rubbed it. "She's going to be okay," she said. "She's going to take over that retirement home. Within one week, she'll be the most popular lady there. I'm calling it right now."

Beth smiled. "You're right. All the men are going to fall in love with her. She'll receive at least one marriage proposal per month."

"All the women will come to her for advice, and she'll memorize the names of every single one of their grandchildren."

"None of the Sunny Acres employees will ever do any work again, because they'll all be too busy telling her their life stories." They laughed together. Ally squeezed Beth's hand.

"We just really have to help her out," Beth said, serious again. "Like, whatever she needs, even if it's kind of a pain in the butt."

"Yeah, of course," Ally said. Was Beth lecturing her? Silently, they went back into the bedroom. Ally tossed her dirty clothes on the floor next to her suitcase and, crouching in only her underwear, rummaged through her bag for some PJs. Beth left her bra on while transferring shirts, then slipped it off under her pajamas.

In the dark that night, Ally lay in the fetal position, facing the wall. She couldn't sleep. Since they'd flicked off the lights, she'd been trying not to toss around, not to disturb her bedmate. For what seemed like the thousandth time, she replayed the argument she'd been having in her mind since Beth first got back in touch, about whether to confront her. Continuing to pretend that nothing was wrong, they'd just keep awkwardly, painfully butting up against that invisible bulwark between them, denying all the while that it existed.

Quickly, before she could change her mind, she turned back to Beth, who lay flat and still on her back. "Hey," she said. "You awake?"

"Mmm." Beth's voice sounded thick and crackly, the voice of a teacher who'd spent the whole day screaming to be heard. "Yup."

"Can we talk for a bit?"

The moon outside the window lit up the room enough that Ally could see Beth's eyes focus on her, but she couldn't make out their expression. Trepidation or impatience?

"Sure," Beth said, sounding more alert. "What's going on?"

"I just—where did you go?"

Beth was silent, so Ally forced a laugh as she continued. "I mean, obviously I know you were in Haiti and you were busy. But I sent you so many e-mails, and you barely wrote me back. Nothing, from December to the end of April."

Still, silence. Ally plowed on. "I just really needed my best friend to be there for me, especially with all the awful shit going on in my life. It felt like I was sending the most vulnerable parts of myself into a void, this blankness, where there used to be so much love and support. I was having a really terrible time, and you weren't there."

She waited, tensed and bare, goose-pimpled, feeling like she'd just cut herself open and proffered her insides in the most haphazard way. Though she'd spent months thinking about this conversation, she still didn't have any clue how it was supposed to go.

"I didn't mean to become a void," Beth said slowly. "Voids are no fun. It's just that I was so busy in Haiti. The nearest Internet café was miles away, and Deirdre and Peter needed me with them pretty much constantly." In her first few months in Haiti, Beth had gushed nonstop in her e-mails about Deirdre and Peter Allen-Fox, the couple who ran the mission clinic, to the point where they'd attained mythical status in Ally's mind—a superhuman power couple who saved the world and also probably had amazing, limber sex at least three times a day.

Ally waited for Beth to keep talking, but she didn't. So finally, Ally said, "Yeah, that's understandable," then immediately wanted to kick herself for making things easy.

"It's good that we're getting to spend this time together now," Beth said.

"Definitely."

"And now, I'm sorry, but I'm completely exhausted so I'm going to be lame and go to bed." Beth turned over, aligning herself toward the door.

"Good night."

So it turns out, Ally thought, *that it's possible to face the bulwark directly, to tap on it, and feel no give at all.*

FOUR

Beth squeezed her eyes shut so hard that patterns burst across the backs of her eyelids. Ally liked to play the victim, and she was leaving out all the parts of the story that didn't flatter her. No mention, of course, of how she had been the first to retreat, the initial creator of the black hole. No apologies, ever, for the crime of being too into her boyfriend and too careless with her best friend. And no recognition, Beth thought to herself, that whatever awfulness that had been so difficult for Ally to deal with alone paled in comparison to what Beth had begged Ally to listen to while Ally had turned blithely away.

Lying there, still and quiet, Beth let herself hate Ally. She screamed a full-throated scream in her mind. *I hate you, I hate you, I hate you.* And, just like that, as the scream reverberated inside her motionless body, it became clear to her, the decision she'd been dragging her feet on for weeks. She had to go back to

Haiti. She had to tell Deirdre and Peter yes. Because she could devote herself to their goodness, no matter how much it hurt, or she could fall into the self-centeredness that Ally so unknowingly espoused, the feeling that one's life was awful even when nothing was really wrong with it. And it was better to be good. You *had* to be good, because if you weren't, where did you put all the guilt? How could you ignore it, as it piled itself higher and higher?

When she opened her eyes the next morning, the anger had crystallized, hardened out of something fragile. Calmly, it waited next to her new certainty. She looked over at Ally, sleeping with her arm thrown over her face and a sheet bunched up in her fist. Beth decided not to wake her up.

She slipped from the bed quietly, excellently, a perfect ten for considerateness. She walked to the kitchen in silence, her footfall defying the floorboards' usual creak. She could see Grandma Stella at the kitchen table, bent over a newspaper. Stella subscribed to both the *Britton Hills Bugle* and the *New York Times*. Together, she claimed, they made one perfect newspaper. "The *Bugle* has my funnies and my silly advice column," she'd always say, "and the *Times* has everything else." Judging by the Comic Sans print so large she could see it from the door, Beth guessed her grandmother was currently concentrating on the *Bugle*.

"Good morning!" she said, brightly. After a little tango of solicitude, in which Grandma Stella insisted on making Beth breakfast, and Beth insisted that she stay seated and relaxed, Beth joined her grandmother at the table and bit into a peach. The juice dripped its way down her chin and, laughing, she wiped it off with the back of her hand before it could reach her neck.

"That is a delicious peach," she said. "Thank you."

"I'm so glad you like it, darling," Grandma Stella replied. "I'm just tickled you're back! Stay here forever."

"I wish. So what's new in town?" Beth asked, pointing to the *Bugle*.

"Well," Grandma Stella let out a big breath, preparing to deliver some shocking news, "today, 'Detesting my daughter-in-law' gave so many details about herself that it's clear to anyone with a brain that she's Penny Joan Munson. She writes all about how her daughter-in-law doesn't appreciate her azaleas, and about how her grandson just started working for an investment bank in New York. Penny Joan never stops bragging around town about her azaleas. And for crying out loud, it's not like someone's grandson becomes an investment banker every year! I swear, that dolt has single-handedly kept *Dear Valerie* in business for years."

Beth made a sympathetic sound of agreement, her usual response when Grandma Stella started riding on the Penny Joan Munson hate train. Grandma Stella loved most people and things with unmatched enthusiasm, but what she hated (line-cutters, people who said rude things about the Red Sox), she hated with an equal and opposite passion. She could rail on Penny Joan, her Britton Hills nemesis, for hours. She'd start small. For instance, "You'll never guess what I saw at the grocery store today. Penny Joan Munson asked the deli girl to make her some more tuna salad, when the store was closing in five minutes and there was some perfectly nice-looking egg salad left." That would balloon into a general indictment of Penny Joan's character. She'd touch on her selfishness—"It just goes to show she has no respect for people's time"—then pirouette over to her snobbery. "I bet she thinks she's too good for their egg salad, just because sometimes it gets a little neon yellow." Variations on this theme occurred, but she always ended with a vigorous headshake and a muttered, "I should stop before I say something awful."

But today, the hate train's route was cut short. Grandma Stella gasped, remembering something. "And oh! Mulberry's Hardware just announced that it's closing at the end of the summer. Such a shame."

"Oh no!" Beth said, legitimately dismayed. She was no hardware connoisseur, but her father, forever DIY-ing his way through Grandma Stella's necessary repairs during family vacations, had taken her along with him on his myriad trips to the cluttered store. Mr. and Mrs. Mulberry had always fussed over her and given her butterscotch-flavored lollipops from a big jar they kept behind the counter. The shop too had an agreeable magic to it. Beth got the sense that you could find anything in the darkness of its shelves. Once, she'd reached for an Allen wrench and pulled out a reindeer-shaped potholder.

The Mulberrys had a son, Owen, around Beth's age. He'd never much registered with her until the summer she and Ally worked at the ice cream store. He had come in nearly every day for an ice cream cone, always two scoops of chocolate chip cookie dough. She'd thought him a bit odd. Who liked ice cream that much? And his face flushed red so easily.

"What would you call that color red? Beetroot? Vermillion?" she'd asked Ally one day, after her fingers had touched Owen's while handing him his cone and, stuttering good-bye, he'd tripped out the door. This was the summer she'd set herself the goal of learning a new vocabulary word each day—it was never too early to start preparing for the SATs—and colors seemed to be popping up a lot.

"I'm gonna go with scarlet."

"Scarlet! Yes. I can't believe O'Hara hasn't gotten tired of cookie dough yet."

"He's totally in love with you, duh," Ally had replied.

"Owen? No!" Beth had said and then, after some consideration, "Well, maybe."

"Definitely."

"No. He probably comes in all the time," Beth had said, "because he's in love with *you*."

Beth tended to assume that guys were in love with Ally because, more often than not, they were. It wasn't that Ally was prettier. Sometimes, Beth even had a sneaking suspicion that she was the better-looking of the two, though she never would have said that aloud. She was taller and thinner, with that luminous red hair that dulled Ally's brown in comparison.

And yet Ally seemed to have some sort of voodoo magic in her smile that, when she unleashed it, caused previously sane-seeming boys to lose their heads. In high school the magic didn't necessarily extend to the football players or the guys whose hands had smelled like pot since the seventh grade, but it proved startlingly effective on the nice, average ones. Ally was just so approachable to them, so they approached. And she encouraged it. She looked at them like they were superheroes, and then she decided after a few months or weeks or days that their powers no longer impressed her. Sometimes when she let them down, they cried. Beth could never get over this fact: *Ally actually makes boys cry*, and she didn't even mean to do it.

In the meantime, Beth stood there and watched her friend get pursued, and felt terrible about herself. She tried to figure out what the problem was and eventually settled on the explanation that the right boys for her just didn't exist in high school. She wanted someone as smart and motivated as she was, someone who didn't make her feel like achieving was a bad thing. And she wanted that boy to care about the world, to have plans for how he was going to make a difference. She pictured a crusading Matt Damon with a high IQ, who volunteered at a soup kitchen after church on Sundays.

Maybe, wanting that, she intimidated the boys around her. Maybe she wasn't as capable as Ally at being friendly and flirty to the cute boys, who seemed to expect fawning as their birthright. Maybe Ally had bigger boobs. Well, definitely Ally had bigger boobs. That might've had something to do with it too.

In high school, whenever Beth allowed herself to complain about her seeming undesirability to Ally, her friend always had the counterexample ready. "What about Jack Flembo? He asked you out like three times."

Beth was nice to the painfully awkward Jack Flembo because she pitied him. She was the only female besides his mother and his teachers who didn't ignore him, who didn't close her eyes and plug her nose when confronted with his acne and his unwashed-boy smell. She'd listened as he'd told her the entire plot of his favorite anime series, and that was enough for him to fall deeply, delusionally in love. He'd asked her to the movies and then, when she'd said no, he'd asked her to Geraldo's Steakhouse and then, when she'd said no to that too, he'd shown up at her front door with six pink roses and asked her to the prom two years in advance.

Jack Flembo didn't count, she always told Ally. She tried to explain that one weird guy being obsessed with her didn't change everything. It didn't make the disparity between their love lives feel any better to her.

So with Owen Mulberry, she suspected that Ally was trying to even the score a bit more. Because Owen Mulberry, despite his blushing and the shyness, seemed too normal to be in love with Beth. He smelled so much better than Jack Flembo, for one thing. And his reedy body showed signs of incipient muscles. Beth hated the idea that Ally was handing Owen to her as a token.

And sure enough, nothing ever happened with him. She went home that summer, her lips still unkissed. In recent years, Owen seemed to have disappeared from Britton Hills. She never saw him around on her visits.

"Speaking of Mulberry's," Grandma Stella said, "I need packing tape. Would you mind going down there and buying some for me today?"

"Sure," Beth said. "I'll head down now."

"Oh, darling, there's no rush! You and Ally can do something first. Maybe you want to go to the shore?"

"No, that's fine."

Grandma Stella fixed her eyes on Beth, and Beth squirmed. Grandma Stella slowly raised one eyebrow. The summer Beth turned eight, she'd begged Grandma Stella to teach her how to move her face like that, overriding her grandmother's concern that the skill couldn't be taught. The two of them had stayed at the kitchen table for two hours, Beth refusing to give up and Grandma Stella trying every possible method of explanation. She'd put her hands on her granddaughter's eyebrows, pushing one down and the other up like modeling clay. She'd asked Beth to visualize marionette strings attached to the hairs, and to try to move with an invisible puppeteer.

When Beth's right eyebrow finally made its solo journey up her forehead, Grandma Stella had pounded the table in victory. Then, spontaneously, the two of them had started dancing around the kitchen. Every few seconds, one or the other would yell out, "Now!" and they would turn to face each other, frozen, except for their right eyebrows wiggling up and down. They'd stayed motionless until their bodies had started to quake with hysterics.

Now, Beth thought for a moment of telling the truth to that eyebrow, and to the woman who possessed it. But instead she said, "Ally's still asleep. I think she's pretty exhausted. I'll go now."

On her walk into town, Beth used her cell to call Deirdre and Peter. They didn't answer, of course, so she left them a quick message. "Hi, it's me. My answer's yes. Say hello to everyone there for me, and that I'll see them soon." She spent the rest of the walk going over her French and Creole vocabulary in her head, visualizing the flash cards she had made. She called up a new one in a regular rhythm, every two steps. *Doctor. Doktè. Médecin.*

Gradually the trees thinned and the sidewalks thickened. The sea-salty smell of the air got stronger, and the distance between houses decreased. Soon, Beth reached the main downtown area, a stretch of three long blocks loaded with stores on both sides of the street. She could picture with total clarity the way that the town opened up into the harbor at the end of the third block where boats waited against seemingly infinite ocean. The sound of waves slapping against rocks mingled faintly with birdsong.

When Beth walked into Mulberry's, nobody sat behind the counter. The tinkling of the bell on the front door rang into silence. The place, despite its clutter, felt deserted, Sleeping Beauty's frozen kingdom behind the briars. She thought about yelling a hello but the stillness seemed too perfect to break.

She wandered throughout the aisles, passing her hands along the shelves. Her fingertips picked up dust and the odd trace of glitter. A warped mirror hung at the end of one shelf and, as she passed it and sneaked a glance, she thought she saw her kid self staring back at her, sucking on one of those butterscotch lollipops. *Well*, she thought, *here goes another piece of my childhood disappearing on me. I could cry about it.* But she didn't. She hadn't cried since Haiti, where, after the incident with the little boy, she'd been crying every day.

Then the door to the storage room in back swung open, and the spell was broken. The guy who walked out of the door, loaded up with paint cans, wasn't a fairy-tale prince but, oh, Beth thought, he was cute.

"Shoot," he said. "Sorry to keep you waiting. Need some help?"

"Oh, no worries. I just walked in."

He put the paint cans down on the floor and turned his attention on her. "Wait—Beth Abbott?" he said, and his face turned a light shade of pink.

Owen Mulberry had grown up.

FIVE

Ally woke to the vibrations of her phone. Swimming up to consciousness, she answered it. "Mmmfggo?"

"Sweetheart!" her mother said in response. Marsha spoke too loudly on the phone, and her voice ping-ponged inside Ally's eardrums, expediting her wake-up process. As she morphed into a real person again, she remembered that she was sharing a bed. She turned toward Beth's side to apologize, but it was empty.

"Hey, Mom."

To say that Ally and her mom talked sporadically would be an understatement. Marsha sometimes went a full month without attempting to contact her daughter (and without returning any of the messages Ally left her). Whenever Ally brought it up, she'd say, "Oh, but you know how I absolutely *loathe* talking on the phone! I much prefer to see someone in person, to touch them, to look at them. Just come home and visit me! Not next week, though, I have a lot going on, but after that, I'm dying to see you!" Then she'd call three days in a row, wanting to talk for hours and protesting when Ally said she had to go.

"Excellent news," her mother said now. "Glen and I are coming up to New York in four days! Surprise getaway for Memorial Day weekend!"

"God, you too?"

"What's that?"

"Nothing. Sorry, it's just Memorial Day mania this year. But that'll be fun for you," Ally said, corralling her tone into pleasantness.

"We *of course* want to see you. Glen wants to take us all to dinner at Jean-Georges, and I read all about this raw Afghan-Thai fusion place that you and I absolutely must try. Apparently, it's very healthy, does wonders with your intestines or something like that."

"Mom, you know I'm in Britton Hills, right?" Ally interjected.

"No! Oh, this is a disaster!" Marsha practically shrieked. "Why didn't you tell me?"

"I did."

"Well, for how long? Can you come back?"

"I'm supposed to stay until next Sunday."

"That's ridiculous. What are you going to do up there for that long? You'll waste away from boredom, and while the early stages of wasting might be a good look on you, I don't want you to disappear completely! Just come back early. I'm sure Glen would be willing to pay for a flight. He is desperate to meet you."

"Beth and her grandma are expecting me to stick around."

"But—" The resentment in Marsha's voice took on a new breathiness. "We have news we want to tell you. In person."

"What?" Ally said.

"In person! I'm not going to tell you over the phone!"

"What? Did you guys get engaged or something?"

On Marsha's end of the line, silence. Ally took a deep breath, orienting herself to a new world. "Holy shit," she said. "You guys got engaged." Her mother, who had sworn after the dissolution of her union with Ally's father that marriage was for suckers, that monogamy was completely impractical and contrary to how human beings had been designed, was getting married to a man Ally had never met. Glen had started popping up in phone conversations about six months ago, but like all of the boyfriends that floated in and out of her mother's life, Ally chose to largely ignore him, assuming that he'd be gone before she had a chance to get attached.

"Well, I wanted to tell you in person. But yes! We're so happy."

"Congratulations," Ally said, mustering up some cheer in her voice.

"So, you see, you have to come back, so we can have a proper celebration. Glen wants to hear you sing. I told him all about how musical you are! Maybe we could go to one of those piano bar places and you could sing us an engagement song. Glen loves 'Til There Was You.'"

"I don't think so."

"Or maybe you could write us a song and sing it at the wedding! You could call it something like 'A Love for All Seasons.'"

"I don't really do that anymore."

"Ooh, how about a lyric like, *Meant to be, Together we're free, Sea to shining sea*—"

"Mom! I don't want to sing you guys a song. I told you I don't perform anymore." Ally sometimes worried that her throat had rusted over in the last month. Even when she tried to sing in the shower, her voice sounded hollow to her, tinny and empty despite the acoustics of her bathroom. Noises came out of her mouth, but they didn't feel connected to anything, so she stopped making them and washed her hair in silence.

"Well, anyway, we just want to see you. I'm sure Beth will understand. Just tell her about the engagement. I'm getting married—I can be selfish!"

Ally didn't say what she wanted to say, that her mother was always selfish, even when she wasn't getting married. Instead, she said, "I'll try."

Maybe, she thought when she hung up, she did want to try. To get to eat at Jean-Georges, without spending any of her own money! She'd probably be able to order an appetizer and a dessert. Or did they do prix fixes there? With wine pairings! She swallowed the excess saliva that rose into her mouth at the thought.

More important, if she went back to New York early to see her mom, she and Tom could get their coffee sooner. And if coffee were to turn into more-than-coffee, they'd have more time for all of that.

That reminded her. Tom. Her heart booming a serious bass line, she checked the rest of her phone.

She had one text message, sent at 1:30 A.M. from a contact labeled *Alex From Bar*, reading, Hey u out? She ignored it.

An e-mail from Gabby, in response to the e-mail from Tom that Ally had forwarded along:

WHAT???????

1] What is this complete inability to stay in one place? He isn't Jesus. There's no need to be so fucking peripatetic.

2] Is "getting coffee" code for the two of you boning and . . .

3] If so, do you want to go with me to get waxed beforehand because it is a full-on jungle down there but you know I hate going to Bella Wax by myself.

Ally could write a *War and Peace*–length tome about Gabby's eating, drinking, and personal grooming habits. If asked to write about Beth's recent doings, she would have trouble filling up a haiku.

Beth went to Haiti.
She wants to be a doctor?
Five more syllables.

Finally, yes, there it was. An e-mail from Tom. It was disappointing in its brevity: Awesome, talk soon!

She stared at it for a second, trying and failing to figure out some nondesperate way of extending the conversation. Then she put her phone on the wicker bedside table next to her and attempted to think about the day ahead, about how she should move forward with her Britton Hills documentary idea, about whether she should go back to New York. Basically, she tried to think about anything that would prevent her from obsessing about Tom. But of course it didn't work. Dwelling on him was the one constant in her life right now.

THE night that Ally met Tom had already been going pretty damn perfectly.

It was her junior year in college, and she'd made a name for herself. She was the singer-songwriter girl on campus now. People she knew only vaguely would stop her sometimes as she walked through the quad in the brisk Massachusetts air and say that they'd loved her last show. "That song," they'd enthuse, "you know, the 'Joys of Being Alone' one, has been stuck in my head all week!"

On this particular night, she'd played a show at Roasters, the coffee shop just a couple blocks off campus. Her hair, steering clear of frizziness, had fallen in perfect waves without her having to do anything special to it. Her voice had come out clear and strong, even more effortlessly than normal. Roasters was full, packed with her friends as well as townies and students she didn't know, who'd been studying or hanging out and seemed (mostly) delighted by the unexpected music. Outside the floor-to-ceiling windows, fat snow-flakes made their way lazily down to the ground. When she played her last song, her friends sang along with the chorus.

"Thanks so much, everyone!" she said as her final guitar strum reverberated and faded away, replaced by clapping and cheers. Then, high on the adrenaline cloud that always enveloped her postperformance, she went to stuff her guitar into its case.

As she zipped the case closed, she felt a hand touching her shoulder.

"Hey, great show," the hand's owner said. Just the sound of the voice, its particular tenor, something about where it existed on the scale, was enough to slow time. She turned around. This guy she'd never seen before stood there, grinning at her. For what seemed an eternity, as she struggled to resume the lung processes she normally didn't have to think about, she let her eyes comb over him. She immediately wanted to run her fingers through the dark brown hair messily topping his head. She looked up at his eyes, a startling shade of blue in his olive-skinned face, and marveled at their force, even behind the shield of dark-rimmed glasses.

"I'm Tom," he said, extending his hand. "And I want to thank you for giving me a distraction from my computer science study group." He jerked his head toward a table in the corner, crowded with three pale guys and one girl, all on their laptops, sneaking peeks in Ally's direction. The girl shot her a malevolent glare, her bushy eyebrows furrowing.

"I'm very happy I could help," Ally said.

"But you've created a big problem for me." She thought she detected in his voice the slightest hint of a twang, like he was desperately trying to leave someplace like Texas behind.

"What's that?" she asked.

He leaned toward her, his face serious. "Well, before I heard your music, coding was boring. Now, after I've heard it, coding will be excruciating."

"Wow. I am so sorry," she said. Behind Tom, Gabby and her burly boyfriend, Jeff, walked by, trying to be stealthy, giving her two big thumbs-up. "There seems to be only one solution here." Tom was still leaning toward her so she moved forward too and lowered her voice. "You should blow it off and walk me home."

They walked back to her dorm through the falling snow. The flakes had started to pile up, covering the dead grass and the concrete walkways. Lampposts glowed, turning into little halos of light. She felt like they were walking through Narnia.

Tom offered to carry her guitar for her. "So music's your thing, huh?" he asked, as he took her case.

"Yeah, it is," she said, loving the certainty with which she was able to answer. "What's yours? Programming the shit out of computers?"

"I don't know," he said, laughing. "Comp sci's okay, but it's not exciting, at least not for me. I think I might currently be thingless. The fact that you know what excites you, though, that's really, really awesome."

They slowed in front of a stone building. "This is me," she said. She turned to face him. Above their heads, party sounds escaped from dorm room windows. Someone yelled something about shots. A Katy Perry song thumped into the night. She looked down at her brown leather boots, and then back up at Tom.

"Want to keep walking?" he asked.

So she ran inside to drop off her guitar. Then they roamed the campus for hours, until the snow piled up into foot-high drifts.

On the eastern side of the athletic field, where bleachers gave way to trees, they made snow angels, rubbing their arms and legs into the coldness. Tom stood up, caked in snow, and drew a thought bubble coming from the head of his snow angel. He snapped a twig off a tree, and with it, he traced letters within the thought bubble. She held her breath as the sentence emerged. *Ally is beautiful.*

"I think my snow angel likes you," he said.

"I think I like your snow angel."

She stood up onto her tiptoes, shivering, and brushed the powder out of his hair. He looked into her eyes until all the snow was gone, and then he wrapped his arms around her and kissed her.

In the weeks that followed, being with Tom made her tick off every cliché she'd ever heard that accompanied falling in love. Her heart actually raced when she was with him. She could feel the Indy 500 zooming around in her chest. Her face got red. She felt herself floating up above the rest of the people on Earth. It was just the two of them, hanging out together fifteen feet off the ground, in their own private patch of air.

She was so crazy about him she even gave up Britton Hills that summer, dizzily agreeing to spend her vacation between school and internship with his family. (Just outside Austin! She'd picked up on his hidden Texas accent just as, she thought, she was able to identify beautiful things in him that the rest of the world couldn't.) His parents had cooed over her, had made sure to buy multiple boxes of her favorite breakfast cereal, and each night after everyone else was asleep, Tom would creep into the guest room where she lay, her whole body alert and impatient for him. He'd get into bed with her, and they'd try so hard to be quiet. "Shh," he would whisper right before he bit down on her ear. He'd set an alarm for six A.M. and they'd fall asleep, exhausted in the best possible way. In the morning, he'd run back to his childhood bedroom before his parents, who probably knew exactly what was going on, woke up.

Except for one brief, weird month in high school where she'd lulled herself to sleep at night designing white dresses in her head, she'd never thought much about weddings. She'd always assumed that a husband and kids would happen someday, far off in the future, and never bothered to think any more about it. But with Tom, she couldn't stop herself from spinning out fantasies.

Some of the details were fuzzy—in the wedding fantasy, she couldn't figure out what she'd look like, how she'd do her hair, or what she'd be wearing. She had no idea how they'd combine their last names. (Could she really hyphenate Morris with his already-hyphenated Mejia-Robertson?) But she knew, in the sharpest relief, how Tom's face would light up when she walked down the aisle. It would be the look of surprise and delight that overtook him sometimes, when she played him a new song he loved or when she wore his favorite dress, the bright blue one that dipped down low in the front and spun out around her legs (and slipped off easily). That look seemed to say, without agenda, *I am the luckiest guy in the world.*

She knew she wore a similar look when she was with him. She felt like the luckiest girl in the world all the way up until the day he broke her heart.

WHEN Ally walked into the kitchen, Grandma Stella was leaning against the counter. She had the cordless phone to her ear—a bulky, tan relic. "No, but I just don't think—" she was saying into it, her voice tight with frustration, when she saw Ally. "Hold on a jiff, Timmy," she said, and covered the phone with her hand. "Morning, dear. Scrambled egg?"

"Oh, amazing, yes. Thank you," Ally replied, and settled herself at the table.

"Let me just finish this," Grandma Stella said, wiggling the phone, "and then we can chat." She took her hand off the receiver and cradled it between her ear and her shoulder, speaking into it once again. "Sorry, darling, I'm back." She opened the refrigerator and took out a blue foam egg carton. "Yes, yes, I know, but you don't understand that I'll *need* it."

As Grandma Stella cracked two eggs and began to beat them

a bit too vigorously in a ceramic bowl, Ally looked down at the newspaper on the table in front of her. The *Bugle* was open to that ridiculous advice column, *Dear Valerie*. Ally winced at how amateur the whole thing looked, with its gigantic print and clip art. Valerie's face, in a misguided glamour shot, peered up from next to her byline. Ally skimmed a letter about strained in-law relations and lingered on Valerie's horrendous response. Apparently, Britton Hills' resident advice columnist was a fan of big romantic gestures and terrible puns.

Then she realized that Grandma Stella had finished her phone call and was standing with her fingers pressed to her temples.

"You all right?" Ally asked.

"Of course," Grandma Stella replied, snapping into brightness. "So. How did you sleep?" She transferred the steaming eggs from the stovetop to a plate with a practiced ease and began to walk them over to the table.

"Really well," Ally said. "You forget, living in New York, what it's like to sleep in total quiet—" A clatter interrupted her.

"Shoot." Grandma Stella said, a mess of eggs and broken plate at her feet. *"Shoot."*

Ally jumped up. In three long steps she crossed over to where Grandma Stella stood, staring fixedly at the ground. "I've got it," she said. Grandma Stella attempted to bend down. "No, don't!" Ally said. "I'll clean it."

"My hands were slippery, from the butter," Grandma Stella said. She grabbed some paper towels.

"Sit down," Ally said, taking the paper towels from her and crouching, picking up pieces of jagged yellow crockery.

"Oh, please don't cut yourself." Grandma Stella hovered. In her right hand, she held the string of her bathrobe uselessly.

"I'll be fine!" Ally said. "Don't worry. Please, sit."

Slowly, Grandma Stella did. "I'm so sorry, dear. Your eggs . . ."

"Oh, I'll just have a piece of the bread instead," Ally said. "Are you okay? Do you want a glass of water?"

"No, no." Grandma Stella waved her hand in the air. "I was just distracted. From the phone call."

"What was it about?"

Grandma Stella sighed. "Oh, Timothy—Beth's father. He's got this crazy idea that I shouldn't be driving anymore. Apparently the world will fall apart if I bring the car to Sunny Acres."

"Do you need the car there?" Ally asked. She dumped the bits of broken plate in the trash. There, they crushed the eggshells that Stella had tossed in so casually minutes earlier. Ally bent back down to pick up the eggs, fluffy and buttery and all over the floor.

"Well if I don't have the car, how am I supposed to ever go anywhere else? If I don't have the car, I'm trapped. I can't go visit anyone, I just have to wait for them to come visit me, and how often will that happen?"

"I'll come visit you," Ally said.

"I know, dear. Thank you. I'm so sorry to go on like this, but Timothy is driving me up the wall. And Mary—you'd never know she was just my daughter-in-law, the way she feels entitled to tell me what to do. I've already let them sell the house. They could at least let me keep the car. But no, they've put up some advertisement on the Internet. Like I want to let some stranger from the Internet come stand in my driveway."

Ally thought she could understand Grandma Stella's annoyance. Beth's mom and dad, a therapist and a high school principal respectively, were wonderful, a deeply-in-love unit. However, they suffered from a bad case of thinking they always knew best.

Grandma Stella gave Ally a halfhearted smile. "It's one of life's cruel tricks," she said, "that your children grow up and treat you like a baby."

"I'm really sorry," Ally said. She finished wiping off the floor and sat down next to Grandma Stella at the table.

"You have nothing to be sorry about, dear. I'm so thankful you're here," Stella said. She leaned forward and rested her forehead on Ally's. Ally could feel her soft skin, the powdered makeup she religiously applied.

Sometimes, Ally caught herself believing that *she* was Stella's real granddaughter, not Beth. She and Grandma Stella shared a certain vivacious smallness that united them. In their midst, long-limbed Beth was an elegant giraffe among cute little prairie dogs. Once, when Grandma Stella had come to visit Wilmington, she'd taken the girls to the movies. Beth had gone to the bathroom, and Ally and Grandma Stella had bought an extra-large popcorn for the three of them to share.

"You and your granddaughter enjoy the film now," the lady behind the counter had said, and Grandma Stella had put her arm around Ally's shoulders.

"We will," she'd replied.

"Will you . . ." Grandma Stella started to ask now, and then hesitated. "Please don't mention all this to Beth. Mary said she was very unhappy in Haiti—well, I'm sure you know all about that."

Except Ally didn't. This was the first she had heard about Beth disliking Haiti. Her e-mails had been immensely upbeat, filled with a sense of purpose. That is, until they'd stopped coming.

"Anyways," Grandma Stella said. "She should be able to have a good time now that she's back, instead of worrying that her parents and I aren't getting along."

If Beth had hated Haiti, Ally wondered, frustrated, why wouldn't she have talked to her about it?

"Is that all right?" Grandma Stella said. "Keeping this between us?"

Ally nodded. "Of course."

SIX

❦

Beth and Owen stood together in the dim light of the store and smiled at each other, each waiting for the other to say something. Then they both started talking at the same time.

"How are—"

"How have—"

"You first!" he said.

"No, no, you go," she replied.

"How are you?" he repeated. But Beth didn't know how to answer that question. Navigating the subject of Haiti required an alert brain. It took full concentration to tell people enough so they'd have some idea of what it was like, but not so much that they'd get depressed.

And right now, her brain didn't seem to be working at full capacity. She tried to force her neurons to slow down and focus on making speech, but they seemed instead to be zooming in on

Owen's gray eyes. One of them had a fleck of brown in it, a little, unexpected dot that complemented all the other freckles lightly dusting his face and arms. Those incipient muscles of his that she'd noticed when they were in high school had arrived in full, but somehow he looked like he spent more time working with his hands than flexing at the gym. A mental image of him carrying lumber lodged itself in her mind.

"I've been good," she said. "What about you? What have you been up to?"

"I've been good too. Just spent the last year working in Acadia National Park, doing park ranger things. If you ever have a hankering for a guided nature walk, I'm your guy."

Aha, she thought, *so the lumber thing wasn't too far off. Acadia National Park has lots of trees.* Then she thought, *A national park has lots of trees? Elizabeth Abbott, get yourself together.*

"And I'm heading off to grad school in the fall for environmental science. But I'm here this summer helping my parents close up the store."

"I can't believe Mulberry's is closing," Beth said. "My dad used to bring me here all the time." It was important to Beth to try to articulate the magic of the place to Owen, to explain how much it had meant to a little girl who had never expected to enjoy trips to buy hardware. At this point, her ability to form complex thoughts seemed to be returning, and she realized that this was the longest conversation she'd ever had with him that hadn't involved ice cream.

"My parents always loved when you came in," Owen said.

"Me?"

"Yeah. They bought a ton of lollipops when the store opened, thinking all the kids who came in would go crazy for them. And then you were the only kid who got really excited."

"I was just thinking about the lollipops!"

Owen paused for a second, furrowing his forehead in thought. The pinkness in his face had faded, leaving his skin tan and smooth. "Actually, we have a bunch of boxes of them in the back. My parents had a tendency to overorder supplies. I think these ones are a couple years old, but those things don't ever go bad, right?"

"What with all the chemicals, I'm sure they're still fine."

"Well, if they don't get eaten, they're going to sit in a landfill somewhere until the sun explodes, probably."

"Oh no!" Beth laughed.

"Any interest?"

"I think it's our duty to reduce landfill waste."

He smiled at her and said, "Hey, me too." Then he went into the back room and brought out a box. He put it on the floor, and they crouched around it. When he opened it up, Beth peered down. A rainbow of colors shone back up at her. The two of them looked at each other over their makeshift candy shop. Beth felt giddy.

"So many flavors!" Beth said. "I always just ate butterscotch."

"Really? You never tried anything else? You were missing out, Beth."

"Hey!" she said. "Don't talk to me about not trying new things, Mr. Chocolate Chip Cookie Dough."

Owen looked up from the tangle of lollipops in his hands then, straight at her, and at first she thought that maybe she'd said something wrong.

But he grinned and said, "Well, it's not too late to branch out.

This box probably covers the entire spectrum of taste." He pulled out a white stick topped with a bulbous black wrapper. "Licorice? Mud pie? Who knows what this one is supposed to be?"

Beth giggled, a sound that surprised her. "It looks ominous. I think it might be poison."

"Maybe we should bury that one at the bottom of the box . . ." Owen said. "So which one do you want?"

"I don't know how to even begin narrowing it down."

"Well, there's no need to limit yourself. We could do a lollipop tasting." He held up a green one, unwrapped it, and waved it around under his nose. He grinned at her and closed his eyes. Then he made a great show of taking a lick. As his tongue swirled around the lollipop, Beth noticed a weird tingle on the back of her thighs. Owen said, "I'm detecting subtle notes of sugar, apple, and corn syrup."

Five minutes later, they were both sitting on the floor, amid a pile of unwrapped lollipops. The candies had gone gummy over time, but that hadn't stopped the two of them from each trying enough flavors to turn their tongues brown. So far, among other flavors, they'd found pineapple, bubble gum, and, as Owen had put it, what pet dander might taste like if a bunch of it flew into your mouth. Beth had kicked off her flip-flops, and her legs, clad in a pair of jean shorts, lay stretched out against the linoleum.

She touched her tongue to a fuchsia sphere. "I think it's supposed to be grape," she said. "Either that, or laundry detergent."

"Oh man, I've gotta try it," Owen said, and laughed. The sound of his laugh traveled across the air to her and enfolded her in warmth. She liked it. It made her break out into a gigantic smile in response and, suddenly self-conscious at how she'd lost control of her face, she looked down at her lap. For some reason, she had no more silly lollipop banter left, and he wasn't saying anything either. A tiny bubble of panic started to rise up inside her at the silence, so she said the first thing that came to her mind.

"You've changed since high school."

"Oh? Yeah. Yeah, I guess I have," he replied. "That's probably a good thing. High school as a science nerd who couldn't stop himself from lecturing people about the dangers of global warming was not exactly fun. Not to mention that my main after-school activity was hanging out with my parents in a hardware store every day."

"No, not every day!"

"Yup. Actually. Every single day."

"Why? I mean, it's great here, but didn't you want to do other things?"

"Um," he said, suddenly quiet and not looking at her. "I guess I just felt like my parents needed me."

Little warning signs went up in Beth's brain, saying *Danger! Potential for Awkward Conversation Ahead! Take U-Turn Now to Return to Easy Banter.* But she couldn't stop herself from plunging forward. "Do you feel really sad about it?" she asked. He looked at her then, confused.

"Wait, you mean sad about—" He let his sentence trail off.

"The store closing," she said. "I can only imagine, if you spent every day here, you must."

"Oh." He picked up another lollipop and started halfheartedly unwrapping it. "Yeah, I guess." He paused, like he wasn't sure whether to go on. She gave him a half smile.

"Well, not 'I guess.' I am," he said. Then the words flowed out easily, as though he'd just been waiting for someone to ask him.

"This store has always been a part of my life. I sat in that corner and did my homework after school, had my first job here, it was probably the thing my parents talked about the most, and now it's not going to exist anymore. It'll just be . . . gone, and fifty years from now, no one will even know it used to be here." He stopped and looked a little embarrassed. "Thank you for listening to that."

"Of course. I understand how you feel," Beth said. "I mean, sort of. Obviously not to the same extent, I mean, but my grandma is leaving her house. Someone will move in and change it, or maybe even tear it down, and it won't be my place anymore."

"Right—you won't be welcome." Owen had been leaning up against a shelf, but now he sat forward in agreement.

"Yeah." She sat forward too, leaning toward him. "And maybe it's childish of me to feel that way. After all, with my grandma, of course the most important thing is her health. Who cares if I don't have my little summer vacation haven anymore? But I guess it's just strange and disorienting to think that this store, that house, they'll be the same physical coordinates on a map as they are now, now when they mean so much to us, but nothing else about them will be the same."

"Exactly. Then, if I have new people who are important to me, or someday when I have kids, and I want to show them this thing that was my whole childhood, I won't be able to."

"I know!" she said. "I think about that too."

He was nodding, inching closer, and she was too without even realizing it, as though his empathy were a gigantic magnet. "It's scary to realize that then there's this huge part of yourself you can never fully share with them," he said.

"Yes! I know with someone like Ally—you remember Ally, right?"

"Yeah, of course. You guys worked at the ice cream store together."

"Right. Anyways, I know our friendship changed completely for the better when she came up to Britton Hills with me for the first time. There was this whole other me that she got to know, that would've just stayed a stranger to her if she hadn't come," Beth said. "I don't know if there's any way to get around that."

"Yeah, I don't know either," Owen said, and was silent a moment. She realized that the feet between them had turned into inches, that her bare leg nearly touched his on the floor now. She could smell him, a pleasant, piney smell. Self-conscious again, she fought an urge to touch his face and tried casually to reverse her trajectory.

"Anyway," she said, leaning back, "what are your parents going to do now that the shop is closing?"

"I don't know. They might get enough money from the sale to be able to retire. That's optimistic, though, so the more likely scenario is that my dad will go work at the Home Depot that's putting them out of business."

Beth felt a deep indignation at imagining Mr. Mulberry, so proud of his own business, in a Home Depot smock. His bushy mustache, his balding head, his genial smile, his potbelly, they all attained an air of elegance when he worked in his store. A customer would ask him a question and he would know the answer, and his whole being would shine with delight. At Home Depot, that pride would have nowhere to go. He'd seem foolish.

"I hate that," she said. "I hate thinking of your dad at Home Depot."

"I know," Owen said. "I hate it too."

"It must be so hard," she said, "to have all of these things you take as guarantees—that your parents are generally in control of their lives, that Mulberry's will always be here—disappearing at the same time."

"It is," he said. "And it also scares the crap out of me—they thought they had it figured out. No matter what else might have happened to them, they had this store that was supposed to carry them through their lives, maybe carry me through my life, not that I wanted that for myself, but still—and all of a sudden it's gone and they have to start over at age fifty. It's just like, did they make the wrong decisions? Did they waste their lives by choosing the wrong thing? And is there any way of knowing that you're choosing the wrong thing? Because I sure as hell don't want to realize I chose the wrong thing in thirty years. I mean, who knows? Maybe there won't be any more national parks left to protect and I'll end up doing palliative care for robots or something."

"No," Beth said. "Well, first of all, I highly doubt you'll end up at a robot hospice, although I'm sure you'd do a very nice job at that if you wanted to. But also, even if your parents made some wrong decisions and things suck now, it wasn't a waste."

"Yeah." But Owen didn't sound convinced.

"It made them happy for a long time. It made a lot of people happy. Hey, I was always over the freaking moon about those lollipops."

"You were," he said, and for the first time in a while, he cracked that sun-filled smile of his. "You legitimately went a little bit insane about them."

"What? Insane? That's not true!" she protested.

"Beth Abbott," he said, "my first memory of you is you walking in here with your dad when we were both, I don't know, six years old? And you were so calm and self-possessed, looking at the tools very seriously, to the point where I thought you were maybe a tiny fifth-grader or something. And then my dad handed you a lollipop, and you went, 'Really?' all wide-eyed, your voice all high, and you started doing this lollipop dance."

"A lollipop dance?" she said, laughing. "What does that even mean?"

"I'm glad you asked. I will demonstrate," Owen said. He threw his hands up in the air and waved them around, then started warbling, "*Lollipoppppp, lollipoppp, I get to eat a lollipopppp.*"

"I did not!"

"I'm telling you, Beth. There was some skipping involved too. One of the best happy dances I've ever seen."

"Liar! I don't believe you." Her stomach hurt from laughing.

"I have witnesses. You can ask my parents. The—okay, maybe this is weird to say, but I'm just going to say it—the Beth Abbott Happy Dance is kind of legendary in our household."

"It is?" For some reason, in the time she'd spent in high school talking with Ally about Owen, it had never occurred to her that he might talk about her too.

"Yeah. I mean, one year, I swear my dad hadn't smiled for a good six months, and then you came into the store and apparently did your happy dance again. He came home from work that night, sat down at the table and said, 'Goddammit if Beth Abbott doesn't still light up like a kid at Christmas when you offer her a lollipop.' Then he and my mom just cracked up for five minutes straight."

He was still grinning at her, but she stopped, caught for a

second on wondering why Mr. Mulberry hadn't smiled for six months. He misread her confusion, and the pinkness in his skin crept back to the surface.

"I'm sorry," he said. "That was weird. I shouldn't have said that."

"No," she said, wanting more than anything else for his smile not to disappear again. "No, no, no, it was good. It proves my point. I can do an amazing, life-changing happy dance. But your parents gave me the opportunity to show it. So therefore they are also amazing and life-changing, and they did not lead a totally misguided existence."

He laughed. "Okay, you've convinced me."

"Yes! Oh, good."

"Thank you for asking me about that. It felt . . . helpful to talk about it."

"Of course."

Owen nodded. She nodded too, and they moved their heads up and down in silence.

"It's really nice to see you again, Beth," Owen said. He was looking at her with such intensity that she feared she was co-opting his trademark blush.

Then the bell on the shop's door rang, and Ally stepped in. She wore strappy leather sandals and a bright red sundress with a sweetheart neckline that tapered at the waist before flowing out to midthigh. She looked so fresh-faced and feminine that Beth, in her T-shirt, instantly felt like she'd been walloped with an ugly stick. Ally's eyes lit on Owen.

"Owen Mulberry!" Ally said, with a huge, easy smile. "Oh my God, hi! Got that ice cream addiction under control yet?"

Owen rose to his feet, and Beth watched the two of them hug. "Hey, Ally," he said. "I didn't realize you were around."

Beth saw Ally look at the lollipops quizzically. She couldn't stand the idea of Ally joining in on the lollipop tasting, of Ally cracking Owen up with a pitch-perfect imitation of a wine snob, of her stealing him away without even trying. "Owen," she said, her voice abrupt, "I totally forgot to ask you if you had any packing tape we could buy. Grandma Stella needs some."

"Of course," he said, and ducked into a shadowy aisle to find it. When he came back, Beth had scooped her lollipop wrappers into the trash can and already had her money out to pay. Ally stood there, her weight shifted onto one leg, her hand on her hip, and kept up an easy stream of conversation with Owen about New York.

"I'll be heading there too," Owen said, "for grad school."

"Oh good, so we can hang out!" Ally said. She grinned, showing those adorable dimples of hers. "Here, take my number."

It felt like an eternity to Beth, handing over her dollar bills and her exact change. When she gave it to Owen, their fingers touched briefly. His were so warm, like they had been soaking in sunlight. "Thank you," she said, and turned to go.

"We'll see you around, Owen," Ally said. "Grandma Stella wants to have a crazy party before she moves, and you should definitely come."

"Sounds great," he said. "Bye, Beth."

"Good-bye," she said, darting a quick, halfhearted smile in his direction.

When she and Ally closed the door behind them and reentered the cloudless day, they walked in silence for a few moments.

"So Owen got cute, huh?" Ally said. "He's kind of got that rugged lumberjack thing going on. I mean, he's not really my type. I like 'em lankier. But still, *rawr!*" She shimmied her shoulders a little bit and made a sexy face at Beth.

Beth fought a momentary urge to throw a bunch of dirt from a nearby planter on her friend's sundress. Instead she just said, "Yeah, I guess he did. His face still turns pink, though."

"Really?" Ally said, her eyes opening wide. "His face was fine the whole time I was there. Well, that settles it, then. I'm giving him to you!"

"I'm sorry, what?" Beth snapped. A crack opened up in the dam. "You're *giving* him to me?" She heard her voice coming out pinched and harsh, but she didn't care.

Ally's face fell. "Oh, no, I didn't mean—"

"How generous, Ally. What a nice little present to give your friend. And my birthday's not even for another month!"

"Beth, no, that came out wrong—"

"Oh, so he's not a birthday present? Well then thank you for your charity. I appreciate your tax-deductible donation."

"Beth! Beth, wait." Ally grabbed her arm and forced her to stop walking. "I'm sorry. That was a stupid way for me to say that. Obviously you're gorgeous and funny and all that wonderful stuff. Plenty of guys like you better than me." She let go of Beth's arm and rubbed her hand over her right temple, like she was trying to coax out the proper words. "I guess I just meant— oh, I don't know how to make this sound right—I meant that I could try to flirt with him because, you know, it's fun to flirt with cute guys, but what would be the point, because he's clearly so much better for you? And, given the face-flushing, he's clearly much more into you than me anyway. So you guys should totally fall in love. And I am an idiot. And I'm sorry. Sorry."

Watching Ally fumble, looking so completely repentant, Beth felt the clenched fist inside her start to relax its grip. Not completely, but enough for her to say, "Okay. It's fine."

Ally gave her a tentative smile, and they started walking again.

"Anyway, it's not like I need to fall in love with Owen Mulberry right now," Beth said. "That's actually the last thing I need." *So it's good that Ally came in before things went any further*, she thought. "I'm going back to Haiti, so—"

"Wait, you are?" Ally stared at her, looking more shocked than Beth had expected. "When? For how long? Like, a few months?"

"The plan right now is to take another month or two at home, and probably get started on some online classes and applications. Then I'll go back to Haiti until med school and then when med school is over, I'll just live there. Deirdre and Peter want me to work with them. They asked me before I came back to the States if I wanted to work my way toward being a third partner of Open Arms." Beth hadn't spoken out loud yet about this plan to anyone since she'd decided to say yes to it.

"Oh." Ally nodded, looking somehow even more deflated than she had when apologizing a moment ago. "Wow."

"Yup." Beth felt a strange disappointment. But then Ally turned on a smile.

"Beth, that's really exciting," she said. "A third partner? You're such a superstar."

"Thank you," Beth said.

"But wait, why didn't you tell Grandma Stella this last night?"

"Um," Beth said, "I haven't really told anyone yet. I'm still figuring out the details. And Grandma Stella already has enough to worry about with the moving stuff. I'll tell her after she's gotten to Sunny Acres. Maybe don't mention it for now?"

"Got it," Ally said. She gave Beth a searching look. "So you really liked it there in Haiti, huh?"

Beth hesitated, not sure how she could answer the question. "I did," she said finally.

"Whoa, calm down now," Ally said. "Enthusiasm overload."

"I mean, it's not really about liking, right?"

"Okay, so you *didn't* like it? Then why are you going back? You could do so many other things."

"Well, yeah, everything isn't sunshine and joy there. But if *I* don't do it, what if nobody does? That's part of the reason that there's so much inequality in this world. Nobody wants to make sacrifices. And it's just getting worse."

"Right," Ally said slowly. It seemed to Beth that she was turning over every word in her mind before she said it aloud. "But you alone don't have to make up for the sacrifices the whole world should be making."

"Well, right, of course I can't do that. But the excuses have to stop somewhere. Thinking that I'm exempt, that somebody else can pick up the slack, that's the line of thinking that leads to everybody doing nothing. We get so caught up in this happiness rhetoric, you know, the idea that the best thing for us to be doing is the thing that makes us the happiest, when maybe what we should be trying to find is the thing that doesn't make us *unhappy* while also putting the greatest amount of good in the world."

"Okay, I hear all that. But I don't know, aren't there other things you can do that help people but don't involve you giving up your whole life?"

"Working in Haiti doesn't mean I'm giving up my whole life," Beth said, adamant. This conversation was making her uncomfortable.

"Okay," Ally said. "Sorry."

They walked silently, passing their little Britton Hills landmarks. There was the ice cream shop where they'd worked that one summer. Mr. Stebbins, the owner, had painted a cartoon version of himself on the window under the pink-and-white striped awning, rotund and stern, Uncle Sam–like, with a word bubble from his mouth saying *I Want You to Eat Ice Cream!*

And there was the pizza place where they'd cried together that first summer of high school, when Ally was convinced she was too fat, and her preoccupation had infected Beth too. They'd eaten only salad for an entire week, and then broken down and gone for pizza. As they'd tearily shoveled slices into their mouths, Ally had said through the great gobs of cheese and grease and mucus, "It's just so ridiculous to not be able to eat what you want." The high schoolers Beth could see through the windows now, waiting for their lunches, looked so young, only partially formed, their limbs long and wild. The boys joked around, throwing napkins at each other, and the girls sat in the booths, giggling, whispering in one another's ears.

A block later, Beth felt Ally stiffen and slow beside her.

"What? Since when has there been a music store here?" Ally asked, walking toward a large storefront window, filled with various instruments and sheet music.

"Hooked on Tonics? I think it opened up a couple years ago. I've never actually been in," Beth said. She watched Ally stop in front of the window as if in a trance.

"Cool," Ally said, her measured voice contrasting with her shining face. "God, look at that guitar. It's gorgeous."

Beth thought the polished, dark wood of the instrument was pretty, but she wouldn't have picked it out of a crowd. Looking through the window, she could see Nick Danner, the store's owner, sitting at the counter and frowning at a magazine in front of him. "Should we go inside?"

Ally turned her head quickly. "Nah," she said, and picked up her pace.

"Hey, wait," Beth said. Seeing Ally close down like that, so rapidly, she felt a familiar sense of protectiveness. Despite her annoyance over Owen, over Haiti, she wanted to do something nice for her. So she asked, "You want to walk along the shore before we go back?"

Ally nodded.

The Britton Hills shoreline moved from harbor to rock beach to sand, finally turning to wild grass with a steep, sloping drop. Beth and Ally had loved each section in turn. Some years, they spent their time at the harbor, wandering among the brightly painted boats and making a game of pointing out the most creative names (*PB and Jellyfish* was their all-time favorite). Other years they concentrated on the rock beach, with Beth trying to teach Ally how to skip the stones. Ally was hopeless at the skipping part, but they spent hours picking up various rocks, feeling their smoothness or their jaggedness, looking at the patterns the sea had made on them. Sometimes they brought towels to the sand beach and dug their feet in, lying out in the sun for full afternoons, sitting up every couple of hours to help each other reapply sunscreen. With the wild grass, they'd stalked through like explorers in their sneakers, checking each other for ticks afterward.

And always, the ocean waited, alternately wild and coy, lapping at their feet and tumbling them around in its surf. They braved its frigidity. The fear of fully submerging themselves never quite went away, whether it was the first day of their trip or the last, so each time, they masochistically isolated the cold shock to each part of their body in turn. First, they forced their feet to feel it, then pushed themselves in up to the thigh. Then came the worst part, when the water hit the area covered by their bikini bottoms. Next, they exposed the soft lower parts of their stomachs, and then they'd finally let their legs fall out from under them and sink down completely in a blind frenzy.

Now, they slowed in the sand. Beth carefully put down the packing tape she was carrying, and the two of them just stood there, tilting their faces to the sky.

"Want to put our feet in?" Ally asked. They kicked their shoes off and walked to the water's edge. Watching a wave unfurl toward them, they braced themselves. As it hit their feet, they both gasped.

"Oh, oh, oh," Beth yelped, and dug her feet in.

"*Shit*, that's cold!" Ally said, and started bouncing up and down.

As Beth looked at her, hopping around like she was on hot coals, she began to laugh, a real, uncontrollable laugh from her stomach. Ally laughed too, with a crazy cackle, doubling over as she continued to hop. The surf leapt up and smacked her in the face, which made the both of them laugh harder. Beth wondered if she could separate this Ally from the one she'd hated the night before, the one she hated still, in that frozen part of her heart. At least until they'd finished helping Grandma Stella move, until she went away forever.

"Want to go in deeper?" she asked, and held out her hand. Ally looked over, her teeth chattering.

"Oh, what the hell," she said, and took Beth's extended hand. Together, uttering a wordless battle cry against the sea, the two of them charged forward.

SEVEN

The following morning, Ally pushed her sweaty hair out of her eyes and took a long sip of her lemonade, surveying the mess of Grandma Stella's attic. Over the past few hours, she'd carried bag after bag of junk down the narrow stairs. She navigated the steps carefully. Each one was a different height, requiring a new estimate of how high to lift your foot, as if the designer of the house wanted to break as many ankles as possible.

No wonder, she thought, that no one ever came up here. She herself had only been once before, her first summer in Britton Hills, when she'd been intent on exploring every inch of the wonderland to which Beth had brought her. Back then, she'd left the attic with an impression of claustrophobic darkness and dust, imagining mice, cobwebs, and bugs skittering in corners.

Now, she was more immune to messiness. She'd endured the

New York City subway system. Attic mice seemed cute in comparison to the mutant rats that scurried around the NYC tracks.

Although she would've rather been in bed, this wasn't a bad place in which to spend the morning. A little window let in the sunlight. The ceiling, with its exposed beams, sloped down on either end to make the whole space into a triangle. And, everywhere, even after hours of cleaning, it was littered with interesting boxes, some closed and others bursting at the tops with odds and ends. Old pieces of furniture were propped in various corners—here a beautiful torchiere, its stained-glass shade chipped at the top, there an ancient-looking rocking horse with a mane of red string. A rack of clothing stood against one of the walls. Ally put down her lemonade and rifled through the fabrics, some of which had gone stiff with age. The hanging clothes ran the gamut from Grandma Stella's old housedresses to a child-sized church suit that must once have been worn by Beth's father.

She began to sort them, laying aside the items that someone could still conceivably want, as Beth walked back up the stairs. "So I think we can do the yard sale Thursday maybe, or Saturday," Beth said. She deposited a box of garbage bags on the floor, then began to look through a box of old photos. "Friday's party day, so we should keep that clear." She continued organizing aloud, talking more to herself than to Ally, making the lists that she loved. Guilty, Ally remembered that phone call from her mom. If she went back to NYC when her mom wanted her to, she'd miss Grandma Stella's party completely. She pushed that thought aside and kept sorting, and, eventually, Beth stopped talking, studying the photos in silence.

When Ally finished with the clothing, she pushed aside a stack of old newspapers and gasped.

"What?" Beth said.

"I found something cool," Ally said, trying to keep her excitement in check. Maybe this, she thought, looking at the box in front of her, the box that she'd forgotten about until that moment, could fix the strangeness that had risen up between the two of them.

"Oh yeah?" Beth said. "I found something cool too, to show you after."

"No, you go first," Ally said.

"Okay." Beth held out a photo. "Isn't this beautiful?" she asked.

Ally walked over and grabbed the picture, then let out an involuntary "Oh!" of appreciation. In it, two women who looked to be in their midthirties sat next to each other at the beach. They wore the early sixties-style bathing suits that Ally wished were still in fashion today (she often thought how wonderful it would be to not worry about cramming her butt into a string bikini, which did nothing to disguise the little bits of cellulite that had already started dimpling her upper thighs). One woman wore a yellow one-piece with a ruched top, and the other, the one she recognized as Grandma Stella, a red bikini with white polka dots and a high-waisted bottom. Their curls blew about in the wind. They'd been captured in a moment of laughter. One woman had her arm around the other, and their faces tilted toward one another, open in glee. They looked glamorous and happy. Radiant.

"God, Grandma Stella was such a fox. Look at her rocking that bikini," Ally said. It struck her as infinitely weird, the thought that in just a few days, the carefree beauty from the photo was headed to a retirement home to live out the rest of her time in a chair, staring at a wall. She shook her head, to clear herself of the unpleasant image. "Who's that with her?"

"It must be my great-aunt Lila. I only met her a couple times before she died, 'cause she lived in Oregon, but my grandma always said that whenever Lila visited, they had the best times together."

"I can't believe that picture's just been languishing up here. Grandma Stella needs to frame it, immediately."

"Yeah. Maybe we could do it for her," Beth said. "There are a few other nice ones too." She passed Ally over a series of Stella and Lila in New York (the two of them standing in front of the Empire State Building with their heads craned up in awe, or tucked into the back of a horse-drawn carriage in Central Park), and one of a group of women at a party, Grandma Stella in the center, luminous in a chiffon dress that Ally coveted immediately. "Anyways, what did you find?"

"Okay," Ally said. "Drumroll, please." She walked back to the box and held it up. "It's the BAAB! Can you believe it?"

The Beth and Ally Box. She and Beth had started it their second summer in Britton Hills, when it became clear that Ally's presence on the Abbott family vacation was no onetime fluke.

"It'll be like a time capsule!" Ally had said.

"And the name is so perfectly palindromic!" Beth had chimed in.

Over the course of each summer visit, they'd compiled mementos to throw into the wooden box Beth's father had made them, which they'd decorated with oversized renderings of their names (in bubble letters, naturally), along with stickers of teen idols (their embarrassing crushes on Carson Daly and James Van Der Beek memorialized long after the ardor had dissipated). Movie stubs mingled with seashells. Photo strips from the booth at Murney's Arcade abounded. And, starting the summer before eighth grade, they wrote each other letters.

Each one, carefully sealed at the end of one summer and opened at the beginning of the next, had to contain at least two pieces of information: a favorite memory from the summer in question, and a prediction or wish for the other. The writing of the letters was a private event, undertaken the day before they left Britton Hills (so that they didn't feel rushed for time, trying to write them while Beth's parents waited in the car). The girls went to separate corners of the house or yard to write, and then came back together to deposit their letters in the box with a great solemnity.

"Wait," Ally said now. "We have unopened letters from each other! We should read them." The letters they'd written to each other after their sophomore year of college lay on the top of the box's contents. She pulled the one addressed to her out of the box, tore it open, and started reading aloud.

Dear Allygator,

I'm really happy we've had these two weeks together. College has been weird. It makes all our time with each other too short—a weekend here, a phone call there. I start to worry that the little details I don't get a chance to tell you are adding up into a big old book you'll never get a chance to read. But then we come here, and it's not just me narrating my life to you or you narrating yours to me. It's us living life together again. That's really important to me.

"Oh Beth," Ally broke off, looking up from the paper, "that's important to me too." This, she thought to herself, was why she had been so weird about Haiti the day before, why she'd felt that sheer terror in her stomach when Beth had announced her plans to go back. She still felt that terror. Haiti had captured Beth before, cut off her communication and buried her in a tangle of vines where Ally couldn't reach her. When she couldn't talk to Beth, her life fell apart. She didn't want Beth to go back. Beth couldn't go back, or she had a feeling she'd never see her again.

Ally went back to the letter.

Anyways, enough sappy stuff! (At least for the moment—who knows what might happen over the rest of this letter?) My favorite memory of you from this summer happened our first night here. We were talking in bed until way past both our bedtimes, and we started to fall asleep. You kept trying to fight the sleep, because there was more that we wanted to say (it's amazing, the number of stories we had saved up for each other), and eventually you just hopped out of bed and did ten jumping jacks to wake yourself up. You, half-asleep, doing exercises at three in the morning just so we could talk more? One of the many reasons I love you.

And speaking of love, here's my prediction/hope for you this year. I predict/hope that you will fall in love with a wonderful boy. It's about freaking time. You deserve someone you're 100% crazy about, not just someone who is 100% crazy about you.

Next summer (this summer? I've never figured out exactly how to qualify time for the BAAB), I hope you read this letter and think—no, not think, know—"Oh yeah, that's _____ (insert name here), my amazing boyfriend of whom Beth totally approves!"

But if not, that's clearly okay too. It will happen some-time, and until then you can just be crazy about me!

Love,
Betharoo

"Wow," Ally said when she finished reading. "Very prescient of you, Beth."

Because that year she'd met Tom, and she had been crazy—one hundred percent, certifiably insane for him, all the way until he'd broken up with her.

That breakup had destroyed her. And Beth, who was currently pulling her hair back into a braid and avoiding Ally's eyes, had never even asked about it.

ALLY was pulling her laundry out of the dryer when Tom texted to ask if he could come over. As she dragged her bag of clothes across three blocks and up four flights of stairs back to her apartment, she briefly considered putting on a fresh bra, or changing out of her sweatpants. But Tom always said that she turned him on just as much in her workout clothes as when she got all dressed up. And, she reasoned, one of the benefits of a long-term relationship was that you could be totally comfortable around the other person. She had yet to poop with the door open, but she sensed that day drawing near. Maybe when they moved in together. They'd started mentioning that possibility every so often. Only abstractly, of course, given that neither one of their leases would be up for months.

She folded her laundry and put it away as she waited for him.

She'd done it all except for matching up the socks by the time he rang her buzzer. When he knocked on the door, she gave him a quick, distracted kiss.

"Hey you," she said. "Let me just finish putting away my laundry." She kept talking over her shoulder as he followed her into her bedroom. "So guess what?" She looked down at the single striped sock in her hand, trying to figure out if the dryer had somehow eaten the other one. "Gabby and Jeff hooked up again. This is, what, the third time since she said they were definitely done forever? I owe you five bucks. I'm gonna go broke soon."

"You shouldn't take my bets on this. They're never going to stop until one of them actually starts dating someone else," he said, but he didn't say, "I knew it!" like he normally did whenever he was right about the ongoing Gabby-and-Jeff saga, and his voice seemed leached of its usual enthusiasm. She turned around and put her arms around him, twining his messy hair around her fingers.

"Hey, you okay? What's wrong?"

He kissed her, squeezing her against him tightly, but not for long. Then he sat down on her bed and stared at her comforter. "I got a job offer in Portland, Oregon."

"Wow!" she said, then, "Wait. What?" She went and sat down next to him. "I didn't realize you were applying for jobs. You know, given that you already have one."

"I'm not, really. I didn't plan on it. I just saw the posting on the alumni list, and it sounded really cool, so I thought I'd apply as a shot in the dark. I didn't think I'd get it. That's why I didn't tell you. I didn't want you to get upset over nothing."

"Well," she said slowly. "I guess it's a good ego boost. It's nice to be wanted."

"Al," he said. "You know I don't like New York that much. I can't get into the 'New York is the center of the universe' mindset that you seem to need to have here. And at Atlas they barely give me anything to do—I just move data from one spreadsheet to another, and I'm so bored. This is a start-up, and it's small, and I'd be really important there."

"New York has start-ups. New York has everything."

"I accepted the offer."

She tried to say something, but she couldn't find her voice. She was angry, angry with him for not consulting her, for unilaterally making this gigantic decision that affected them both. They were a disaster at long-distance—over the breaks at college when they'd been apart for longer than two weeks, she'd moped around in a swamp of despair. They'd eagerly scheduled Skype sessions, but the video always seemed to freeze, or somehow an awkwardness would spring up between them, lasting until they were able to see each other in person again.

"Okay," she said finally. "So, Portland. I've always thought it could be a cool place to live." She grabbed his hand. It felt a lot warmer than her own. Dimly, she registered that he wasn't really holding hers back.

"Come on," he said. "Don't move to Portland for me. You love New York. You have all the inroads you've been making with your music career here."

"What? Projected Trajectory? Please. I don't care about them. It's not like we're going anywhere as a band. I could quit, easily."

He pulled his hand away, took off his glasses, and rubbed his eyes. Then he put his glasses back on and said quietly, "No. I don't want you to move to Portland for me."

"Oh." Understanding flickered through her body. This wasn't a problem-solving session. This was a breakup. "Why not?"

"It's just . . . so big, you moving across the country for me. I'm not ready. I love you, but it just feels too soon to tie our lives together like that."

"Too soon in our relationship? We've been together almost two years."

"Too soon in my life."

He looked so unhappy as he said this, and she knew her face mirrored his in a mask of misery. She didn't know what to say, so she didn't say anything. She was about to cry, but she tried to hold off for as long as possible. She looked straight ahead at her white wall, with its posters and pictures she'd never bothered to frame, stuck up with Scotch tape. Eventually, her phone started ringing, across the room, on top of her dresser. Silently, she and Tom waited for it to stop. But as soon as it did, it began again, that stupid strumming guitar sound filling the room. Finally, the third time it happened, she got off the bed and strode over to her phone, wanting to throw it out the window or smash it on the ground and jump on it until it broke into pieces smaller than dust. But as she picked it up and saw a blocked, unknown number on the screen, the absurd thought flashed through her mind: *Maybe it's someone calling about my music career.* So reflexively, she answered it.

"Hello?" As soon as she answered the phone, she knew it was a mistake. She should've just turned it off. Tom looked at her in disbelief.

"Allygator?" The voice on the other line barely sounded like Beth's—the connection must have been bad—but no one besides Beth had ever called her that silly childhood nickname. She hesitated, considering just hanging up and pretending later that she'd lost the signal. The last thing she wanted to do right now was have a long catch-up session.

"Beth? What's up?" she said.

"Oh, Ally. I really need to talk to you—"

"Look, love, I'm so sorry, but this isn't a good time. I kinda have to go."

Beth started speaking again, saying something, but Ally didn't even hear it. She took the phone away from her ear because Tom was talking to her too and she was looking at him, at how handsome he was, thinking about how impossible it seemed that she wouldn't get to kiss him every day.

"Tell her to call you back later," Tom said, urgently, frustrated, and she couldn't believe she still had the phone in her hand. She pressed it back to her ear.

"I'm gonna go, but call me back tomorrow, maybe," she said, and hung up. She turned her phone off, opened the door, and threw it out into the hallway. Then she burst into tears. She crawled back onto the bed and curled up against Tom. He put his arms around her, and they spooned there together. He cried too (she'd only ever seen him cry one other time, when his grandfather died the year before), and when she felt his tears on the back of her neck, she said, "You don't have to do this. Are you sure you want to do this?"

"Yes," he said, muffled, into her hair.

What felt like hours later, he finally withdrew his arms from around her body. "I should go," he said.

"Wait." She pulled him back down to the bed and kissed him, then tugged off her sweatpants.

In the past when she'd had breakup sex, it had been hot, filled with a last-chance passion. But with Tom, it just made her sad, like every movement he made inside her was tearing her heart even further. She turned her head so that he wouldn't see her start to cry again. But it didn't work.

"Shit, Ally, I'm so sorry." He pulled out and drew away from her quickly, like he was scared of her sadness. From his position half off the bed, his nakedness suddenly seemed foreign.

"Just go," she said, and turned her back to him, drawing herself up into the fetal position. She squeezed her eyes shut.

"I don't want to leave you like this . . ."

"Just go!" She heard him hesitate, and then eventually, the door to her room opened and closed. As soon as she heard her front door shut too, she wished she hadn't told him to leave. She should have fought harder for their relationship and then, if that had failed, she should've at least kept him with her as long as he'd been willing to stay.

She lay there in bed awhile longer, nearly comatose, unable to believe that he'd never again lie there with her. And then, as her body ran out of tears, she needed to tell someone. Gabby would probably be home soon, but she didn't really want Gabby. The first person she wanted to talk to, the first person she *needed* to talk to, was Beth.

ALLY breathed out quickly in the hot attic air. "I'm still really sad about him," she said to Beth, inwardly chanting *ask me about it, ask me about it, ask me about it.*

"Oh yeah?" Beth replied, uncovering a pile of old magazines. Ally decided that was good enough.

"Yeah. It's like we're broken up, but not fully because he still texts me sometimes, and wants to be friendly, and sometimes I'm like, well, maybe the only reason we're not together is because he had to move away, and other times I'm like, no, idiot, he just didn't love you enough." She stared at Beth as she talked, gratified when she moved away from the magazines and sat down. She took a deep breath. She was ready to give Beth another chance to be the friend that she'd needed her to be. "And now . . . he's coming back to New York soon for a job interview, and he wants to hang out. I'm worried that seeing him again is just going to throw me into an emotional tailspin."

"He's coming back? Maybe you shouldn't see him. Make some excuse. Or tell him the truth, that you need a little break from communication."

"I don't think I can do that."

Beth sighed. "It just seems like you do the work of trying to get over him, and then he undoes all that hard work every time he contacts you. I think you need to stop talking to him for a bit."

Ally bristled at the commonsense suggestion, one she'd heard so many times before. She herself had said it to friends going through bad breakups in the past, wondering why they couldn't just do the obvious thing that would make them feel better. But she hadn't under-stood then how even limited contact with Tom could lift her out of a week's worth of feeling deadened and numb. She'd walk around at a remove from everyone and everything else, forgetting that she was fully alive, and then he'd send her a text and remind her.

"That's easier said than done," she said. "He's still really important to me. And now that he might be moving back to New York, who knows? Maybe we *will* get back together. The whole situation is just really awful."

"Okay," Beth said, starting to stand back up. "That's hard."

"I mean," Ally said, wanting to draw Beth back down to the floor with her, "I haven't been able to hook up with someone since we broke up—at least not sober— and it's been half a year."

"Wait, how many people have you been hooking up with drunk?"

"I don't know." Ally cast her mind back. "Okay, so I kissed those two guys like a week after the breakup."

"Two?"

"Yeah." Ally laughed. "I got super drunk at this bar and made out with one guy for a while, and then wandered away when I got bored of him, and made out with another."

"I'm impressed," Beth said. "I'm no good at that, going up to a random guy and kissing him."

"Oh, it's not so hard. Over the course of my painstaking research the past six months, I've discovered that most straight single guys will hook up with you if you throw yourself at them."

"Well, good for you, getting back out there. Were you interested in either of them?"

"Like for dating? God, no. They were cute enough, but I didn't really want to know anything about them."

"Ah. Okay," Beth said carefully.

"Then at Gabby's office holiday party a week or two later, I had sex with some guy in the janitor's closet."

"Whoa," Beth said, blinking rapidly. "Um, in the janitor's closet?"

"Yeah, it was nearby, and it had a lock." They'd knocked over a mop and broken a carton of lightbulbs, although she'd barely noticed at the time. She'd been so wasted that everything happening had taken on the blurriness of an Impressionist painting.

"Weren't you nervous that people would hear you?" Beth asked. "Or know what you were doing?"

"Well," Ally retorted, "I wanted to have sex with him, but I didn't want to go home with him because he could have been a murderer. So no, I was fine with the closet."

"I just feel like that's kind of risky," Beth said. "On so many levels."

"Oh, so you'd rather I go home with strangers? Well don't worry, I did that once too, and it was an awful decision."

"Ally." Beth sat down close to her. "Are you okay? What happened?"

Ally hadn't meant to bring this up. She didn't want to talk about it. "Well, nothing, really." Beth raised an eyebrow and didn't look away. "I was just blackout drunk, and we had sex and I don't remember it. It . . . it was a mistake. I shouldn't have done that. I'm not happy I did."

She'd woken up the next morning with her eye makeup smeared beneath her eyes, the unfamiliar sheets rough against her nakedness. She had no idea whether they'd used protection, and no memory at all of his name or why she'd been attracted to him. She'd hurled herself into her clothes, hoping he wouldn't wake up, and left, calling Gabby on her way to the subway. Gabby had gone with her to the pharmacy to get Plan B. Gabby had exhaled with her in relief when all her STD tests came back negative. Beth hadn't been responding to her e-mails at this point.

"Ally . . . that's rape," Beth said *rape* softly, nearly whispering it. She looked into Ally's eyes with total concentration.

"No," she said. "No. I mean, I was into it at the time. I remember being all excited leaving the bar with him. It was just the next morning I felt weird about it."

"But technically if you were really drunk you couldn't consent—"

"I'm aware of that, Beth. I've read a fucking Jezebel article. But maybe he couldn't tell I was as drunk as I was. I can appear pretty coherent when I'm wasted. So it happened, and now I just don't go home with strangers from bars. Okay?"

"Okay," Beth said. She reached her hand out and held Ally's in silence for a minute. Then she said, "If you want to talk about it—"

"I don't."

"Okay." Beth rubbed her thumb along Ally's palm. Then she asked, "But the making out, and the anonymous sex in closets, you're fine with?"

"Yeah, totally." Ally said.

"Really?"

"What?"

"I just worry that if you can't do something sober, maybe you shouldn't be doing it at all. Or not so much, anyway." Ally thought she saw a hint of Beth Superior lurking on Beth's face.

"Oh, I'm happy when I do it. I have a fucking fantastic time." She pulled her hand out of Beth's grasp. "But thanks anyway for the thorough slut-shaming." Ally felt the attic closing in on her. She needed to get away from Beth looking at her with mingled pity and judgment. She had no right to judge. If she'd bothered responding to Ally's e-mails, Ally might not have felt the overwhelming need on that lost night, the total loneliness that made her keep pouring back tequila shots until she couldn't remember anything.

"No, I didn't mean to slut-shame you," Beth said. "That's not—"

Ally stood up. "I've got to take a break from this. I'm going to walk into town." She walked toward the stairs as quickly as she could, stepping over the remains of Grandma Stella's storage cartons. She'd thought that going through the BAAB would help things. But instead, it had given her discomfort a steroid shot.

"Ally, wait," Beth said. "Come back."

Not caring that she was sweaty, not caring that she had dust on her hands, not even caring that she was wearing smelly sneakers and shorts with a gaping hole in them, Ally powered down the stairs and out the door.

EIGHT

Beth pushed herself to her feet to run after Ally. But then she looked at the mess in the attic. She'd come up to Britton Hills to help Grandma Stella, not to run after her friend. She got back to cleaning.

At least, she tried to get back to cleaning. But she kept looking at the BAAB, at the letter Ally had just read aloud and then discarded on the floor, at the unopened letter addressed to her, waiting impatiently for her eyes. When she'd brought the BAAB up to the attic, alone, the summer Ally had abandoned her, she'd thought about opening her letter, reading it by herself out of spite, but she hadn't. *We'll be back here next summer*, she had thought then. *I'll wait*.

Now, she carefully unsealed the envelope and unfolded its contents, smoothing out the paper on her leg before she let herself read it.

Beth,

Hey, lovely lady! Happy BAAB Opening Day—cue the
parades and timpani, welcoming us back to Britton Hills!
As I write this, I'm sitting under a big old tree in the sun,
just thinking how lucky I feel that you volunteered to be
my special friend back in fifth grade. What if it had been
some kid who wasn't willing to cart me along on family
vacations, or what if all their family vacations happened at
the Jersey Shore? I mean, I'd have an excellent tan, but I'd
also probably be hopelessly addicted to fried Oreos and
weigh roughly 352 pounds. What if that kid in fifth grade
had been mean, or boring, or had thought N'SYNC was
better than the Backstreet Boys? What would I have done??
    But all my sacrifices to the pagan goddess of
friendship and joy—don't worry, I didn't sacrifice any
animals—paid off when you raised your hand in class.
I'm so happy to be your friend, and every time we hang
out, I'm reminded of that fact. These past couple weeks,
I've been thinking about it lots. You do something
considerate and wonderful, and a little angel in my brain
starts bouncing around going, "Hey girl, you are lucky
to have Beth in your life!"
    So, favorite memory of you: When Murney's Arcade
was closing, and we were super-sad, and then you decided
we should organize a thank-you/good-bye potluck for Mr.
and Mrs. Murney, my brain angel went haywire. It was
really delightful to see you in your element, going around

to all the people in town to get them to contribute food and stories. And then to see Mrs. Murney at the potluck so moved that she started crying and laughing at the same time, and getting her tears and snot all over you when she hugged you, it was just confirmation that you're going to make a lot of people happy.

And that's actually my prediction for you. Since you're a total badass and got elected president of your student volunteers thingy as a rising junior—congratulations again, by the way—you're going to spend this year changing a lot of people's lives for the better, until everyone in the greater Philadelphia area is just like, "Oh yeah, Beth Abbott? She's basically the best ever." Okay, maybe that's a tad hyperbolic, but you know what I mean.

I love you more than anyone in the world. That part's not hyperbolic.

Hugs and snotty Mrs. Murney kisses,
Ally

Beth put down the letter. She ached for the Ally who had written it, and for the Beth who would have read it with Ally by her side. *That* Beth would have felt pure warmth filling her up to her hairline from Ally's words.

But this Beth, this real-life person she was now, stood up and continued to clean, thinking that everything she had done with her "student volunteers thingy" hadn't been enough. It hadn't been anything compared to Haiti.

WHEN Beth arrived in Port-au-Prince, she stepped off the airplane and into a wall of heat. As she walked from the jet bridge into the main airport, she heard faint music, a makeshift band of men playing in welcome.

Peter Allen-Fox met her at the baggage claim. He pressed his way through a crowd of taxi drivers and chauffeurs holding up name signs, waving so hard she worried his arm might pop out of its socket. He flicked a sweaty lock of sandy hair off his forehead and grabbed one of her bulging suitcases. He lifted it with an easy, fluid motion. "Let's get you back to Open Arms," he said, "so you can see where you'll be spending the next year." Together, they climbed into a pickup truck that Beth guessed had once been white.

"It should only take us about four hours. But once we get out of Port-au-Prince, the road gets real bumpy." He grinned. "Hope you don't get motion sickness!" Beth smiled back at him, momentarily at a loss for words, wondering if turning down graduate school had been the biggest mistake of her life.

She'd been deciding between three schools for English literature—all top-ten programs, all offering her generous living stipends. And yet she'd dragged her feet on deciding. It didn't feel like her calling, and more than anything else, she longed for even a feeble, dawning awareness of what she'd been put on Earth to do. Sometimes she thought she could feel it fluttering around her head, buzzing intermittently in her ear, but it proved impossible to catch. Then one day, walking aimlessly, debating the merits of Charlottesville versus New Haven, she'd wandered into a church off-campus and heard Deirdre—home in Philly for a rare vacation—speak. She'd asked the congregation for money to help build a new water purification system so that the people in the Open Arms catchment area wouldn't keep dying from drinking stagnant water and given a relatively standard speech about the horrors of poverty in Haiti. They were facts Beth thought she already knew—that Haiti was the poorest country in the Western Hemisphere, that the 2010 earthquake had dealt a crippling blow to everyone there. But as Deirdre had talked, she'd glowed, her chestnut skin suffused with certainty from within, and somehow Beth seemed to hear the facts anew, to feel the injustice of them for the first time.

At the end of her speech, Deirdre had said, "If anyone knows any idealistic kids who want to make a difference and don't mind living without indoor plumbing, please send them our way. We can always use some extra hands." That had been enough for Beth to tilt her life off its course.

Peter hadn't been exaggerating about the bumps. The central highway quickly turned into a succession of ruts and mud puddles. Beth winced each time the backs of her thighs slammed into her seat. Out the window of the truck, bits of rubble still left over from the earthquake (*still!* Beth thought, incredulous) dotted the Port-au-Prince landscape. She saw shacks, huts with tin roofs and lean-tos with roofs made of tarps, and then they left those behind. Breathtaking greenery whizzed by, alternating with views of dry, barren brown. Peter stopped twice to help pull other cars out of the ruts they'd gotten lodged in. The first time, he'd told Beth to stay put, he'd only be a minute, but when he stopped for the second car, Beth clambered out of the truck too. She stood next to Peter and they applied their shoulders to the rear of the old, rusty Nissan, pushing as the Haitian man who owned it steered it back onto an even stretch of road.

"Good karma," Peter said, winking at her, in between deep breaths. "You drive these roads enough, sooner or later it's you stuck in the mud." The Haitian man gave them mangoes, and said something emphatic to Beth in Creole. She smiled back at him, dumbly, and he threw back his head and laughed.

"*Mon blan!*" he said.

"What's '*blan*'?" she asked Peter when they got back into their truck.

"Foreigner. White foreigner, in particular," he said. "Get used to hearing it. I did."

Sherbet pinks and oranges were streaking their way across the darkening sky by the time they turned onto the dirt road leading to Open Arms. Deirdre had sent Beth a picture of the building a couple months before, tucked into the envelope with instructions on what to bring and how to prepare (items on the checklist had included all her immunizations, huge tubes of extra-strength sunscreen for her milky skin, a big flashlight, clothes she didn't mind destroying), and Beth had carefully pressed a loop of tape on the back of the picture, then stuck it on the wall next to her bed, opening her eyes to it first thing every morning. She'd looked at the picture and tried to memorize every detail of it. There was the open patch of concrete at the front where people gathered and patients waited, scattered with assorted chairs and benches. And there, the tall structure set slightly aside from the rest, where Deirdre said that Peter led the worship each Sunday. She'd thought that if she memorized the details, she'd know what to expect, but of course (she mentally smacked herself now), of course there was no real way to prepare.

Now that she was here, up close, she could see that the concrete blocks crumbled at the corners. Peter noticed her looking, and said, "I know, I know, but repairs don't exactly come in at number one on our priority list here." He led her toward the main building. Her rolling suitcase rattled an uneven drumbeat on the ground.

As she walked, Beth stared at the chairs—deck chairs, folding chairs, some covered with a light fur of rust. A few people waited on them, playing dominoes. Peter called out a hello to them as he and Beth walked by, and they waved back enthusiastically, wiggling their fingers and staring at Beth with curiosity. Peter swung open the front door, over which hung a sign. *To All in Need, We Offer*, it said in small letters and then, underneath, in a bold twisting print, *Open Arms—Bra Louvri*.

There, at a behemoth desk that looked once-removed from a tank, Deirdre sat, leaning toward the thin young Haitian woman in the chair next to her, inserting a needle into her arm. At the sound of the door, she turned her head and smiled a slow, easy smile. "Beth," she said. "Welcome! Give me just a sec."

She withdrew the needle from the woman's arm. The woman made a low sucking sound through her teeth, then said something to Deirdre in Creole. Deirdre laughed and said something back, and then stood up to her full, Amazonian height. She walked the woman to the door.

"*Na we pita*, Nathaly," she said.

"*Na we pita*, Didi," Nathaly replied. She smiled shyly at Beth and nodded her head, her braids swinging.

"The birth control shot," Deirdre said to Beth, as Nathaly walked out the door. "She's your age, and she had baby number four a few months ago." Then she reached out her Michelle

Obama arms. "All right, it's time for a proper hello." She enfolded Beth into a steely hug. Beth, sometimes stiff in hugs with people she didn't know well, leaned into the steel, and they stayed like that for a minute, until Deirdre leaned back out and said, "Let's send the next patient on in."

THE next morning, as Beth was getting dressed, she glanced over her shoulder into the clouded mirror on the wall. Eggplant-colored bruises ran down the backs of her thighs, from the car ride the day before, and she smiled at the sight of them. She pulled on long shorts over the bruises and walked out to start her day.

During those first few months at Open Arms, Beth did many things she'd never done before. She walked fifteen miles in one day to bring a basket of food to a family on a remote hillside. She checked in on patients as they recovered from the flu, back in their own homes after a couple of hours in one of Open Arms' two hospital cots. Deirdre, the half of the Allen-Fox power couple with a medical degree, taught her how to bandage a sprained ankle, and how to identify the early stages of malaria. Together, they took the car forty miles down the road to the nearest hospital and picked up supplies. Beth wrote a lot of letters soliciting money, and drove them to the nearest post office. "You're a life-saver," Deirdre always said to her as she drove off.

Peter called her up to the front of a congregation of Haitians one Sunday, after he'd finished his sermon, and asked her to read a passage she'd chosen. She looked out at everyone she'd gotten to know over the past couple of months, dressed in their Sunday finest, smiling with affection at their *blan*. There was Emmanuel, the grizzled, ancient man who had taught her how to play dominoes. There were Leila and Claire, giggly teenage girls who went everywhere together, often hand in hand, reminding her of herself and Ally. There was Jean-Claude, who played the tanbou drum and was so handsome that she had trouble looking him in the eye. She ended up focusing on Deirdre in the front pew, sitting up with the straightest posture she'd ever seen, and spoke in a voice that grew stronger and stronger as it pushed against the humid air. "Whatever is true, whatever is noble, whatever is right, whatever is pure, whatever is lovely, whatever is admirable—if anything is excellent or praiseworthy—think about such things."

Beth was gulping down the Allen-Fox Kool-Aid, and to her it tasted delicious, satisfied a thirst she hadn't been able to name. She felt useful, needed. Every night she stumbled into her narrow bed, closed her eyes, and fell asleep within seconds. No need, like in college, to turn over and over, or to count backward from one hundred. And in the mornings, no tangled sheets, no quilts pulled out from where she'd tucked them in. She awoke now in the same position in which she'd fallen asleep the night before. She imagined her body, in the dark, turning into stone, a peaceful sculpture of herself like a Buddha.

For the first time, she could see the insect buzzing in her ear and, though she couldn't fully identify its markings or redraw the filigree of its wings, she had a general sense of what it was called. She knew the genus, if not the species, and the genus was *Helping*. She thought to herself, *When I get back home, I can do more good things there, and I can be happy*. She saw herself flying back to the United States when her year in Haiti was up, carrying an invisible suitcase filled with Deirdre's unflappable efficiency and

Peter's limitless energy. How much more she'd be able to do now than before! How much she could fix, how many people she could help, armed with this adventure to which she'd said yes.

She biked to the Internet café once every couple of weeks, ten miles of gravel that turned into pavement that turned into sand, constantly afraid that her tires would pop. She sat in the hard chairs at the Internet café and sent out long group e-mails, composed in her head on the bike ride and filled with enthusiasm. She wanted to share her newfound sense of purpose, to get her readers as fired up as she was. She also sent separate e-mails to her parents, to Ally, and to Dean and Sophie, her two best friends from college. She used the Allen-Foxes' emergency phone, with its outrageous international rates, to call home. Her parents, relieved to hear her voice, put her on speakerphone, turning their declarations of love for her into far-off echoes. They missed her so much, she knew. It had been tough enough when she'd gone off to college an hour away. But now that their little baby bird had flown off to a whole new country (not to mention an impoverished and potentially very dangerous one), their empty nesting took on a whole new dimension of fear. Still, ever supportive, they cheered her on in their certainty that all they had to do was wait it out. Soon, this year would be over, and they would get her back. When she said good-bye, she heard her mom start to cry on the other end of the line.

Two weeks in, Beth called Ally. She dialed the number, one of the few she still knew by heart in the cell phone age, and drummed her fingers on the oak desktop that held the rotary phone.

Then a click, and Ally's voice, uncertain and hopeful. "Hello?"

Beth felt her own voice go uncertain and hopeful in return. "Ally?"

Ally emitted a garbled shriek. "Oh my God, it's good to hear your voice."

"I know," Beth relaxed into the phone, leaning against the desk in joy at the sound of her friend.

"How are you? How's Haiti? Tell me everything."

Beth wanted to talk forever. She wished that the phone were cordless, that she could take it into her bed and stay there for hours, listening to Ally joke and comfort and chat. "I'm really good, actually. It's crazy here—so different—but I like it. I think—"

Beth heard a muffled laugh, then Ally's voice saying, teasingly, "Stop it, you jerk."

"Ally?"

"Hey. Yeah, sorry. Tom is being a pain in the ass. Apparently now is the perfect time to tickle my kneecap." Again, the muffled sound. "Go away! I'm talking to Beth and I like her better than you."

"HELLO, BETH," Beth heard Tom shout, then an "Ouch!" as, she guessed, either he fell off the bed or Ally whacked him with a pillow.

She straightened up from her comfort slump. "Um. Hi to Tom," she said. Tom was nice. He'd been sweet to her, the one time she'd actually met him in person, when she'd gone up to visit Ally in Massachusetts the fall of their senior year.

She'd carried her backpack into Ally's single room and had realized right away that it effectively functioned as a double. She'd known from the way an Old Spice deodorant sat next to Ally's toothpaste on the top of her dresser, and from how Ally had casually picked up a pair of plaid boxers crumpled in the corner and tossed them into her hamper as she showed Beth around.

And then Tom had joined them for dinner, saying things like, "Oh, it's great to finally meet the famous Beth," things that were so kind, but that implied lots of long conversations with Ally that she'd never be a part of, and it just made her feel alone.

"Sorry, love," Ally said now, on the other end of the line. "Okay, go on. What's it like there? You said it's crazy?"

"Um, yeah, it is. Is now a bad time for you?"

"No, no, no, no! Please. I've been missing you and thinking about you. Here," and now Beth heard footsteps, then a door closing. "I'm shutting myself in the bathroom. It's just me, you, and a toilet."

So Beth told Ally everything, until she looked at the clock and realized that they'd been talking for almost an hour at $1.15 per minute. After a quick exchange of "I love yous" and "Talk soons," they hung up.

Beth was determined to keep in touch while in Haiti. She wasn't going to disappear, no matter how sore her butt felt after those Internet café bike rides.

But that was before the day Deirdre and Peter drove off to deliver malaria medicine to a cluster of families in the mountains, leaving her in charge. That was before, sitting idly at the desk in the damp stillness, she heard screaming rip apart the morning air.

NINE

Ally slammed her feet on the road into town, and her steps stirred up the heat captured by the asphalt. It shot up her legs and danced, forking itself all around her.

She'd been walking like this for only a few minutes when her cell phone buzzed. Working it out of the pocket of her shorts, she saw her mother's name on the screen. Clearly, Marsha was in one of her manic communication modes again. She slowed her angry pace ever so slightly to catch her breath before answering.

"Hey, Mom, what's up?"

"Beautiful, glorious daughter of mine, I'm not going to beat around the bush. Are you coming to New York to see me?"

"Oh, shit, Mom," Ally said, "I haven't really thought about it since we spoke. Things have just been crazy here. There's been no chance to bring it up with Beth yet." Ahead of her, she saw a figure approaching, traveling the opposite direction on the wooded road that led from Grandma Stella's house to the center of town. As he neared, she recognized Owen Mulberry. He waved at her as he passed, carrying a load of cardboard boxes, little half moons of perspiration showing in the sleeves of his neat gray T-shirt. She turned her head to watch him after they passed one another, admiring his ass in a dispassionate, impersonal way.

"All right, sweetheart," her mother said. "I'm not going to beg. I won't throw myself at your feet. But I talked to Glen and we agreed that it would be nice to get you a plane ticket just in case. That way, you don't have to worry about logistics or any of the gory details."

"Wait, you bought me a plane ticket back to New York?" Ally asked.

"Yes, the early flight out of Bangor on Thursday."

"But, Mom, I didn't tell you I was going to come."

"Well, you don't have to use it! Glen has so many miles built up, and he wants to meet you so badly, we thought we should just go ahead and have it waiting for you if you want it. If you don't use it, we won't be angry. We'll just miss you, and I'll cry."

"Oh my God," Ally sighed. "Okay, I will strongly consider it."

Marsha emitted a squeal, somehow throatier than Ally had thought squeals could be. "Do! Do consider it! Glen made the Jean-Georges reservation for Friday night. He said just take a taxi from the airport back to your place, and he'll reimburse you! Oh, I'm just dying to see you."

As trees turned to town and Ally entered the first block of shops, she stopped to smell the flowers in one of the planters that lined the sidewalk. These blossoms, rich purple something-or-others (she was no good with flower varieties), still had water droplets on their little petals. She knew that various townspeople volunteered to plant and tend the flowers, and looking up a couple planters ahead, she saw one of them making the rounds, watering with zeal. The woman—older, tall, with a birdlike thinness—wore a floppy tan hat to protect herself from the sun. As Ally got closer, she peeked into the planter. Once again, she had no idea what the flowers were called, but they were plentiful, and shockingly red.

"Wow, those are gorgeous," she said to the woman.

"Thank you!" the woman said happily, turning her head briefly to give a satisfied smile. "I worried about these babies— we've had such a cool season so far, they were holding out on me a little. But I think they've come through nicely."

"What are they called? I love them."

The woman stopped her watering and pushed back her hat, turning to Ally to answer, and that was when Ally realized who she was: Penny Joan Munson. Ally had never actually held a conversation with Penny Joan before, though she'd been aware of her for as long as she could remember. Grandma Stella generally ranted about the latest Penny Joan annoyance at least once a summer. Apparently, Penny Joan was aware of Ally too, because she squinted at her, and then, having identified her, suddenly appeared to perch on the sidewalk, ready to fly away at any minute.

"They're coreopsis. Limerock Ruby variety," she said, curt, and turned back to the planter.

"Ah," Ally said. "Would they grow well farther south too?"

"Oh yes," Penny Joan answered. She watched the water as it streamed from her watering can into the planter, and then she turned back to Ally and said quickly, "They actually do better in slightly warmer climates. Maine is probably too cold for them, but I had to try."

"Good to know," Ally said.

"Yes," Penny Joan replied. She hesitated a little, then asked, "Do you garden? Are you interested in flowers?"

"I had a basil plant on my windowsill in New York but, um, it died." Of course Ally realized that watering plants was generally the first step in keeping them alive, but sometimes it was hard to put that knowledge into practice.

"Marigolds are good starter flowers. I'd recommend those if you don't have much space and time," Penny Joan said.

"Thanks so much," Ally said. She smiled big at Penny Joan and, automatically, Penny Joan smiled back. Her smile struck Ally as familiar—the crookedness of one of her teeth, the greater-than-average amount that she opened her mouth.

"Now, excuse me. I should . . ." Penny Joan gestured vaguely toward the rest of the planters and waved her watering pot around.

"Oh, of course," Ally said, and Penny Joan hurried away, crossing to the other side of the street. Ally stared after her, her mind fitting the pieces together.

It wasn't Beth's great-aunt Lila in those photos from the attic.

Ally turned and sprinted into the closest shop. A tinkling bell announced her arrival.

"Ally! Oh my goodness, hello!" Sarabeth, the counterwoman at the knitwear store, stood up and opened her arms for a hug. The knitwear store never had many customers in the summer, so Sarabeth was always overly perky when Ally and Beth came in, starved for both attention and business.

"Hi, Sarabeth," Ally said. As Sarabeth hugged her tightly, a familiar smell emanating from her, Ally suspected that she'd taken to spiking the mug of tea she always kept on the counter.

"How the heck are you doing? You've gotten so beautiful and grown-up." Sarabeth grabbed Ally's hand and tugged her over to a display. "Here, try on some hats—"

"Thanks," Ally said. "Listen, sort of random question—do you know if Penny Joan Munson and Beth's grandma used to be friends?"

Sarabeth paused in the act of plopping a green beret on Ally's head. "Oh, you know, I haven't thought about that in forever." She frowned at the beret, then pulled it off and sorted through a pile of other options. "Let's see. Well, I know that they used to meet up every Wednesday night for dinner across the street here, at Monroe's. I'd walk by the restaurant after closing up the shop and wave to them. Yes, I remember they always sat at the same table in the window, with a bottle of Merlot and a basket of bread."

"Why did it stop?"

"Oh gosh, no idea." Sarabeth wound a puce-colored scarf around Ally's neck. "That's nice on you, right? It's still chilly here at night. You don't want to catch a cold!"

"Very pretty," Ally said. "But, sorry, do you remember *when* the dinners stopped?"

"Oh well, when Stella's husband died, they didn't have dinner that week, I know that. But of course I didn't expect that they would after such a loss. If, God forbid, Martin goes before me, I just don't know what I'll do. I've told him, I would like to die first, or we can do it at the exact same time, like in that wonderful Nicholas Sparks novel, but him leaving me here alone? No sir!"

"Did you ever see them together again?" Ally asked.

"I don't remember," Sarabeth said, adjusting a soft red winter hat on Ally's hair. Then she suddenly gasped, "Oh!"

"What?" Ally felt her whole body stiffen with anticipation.

Sarabeth pointed one finger toward Ally's nose. "That hat just looks darling! It does wonders for your complexion. I'll give you a discount, as long as you tell everyone in New York to come up here and keep me in business."

She tried a few other stores after Sarabeth's, but no one had any extra information. She ambled by Hooked on Tonics a few times, her stride slowing almost imperceptibly as she passed those full windows, calling to her with their siren song. Finally, popping the last bites of an ice cream cone she'd gotten for free from Mr. Stebbins into her mouth, she decided to go in. *Leave no stone unturned*, she thought to herself.

The store smelled wonderful, like varnish and the metallic tang of mesh on a microphone. She didn't recognize the guy at the counter, who was immersed in his magazine, scratching the scruff on his cheeks. With his eyes still cast down he said, in a voice devoid of enthusiasm, "Hey, let me know if you need help."

She decided to wait to bother him until he seemed a little less invested in his reading, and looking around, her eyes were drawn to the array of guitars on display. *Really reasonable prices*, she thought, her attention locked on a mahogany acoustic Fender. It reminded her of her own guitar, which was still underneath her bed, useless, accruing dust. She hadn't had the heart to throw it away.

"You're allowed to try it out," the guy said. "We're not a museum."

He continued looking at her, half-expectantly, tapping a pencil against his chin, so she reached out, her fingers stretching toward the guitar neck.

"Don't drop it!" he yelled sharply, and she let out a gasp, spastically drawing back her hand. He snorted, and she turned to him. Her relief expelled itself from her body in a breathless laugh.

"Don't be an asshole!" she said, smiling.

"Sorry. I'll leave you alone now," he replied, his eyes still glinting, and he sent his attention back down to the magazine— the *New Yorker*, she saw.

Shaking her head, she grabbed the guitar and sat on a nearby stool, resting it on her knee. She placed her fingers on the strings and pressed down, forming a C chord. The strings bit into the pads of her fingers, fleshy and vulnerable without the calluses she used to have. She winced at their sensitivity. The pain felt good, right, and she pressed down a little harder. *I can build these calluses up again in no time*, she thought, as she strummed a random selection of chords. As soon as she caught herself thinking it, she fanned her fingers out and curled them into a fist, cutting off the music.

"No need to stop," the guy said.

"No, it's okay. Actually—"

"You a musician?" he asked.

"I used to be. I haven't played in a while, though. I actually came in to ask you if you knew Stella Abbott or Penny Joan Munson."

"Who are they?"

"Okay," she said. "Guess not, then. Thanks." As she talked, she hung the guitar back up and started toward the door.

"Wait, lapsed musician," the guy said. "Play me a song." She hesitated, then shook her head. "Come on," he pressed. "It's the price of admission to the store."

"I didn't know stores had admission prices."

"This one does."

"You know, I'm not even sure if I remember anything. I haven't played in a really long time."

He moved out from behind the desk then and, in just a few strides, loped over to the guitar display. Standing, she could see how rangy he was, taller and leaner than he'd appeared while sitting. He looked to be in his early thirties, with a few threads of gray nestled among his dark, shaggy hair. He wore a faded brown T-shirt with Jeff Buckley's face on it. He must have owned that shirt for years. It seemed like it had been through the wash so many times that whatever shape and thickness it might have once possessed had long since been worn away. He had the slightest hint of a beer belly, but a delicate one that fit in with the skinniness of the rest of him. Attractive, she thought, in a halfhearted, aging-hipster way.

"Then just make something up," he said. "I'm bored. Already to the critics section in the *New Yorker*, and there are still so many hours left in the day."

He foisted the Fender on her and then, in response to her self-conscious protestations, grabbed one for himself. "I'll play too," he said. "But you start."

Thinking that she was tired of protesting, and that it would probably be easier to leave if she just played something and got it over with, she sat back down on the stool.

"Fine," she said. "But I'm warning you, do not get your hopes up."

He smiled a crooked smile at her. "No promises."

She took a deep breath in and heaved it out, her mind casting about for a song to play. Preperformance nerves did belly flops in her stomach.

Just play something, she instructed her fingers silently, and, obediently, they started to strum. Thankful, she switched to a second chord, one she thought might sound pretty after the first. It did sound nice, she realized, as she switched to another, then another, and then repeated the pattern over again, strumming louder. Counter Guy stared at her fingers, and then he started to move his own, picking out a melody on the strings of his guitar. It swooped delicately high, and then full and low. She stopped looking down at what she was doing and concentrated on his movements, trying to answer them with her playing. When it didn't feel like enough anymore, when she wanted to add in more harmonies, she started to hum almost without knowing it. It felt good to hum, her body vibrating from the guitar's reverberations and the noises coming from her own throat.

Then Counter Guy started to sing. "Oh, we're sitting here playing guitar," he crooned, in a rasp that she wouldn't exactly label "pleasant," but that bounced nicely against her eardrums anyways. He stopped singing and cocked his head toward her.

Quickly, she ran through rhyming possibilities—*star? par? mar?*—and then, her voice coming out easily, sang, "We haven't played very much so far."

He smiled, his eyes focused up toward the ceiling as he searched for the next line. "But you just wait, because before very long . . ."

Easy, she thought. "We'll have made up an entire song, an entire song."

They played through a few bars of just guitar, and she loved the way her whole body felt like it was dancing even though she was anchored to a stool, a big instrument weighing down her lap.

"Hello, my name is Nick," the guy sang again, starting a new verse. "Sorry that at first I was being a dick."

"Hi, Nick, my name's Ally," she answered, "and I forgive you for fucking with me." Then she slowed and, resolving the chords, sang one last time, very sweetly, "for fucking with me." He harmonized with her on the last "fucking with me," the both of them looking into each other's faces with total concentration as if they were playing a game, trying to discern the next steps simultaneously without speaking them aloud. They held out the last note. Ally cut it off. Nick added one final *cha-cha-cha* on the guitar, catching her off-guard so that she only got the last beat of it. They laughed at the nearness to improvised perfection they'd reached.

"Well, Nick-the-Dick," she said, "that was fun."

"Yes it was, Ally. Nice voice."

"Really? Thanks," she said. "You have a nice voice too."

He snorted. "Thanks. I consider myself more a guitarist-slash-drummer-slash-pianist who can carry a tune, but I'll take the compliment. We should jam more sometime. I got a makeshift, semicrap recording studio back there." He jerked his thumb toward a doorway by the drum sets.

"Wow, a semicrap recording studio? How could I resist?" Ally teased.

"Seriously, we should. You home from college or something?"

"Oh no, I graduated already. And I don't live here. I'm just visiting. I live in New York."

His face sparked with the same luminescence she'd seen when he was playing, a joy tinged with wistfulness. "Man, New York! I used to live there."

"Ah! Really? Where?"

"Lower East Side."

"Oh, I wish I could afford the Lower East Side. I'd live there in a heartbeat."

"I know, it's sick, right?" he said, talking faster than she'd heard him speak before. "So many good music places. You ever go to Arlene's Grocery? Or Rockwood? Jerky always gets guitarists so good, they'll make you weep."

"Yeah! Those places are amazing. I'd sort of like to live in them, you know, just sleep on the floor and drink all their beer for breakfast and get to see free shows every night."

He laughed. "So assuming you don't live on the floor of dirty music clubs, where you located?"

"Queens. Sunnyside. It's cheap. Why'd you come to Britton Hills? That's a big move."

The enthusiasm leached out of his face and voice. "My wife's from here, and her dad got sick so we moved to take care of him. Plus, she never wanted to stay in NYC. Too expensive, not enough space for hypothetical future kids to run around, all that shit."

For the first time, she registered the slim silver band on his left hand. She'd been too busy watching his right as it leapt from string to string while he played. She resolved to tone down the flirting.

"But hey, Britton Hills is awesome. Plus, you get to have a cool music shop." She tried to sound sincere as she said, "Hooked on Tonics!"

"I know, I know," he groaned. "It's a terrible name. My wife thought all the townies would like it, and they do, but I think it sounds like a piss-poor college a cappella group trying too hard to be witty."

She didn't have much to say to contradict him.

"So, who are you visiting in Bumblefuck, Maine?" he asked.

"Oh, my friend's grandmother. We're helping her pack up her house. I spent all morning carrying boxes down stairs. Hence the sweatiness," she said, indicating her limp hair, the slightly stained armpits of her shirt.

"You're not that sweaty."

"Thanks," she said, letting out a little laugh.

"So helping out your friend's grandma? That's nice of you."

"Well, it's nice of you to help out your father-in-law. Besides, it's also about spending time with Beth—my friend—since apparently I'm never going to see her again after this." She tried to smile to counteract the bitterness in her voice, but it hurt, just thinking about how Beth so easily could choose a life without her. She realized now that, even though Beth had stopped communicating with her, even though she'd warned herself that Britton Hills this time would feel different, she hadn't fully believed it. She'd thought that things would get back to normal. But there was no way they could when Beth was just going to disappear again. How could you want to repair something so temporary?

She didn't want to be temporary to another person. She'd been expendable to Tom (well, maybe—she still clung to the hope that their breakup was a mistake that he'd want to unmake as soon as they were in the same place again). Her father—after the divorce, he'd taken off to California, where he lived with a stiff, polite woman Ally had never really gotten to know. Throughout the rest of her childhood he'd sent regular checks to support her and Marsha, whose focus on two creative *P*s—pottery (lumpy) and poetry (abstract)—didn't do much to pay the bills. Thanks to his dot-com money, he'd been able to put Ally through college, for which she was grateful, of course. But that wasn't love, not really. He knew the highlights version of her life and didn't seem interested in anything more. And Marsha. Ally could never quite get a read on how much she mattered to her mother.

Beth had been the constant factor, the symbol that was always supposed to equal the same thing—support, stability, love. She had as good as promised it, ever since that day at the end of eighth grade. They'd gone on a field trip to a Revolutionary War battle-field with their class, the teachers doing everything in their power to kill time until the school year ended, driving on a cramped bus from Delaware into New Jersey, and Beth and Ally had, of course, been bus partners. They'd stuck together the whole day like they normally did, but on this day, Ally had been ornery. She'd turned fourteen the day before, and while a lot about her birthday had been very right (her mom had baked her a dark chocolate cake with rich icing, and Beth and some other friends had surprised her at school with balloons and little presents like lip gloss and nail polish), her dad hadn't called her. He hadn't sent a card either. He'd clearly just forgotten. It felt to her, after the divorce and his move away, like he'd halfheartedly tried to stay in her life for a couple of years, doing the requisite divorced-dad things, but now he was starting to give up. He was letting go of his duties slowly but intently, and pretty soon she'd have nothing left of him. Lit-tle things about being with him were starting to recede in her mind. The snort that crept into his laugh whenever she did some-thing he found genuinely funny, the way he fought against his natural competitiveness when they played Clue together so that she could win, these were now things that she told herself about rather than things she actually remembered experiencing.

The class had listened to a presentation from a historian Ally considered far too chipper, and they had eaten a Colonial-themed lunch of apple butter and roast beef. After everyone split up to wander around for the last hour before their buses came back to take them home, Ally had just wanted to be alone. But Beth had followed her as she walked silently into the field, chatting along about facts from the worksheet the historian had passed out, as if Ally couldn't read them herself.

"Did you see this—that nearly three hundred men died here? Oh man. And they think maybe more people would have died, but the British couldn't get some of their cannons to work . . ."

The trees around them hung heavy with mid-May blossoms, whites and pale pinks nestled among the green leaves, and the sky above them stretched out clear and uninterrupted by clouds. Birds sang to one another with lilting melodies. Ally felt like she'd stepped into the most beautiful landscape painting she'd ever seen, but the canvas was smothering her. She sat in the grass, pressed down by an invisible weight.

"It's so weird," Beth was saying as she sat down next to her, her voice drilling into Ally's ear, "that all these people died here, but now it's so beautiful, right? Kind of crazy!"

"Beth," Ally said. "Shut up."

"What?"

"You're being really freaking annoying. Shut up. I don't care about that stupid stuff. You're acting like such a big nerd." She put on a cartoon nerd's mocking voice, and said, "Oooh, isn't it pretty here even though people died?" She was being mean, like one of the popular girls, and for a second she liked seeing how Beth's face whitened and her eyes registered a deep betrayal, so

she pushed it even further and started to yell, something she'd
never done in front of Beth before. "I. DON'T. CARE. I just want
you to go away!"

But then Beth got to her feet and started to run away, and Ally
couldn't stop herself from calling out after her. "Wait—I'm sorry."

Beth whirled around. "That was really not nice of you."

"I know. I just—my dad forgot my birthday yesterday."

Slowly, Beth started back toward Ally. "Really? He forgot?
Are you sure?"

"Yeah. He didn't call or anything."

"Maybe he sent you a card, and it's late getting to you."

"I don't think so."

"That really sucks." Beth sat back down on the grass again,
not as close as she'd been sitting before.

"Sometimes I hate him."

"Well, yeah, that makes sense."

"No, but sometimes I *really* hate him. Like, like I want him
to die. Like he could just die some painful death. Be, I don't know,
bayoneted by a redcoat or something, and I wouldn't care. I would
say, 'Serves you right for leaving me.'" Ally couldn't look at Beth
as she said this. She'd never told anyone before about this ice in
her veins. "And sometimes that hate just takes over and gets bigger and bigger, and then I hate everyone."

"Even me?" Beth said in a little voice.

Ally met her eyes then and nodded, ashamed of herself. "Yes.
Even you."

"Oh."

"Don't you hate me sometimes?"

Beth considered this as Ally held her breath. Then she shook her head slowly. "No. No, I don't hate you ever. Sometimes I get really annoyed with you, but I always still love you."

"I'm sorry," Ally said. "I'm sorry I'm such a bad person. I understand if you don't want to be friends with me anymore or anything."

"I'm a bad person too sometimes," Beth said.

"No you're not. You're perfect."

"I'm not perfect." Beth looked around to see if anyone was nearby. "And sometimes I get so annoyed with acting like I am that I just want to do bad things on purpose."

"But you don't actually do them, right?"

"Well, yeah," Beth said. "Except—except last weekend when my mom and I went to the mall—we were at Isabel's Closet and there was another mom with her daughter right by us. The daughter was throwing this fit 'cause her mom said she couldn't get a skirt she wanted. And my mom turned to me and patted me on the head like I was a dog and said, 'Thank goodness for you, my good girl.' So, when she went to a different part of the store to look at the scarves, I went to the earring section and"—she fixed her gaze on Ally, worried—"I stole a pair. I just slipped them in my pocket, these little smiley face earrings. I didn't even like them that much. I threw them out when I got home—buried them in the bottom of the trash can. I just did it, I don't know, for fun or something, or because I had to." She blinked down at the ground, her face white. "I *stole* from them. I'm a criminal. So I understand if you don't want to be friends with *me*."

"But I do," Ally said, and grabbed Beth's hand. They lay back with their heads against the grass and stared at the sky until Ms. Mandrino blew the whistle, summoning them back to the buses.

Something had shifted between them that day. They'd been

best friends before, but now they were more than that. Ally had shown a secret, unlovable part of herself to Beth, and Beth had shown her own in turn. And they'd looked at these half-formed shames and said, "Okay. I love you anyway." So Ally had thought nothing could change that.

But now it *had* changed, and figuring out how to switch it back, now that the givens of her life had mutated on her, felt insurmountably difficult.

She could feel Nick looking at her. "Well, if you can tear yourself away from your friend, come here and we'll write songs," he said, calling her back to her stool.

She smiled at him. "Maybe I will," she said.

TEN

Beth yanked herself back to the attic, hurtling across the ocean to rest on Grandma Stella's floor. She didn't want to think about that morning at Open Arms, not now. Instead, she finished cleaning like someone hopped up on speed. Not that she knew what that felt like. She'd never considered doing drugs. Even alcohol sometimes made her nervous. She worried at the way it coursed through her body, leaving a looseness that convinced her she could sleep for an entire day or dance for an entire night. She only thought about herself and what she wanted when her body unknotted itself like that.

She swept the last of the cobwebs out of the attic, now cleared of everything except the BAAB, the pictures of Grandma Stella, and an old dark wood picture frame she'd found in a dusty box. Then she grabbed the beach picture, of Stella and Lila radiant in their bathing suits, and fit it into the frame. She marched downstairs, stepping over the rejected odds and ends encased in their trash bags, and walked into the kitchen.

"Cleaning's done," she trilled. "I'll drive over to the dump in just a little bit, so the trash won't be in the way for your party."

"You're a lifesaver!" Grandma Stella replied from her seat at the kitchen table.

"Oh, no, I'm not."

"Yes, you are. You're my angel, my sweet, sweet doll! Now take a break." Grandma Stella patted the chair next to her, and Beth came and sat down.

"I have a surprise for you. Ally and I found this in the attic and thought you might like to take it with you to Sunny Acres." She pulled the photo out from behind her back and set it on the table.

"Oh?" Grandma Stella said, her face filled with love as she looked at Beth. Then she leaned forward to see the photo. Her eyes focused on it, and her smile drained away. Beth waited for exclamations of joy, but they didn't come.

Finally, after a few seconds, Grandma Stella said, "That's nice."

"It's such a lovely photo," Beth said. "You both look beautiful." Grandma Stella shot her a wary look, one that Beth wasn't used to seeing, so Beth kept talking. "I don't think I've seen pictures of her that age before. Lila, I mean."

Grandma Stella let out a quick exhale when Beth said Lila's name. "Oh. Yes," she said. Then she stood up and headed over to the refrigerator, burying her face inside it. "Thank you. Now, do you want something to eat? I have oranges so juicy, you'll think you hopped in a swimming pool."

"No, I'm fine," Beth said, remaining at the table. She looked at the photo again, then at her grandmother's stiffened back. She walked up to join her at the fridge. "I really don't need any—"

The sight of Grandma Stella's face cut off the rest of her sentence prematurely. Her eyes were wet and red, and she was biting her lip as if doing so could prevent her eyes from getting any wetter and redder than they already were.

"Oh," Beth said. "I'm so sorry. I thought you'd like it."

"No, no, I do." Grandma Stella dabbed at her eyes with her pointer finger, then blinked rapidly. "I guess I just miss her." She let out a deep breath and gave Beth a half smile. "Now, are you sure I can't feed you?"

Just then, someone rapped on the door. Grandma Stella scooted off to answer it. A few moments later, Beth heard her chatting excitedly as she led the visitor into the kitchen.

"Beth, darling, look who it is!" she said. She seemed to have shaken off her prior distress as she tugged Owen Mulberry by the hand. His hand, callused and strong, nearly swallowed hers whole. She moved her eyebrow up and down in a lascivious wiggle meant only for Beth, but Owen had no trouble seeing it. He bit down on his lip to keep from laughing.

Beth felt like the air-conditioning had decided to take a lunch break. All of a sudden, she was far too hot. "Hi, Owen," she said.

"Hi, Beth." He smiled a colossal smile. Grandma Stella looked back and forth between the two of them like a hyped-up Jack Russell, and Beth remembered that, generally, in a conversation, a person was supposed to say something.

"What are you doing here?" she asked. He held up some flattened cardboard boxes.

"I thought you might need these to go along with your packing tape. We have a bunch of extra cartons sitting around the store."

"Oh. Thank you. That's really thoughtful of you."

Grandma Stella chimed in. "Coming all this way, when it's so warm outside! Owen, that's over a thirty-minute walk."

"Well, Grandma," Beth said, "I think Owen probably walks a bit faster than you do."

Grandma Stella nodded approvingly at Owen. "Yes, long legs," she said, admiring them shamelessly. "And you seem very athletic. I bet you can lift heavy things!" Again, Owen bit down on his lip and made eye contact with Beth, who stuck her knuckle in her mouth and put her teeth on it, hard, stifling the breathless laugh that often betrayed her in moments of embarrassment.

"How long did it take you to walk?" Grandma Stella pressed.

"Oh, I don't know. Fifteen, twenty minutes?"

"Owen!" Grandma Stella clapped her hands together and widened her eyes, as though he'd just told her he'd saved the lives of a thousand kittens and would be giving her the cutest one. "That's so fast! You must be thirsty. Lemonade? Ice water? I think I have cold white wine around here somewhere, and you should know that I don't offer my good wine to just *anyone*."

"Please, I'm fine," he said. "Actually, do you mind if I use your bathroom?"

"Of course, of course, of course! Any time you want it, my bathroom is yours," Grandma Stella replied, and gave him some effusive directions on how to navigate the fifteen feet to the toilet. He stepped out of the kitchen. Grandma Stella waited about three seconds, then turned to Beth.

"He is so handsome," she stage-whispered, beaming. "And I

think he likes you! Well, why wouldn't he? He's smart, that's what he is. Smart and handsome. And a fast walker!"

Without warning, irritation cut into Beth, irritation at Grandma Stella's blithe matchmaking, at Owen's unthinking certainty that he could bring over some cardboard boxes and complicate her life. She hated her own body for the way her blood started humming the moment he appeared in Grandma Stella's kitchen, making her flush. With her body acting like that, it was difficult to remember that she had important things to do far away from Britton Hills, duties that she could force herself to do much more easily if she didn't fall in love, or in crazy lust, or whatever you could call this novel, overwhelming sensation.

So when Owen came back from the bathroom and asked about all the trash in the hallway, and Grandma Stella said, "Oh, Beth is taking it to the dump. It's certainly a lot for one person to handle, even if she is as capable as my granddaughter," and Owen offered to drive with her to help, she knew she should say no. She opened her mouth to do just that, as politely as possible, but Grandma Stella cut in.

"Owen Mulberry, your parents have raised you right! What a nice offer. This will make it go so much quicker, don't you think so, Beth?"

Grandma Stella's car had a bigger trunk than Beth's. At first, Grandma Stella fretted about letting them take it. "Oh, but you'll have to bring it back by two," she said, "because someone's coming to look at it. What if you want to stay out longer? Maybe you should take yours instead." But Beth insisted that they needed the extra room, so she and Owen swung the trash bags into Grandma Stella's car and climbed in.

Beth buckled her seat belt, checked her mirrors, and resolved to keep things friendly. It helped when she concentrated on the smell of a particularly rank bag of trash Grandma Stella had asked them to take, filled with the remains of last night's seafood dinner. On the way to the dump, they talked about nothing things. Beth brought up the weather at one point. Owen fiddled with the radio, eventually settling on an oldies station playing Hall and Oates.

As they pulled into the dump and opened the trunk, Beth silently congratulated herself for staying removed, aloof. Then she and Owen reached for the seafood bag at the same time and, as they both tried to pull it to their respective chests, she thought, *No, we're too close*. She was about to let go when a hole in the bag split fully open. Day-old lobster juice, gnawed corncobs, and splintery cracked shells spilled out all over them, and for a moment they simply stared at each other, unsure of what exactly had happened.

Then the smell, now free of the bag's shield, hit their noses simultaneously, and they recoiled, dropping the torn plastic on the ground.

"Oh, ugh!" Beth said, half laughing.

"That's appetizing," Owen said, shaking some of the trash off the front of his shirt. He looked at her and laughed, a laugh he tried to politely stifle halfway through. "You, uh, there's a lobster claw trying to get a little friendly with you."

She cast her eyes down over her body and noticed the lobster claw perched right on her breast, stuck there as if magnetized. Hurriedly, she flicked it off. "Sorry, lobster. Take me to dinner first," she tried to joke, and then she kicked herself for even bringing up the subject of dating. "I guess we should just push this onto the trash pile? And then we can figure out what to do about getting clean," she went on, indicating the bag's debris all over the ground. Quickly, with their feet, they shuffled it away.

"Bet you weren't expecting to get a garbage shower when you volunteered to help me out." Her exposed skin felt slimy, and she wiggled her shoe to dislodge a stubborn peach pit. Even better, she thought, to be covered in garbage around him. Any air of mystery and romance had officially been destroyed.

"Are you kidding? It's the only reason I offered! For an environmental nerd, visiting a dump is generally a pretty depressing prospect," he said. Then he hesitated. "Actually, uh, I wasn't going to say this 'cause I was hoping you would find me devastatingly cool and attractive, but that's clearly gone out the window so I might as well, because it has been driving me crazy. Can we *please* separate your grandma's recyclable material from the rest of the trash?"

"What?" Beth stared at him, and he turned pink again.

"I just—Britton Hills is so terrible about recycling, and I've tried talking to the town council about starting a recycling program, but they say it's too expensive and there's not enough interest."

"But wait, if there's no recycling program, then what are you going to do with the stuff if we separate it?"

He looked down. "Um, I've been driving over to Hancock every Saturday to drop off my family's stuff and stuff from the store at their recycling center there, since it's the closest one. So I'll bring this along next time I go. I know it's kind of weird. And the gas I use driving over there probably almost negates the positive effect I'm having. I just really hate seeing stuff that could be reused sitting on a trash pile forever, taking up space, and I feel like I have to do something."

"I don't think it's weird," she said. At that moment, she was almost overwhelmed by how much she liked him, as he stood there, a little embarrassed but firm in his belief that he had to try to save the world. "Of course we should separate it."

Together they knelt down and rooted through the trash bags, pulling out anything plastic or paper. Almost immediately, Beth's whole arm felt sticky, but the trash smell ceased to bother her. Owen, on the other hand, squinted at the trash as he sorted it, his nose wrinkling. She couldn't help laughing.

"What?" he asked.

"Your face," she said, and demonstrated, mirroring him.

"I'm sorry we can't all be as calm and collected as you when reaching into trash bags," he said, faux-offended. "Tell me the truth—you've got to be a secret Dumpster diver or something."

"Hah. No Dumpster diving for me. But Haiti isn't exactly the cleanest place in the world, so I've experienced worse."

"Haiti, huh? I'd like to hear about that." She didn't say anything, just moved a sheaf of magazines from one bag to another as she tried to figure out what she wanted to tell him. "I mean, if you'd like to talk about it."

"Yeah, I think it's a longer conversation. Maybe not right now."

"Okay." They finished sorting and turned back toward the car, bags full of recycling in hand.

"Oh no, we're going to stink up Grandma Stella's car," Beth said. "And someone's finally coming to look at it this afternoon, 'cause it makes no sense for her to have it at the retirement home. Shoot."

"Hey, we're not too far away from Carvey's Pond," Owen said. "I'd guess half a mile, a mile, maybe. Want to run over there and jump in to clean off? It's much better to smell like pond than like rotting shellfish."

"All right, let's do it," she said.

They jogged over to the pond, silent except for their breathing and the thuds of their sneakers on grass. The sun on her face felt like something out of an advertisement for a perfect day. As they straggled up to the top of a hill, the pond came into view ahead of them, their salvation from stinkiness. Owen let out a yell, suddenly boyish.

"Race you the last bit," he called. He powered down the hill and plowed straight into the water, spray arcing up on either side of him. Caught off-guard, Beth lagged behind. When she reached the pond too and sank completely down into it, the water blissfully cool, he turned to her and smiled.

"Looks like I beat you."

"I didn't know we were racing, cheater! I'll get you on the way back."

"Are you sure about that? Your own grandmother vouched for my speed and my strength, so I think I'm going to win again." Jokingly, he flexed, and Beth found herself temporarily distracted by the way his arm hair glinted golden in the sunlight. Water droplets clung to his muscles, slowly streaking along his skin.

"Uh. Yeah. Yes. I'm sure," she said lamely.

He laughed. "You're gonna have to step up your smack-talking. The only thing you've convinced me of is that I'm going to be leaving you behind in the dust."

"Hey! Not going to happen. I'm ruthless," she said, and to prove it, she splashed him. The water, more than she had intended, temporarily blocked him from her view, and when he reemerged into her sight, he was shaking his head side to side, his face a perfect mixture of outrage and joy.

"Oh, you are in for it," he said, and launched into a counterattack. She screamed and tried to swim out of range, and he followed. They circled each other warily, panting, then slapped at the water simultaneously, great jets of it spraying into the air and at each other. As she ducked and attacked, shrieking and giggling, Beth realized that she'd spent more time being goofy in the past few days than in the entirety of the last year. "Okay, okay," she said, and held up her hands, palms toward Owen. She backed out of the water and lay back on the grass, letting the sun dry her body and clothes. Owen scrambled onto the grass beside her and set himself down less than a foot away. She could sense the warmth rising off him, the air carrying it from his body to hers.

"I never thought I'd say this, but I'm glad that trash bag covered us in crap," he said. He stretched his hand out so the side of his pinky touched the side of hers. The entirety of Beth's attention shot to her little finger, an infinite amount of sensation and awareness concentrating itself in one tiny digit. Owen moved his hand over farther so it laced completely with hers. She allowed herself two seconds of that sweetness, then pulled away, jumping to her feet.

"I'm going to win," she said, and started running. She heard his feet behind her. They ran through the high grass, crickets and bumblebees singing whispery insect songs around them as their legs swished along. Beth put thoughts of Haiti and obligation and attraction out of her mind and just focused on breathing, on lifting her feet up and over. Her calves started to ache. Owen pulled ahead, just slightly. The dump appeared, and Owen shouted back at her, "First one to touch the car!"

She ignored her body's complaints and pushed it faster, letting the pain embrace her. She changed the pain from her enemy to her partner, and they worked together in a beautiful symbiosis. Just fifty feet more, then twenty, then ten, and she passed Owen, running straight to the side of the car and slapping it hard.

Her breath expelled itself in a *whoosh* from her body, and she hurled her arms up toward the sky. "I won! I won!" she crowed. "Bow down to the champion!"

Owen threw himself on the ground in front of her. "Ah, Beth," he gasped in defeat, "you superior goddess, you are the fastest lady in the world and I am not even worthy to kiss the ground at your feet."

"Oh shush," she laughed, pulling him up, and then, before she even quite knew what was happening, his lips were on hers, full and warm, and she was returning the kiss, her whole body alight with the sun and with him. They drew in deep, shuddering breaths, and he wrapped his arms around her, his fingers tangling in her hair. She pressed herself into him and he pressed back, the great expanse of trash around them disappearing. She could have stayed like that forever.

A horn honked, startling them apart. An old man with about four teeth leaned out the window of his pickup truck and screeched, "Hey, lovebirds! Move your car. I gotta dump my crap."

Half-chastised, half-delighted, they hustled into the car, calling out apologies to him as they buckled their seat belts. Beth started driving, and as they moved down the dirt pathway from the dump to the main road, they imitated him. Beth felt lightheaded. Time seemed to be *whoosh*ing by at twice its normal speed. Her heart thudded heavily, and she wasn't sure whether it was from the running, or from how completely happy she felt.

"Hey, lovebirds!" Owen called out in a high-pitched voice.

"Quit your necking! I'm a busy man," Beth quavered, and giggled.

They calmed their hysterics, and in a pause from her laughter, Beth thought to herself, *Oh no. What have I done? This was not supposed to happen.*

Owen rubbed away tears of laughter from his eyes. "Young lady, I want to take you on a date," he said, still in the screechy voice.

"Ha-ha, old man," she said.

"No, but really," Owen said, his voice suddenly serious. "I would like to do that, very much."

Beth panicked. "I might be too busy helping Grandma Stella pack up," she said. "There's so much to do, and I'm not around for very long."

"Oh. Okay," Owen said. There was an uncomfortable silence. "Beth, if you don't want to go out with me, you can just tell me so. I can leave you alone, but I'm getting a lot of mixed signals from you. I'm confused here."

Beth pulled the car over to the side of the path and turned it off. The kiss had changed things. She was tired of herself, of her evasions that accomplished nothing.

"This isn't me," she said, angling in her seat toward him.

"What isn't you?"

"I can't be a silly, splashing girl."

"I don't think you're silly," he said. "Or, well, maybe sometimes, but in a good way."

"I don't normally sit around tasting lollipops and making fun of old men and having dance parties all day."

"Wait, having dance parties?"

She kept talking, quickly, the jumble of words fighting each other to exit her mouth. "I like doing all this stuff, I do, I really do, and that kiss was, well, it was amazing—"

"I agree."

"But I've made a commitment to go back to Haiti. Because I can't live in a world filled with such inequality and sadness, and not do my best to try and fix it." He was looking at her, his eyes grayer than ever in the day's brightness. He had long, light lashes. "Like how you feel about the recycling, I think. Recognizing that you probably won't make much of a difference, but that you have to try anyway. So my life is not going to be able to include a lot of this fun, silly stuff."

"Okay," he said. "First off, I think it's awesome that you're going to do good stuff for the world in Haiti, if that's what you want."

"Thank you."

"But are you saying that spending time with me is silly and pointless? 'Cause that makes me feel kind of bummed."

"No, no, no, I'm not trying to say that. It's not that being with you is silly, it's that it's something that's totally for myself. And I like it so much that I could start only wanting to do things that make me happy, and then I'll never end up helping other people the way I think I should. No, not think. Know. The way that I *know* I should. What if I get sucked into it, and then realize that all these years have gone by, and I haven't done anything with my life except amuse myself?"

"Would that be so terrible? What if it's just as bad to be bored with your life?"

"Oh, I'm not bored in Haiti. I'm just—" She stopped herself, aware that she'd been about to say *miserable*.

"Just what?"

"I don't know." She couldn't dwell on the word that had danced, unbidden, to the tip of her tongue. "Anyway, given the circumstances, and the fact that I'm not really a one-night-stand or even a one-week-stand kind of person, I think it's best to say no to a date. I'm sorry."

"You don't have to apologize," he said.

She turned the car on again and drove back along the main road. They sat quietly. He gave her brief directions to his house. She dropped him off and thanked him for his help. He got out of the car, the bags of recycling clanking in his hands, and started to shut the door. Then he stopped himself, and leaned his head back in.

"Have dinner with me," he said, "as friends."

She stared at him, taken aback. "Um, I think that's a bad idea."

"I won't offer to pay for your meal. And I promise I won't try to kiss you." He held up his fingers in the scout's-honor salute, and she felt certain that he'd been the most adorable Boy Scout in the world. "But I like you, and while you're still in this country, before you begin your grand renunciation of silliness and fun, I'd rather hang out as friends than not at all."

"I— When? Where?"

"Tomorrow night. Meet me in front of Mulberry's at six."

She tried to corral the goofy smile yanking her lips upward, but it was too strong for her. "Fine," she said. "No romance."

"Okay," he said. "It's a friend date." Then he shut the door and walked up the driveway to his house, carrying the bulky recycling bags effortlessly.

She put her head on the steering wheel for a minute, took some deep breaths, and then drove back to Grandma Stella's, barely seeing the road (which was blessedly devoid of traffic). As she pulled into the driveway and got out of the car, Ally opened the front door and ran out to her, her big eyes bright, her anger from before replaced by what seemed like anticipation.

"There you are!" Ally said. "I have something I really need to tell you."

Beth walked straight up to Ally and leaned into her, holding on for dear life. "Oh, Ally," she said, "I'm so confused."

ELEVEN

No, no, I told you that you could review a movie for adults, *not* an adult movie! This is a family newspaper, goddammit! I won't run it!" August Niederbacher, roly-poly editor and owner of the *Britton Hills Bugle*, slammed down his telephone and turned to Ally and Beth as they walked through the door of the *Bugle* headquarters. "Good afternoon," he said, suddenly formal. "How may I help you?"

"Is Valerie around?" Ally asked.

"Right in there," he said. He pointed toward a door in the wall, with a sign posted on it that said *Home of Britton Hills' Favorite Advice Column* and, underneath, a gold plaque with the name Valerie Niederbacher. (Ally suspected nepotism played a large part in *Dear Valerie*'s continued existence.)

"Thanks so much," Beth said, and together they walked over to the door and gave it a knock.

When Ally had told Beth about her Penny Joan Munson discovery, and Beth had shared Grandma Stella's comment about missing the woman in the photo, they'd sat in perplexed silence for a moment.

Then Ally had blurted, "We need to get them back together!" She'd realized immediately after she said it how childish she sounded, so she said, rolling her eyes, "Coming soon, direct to DVD, *The Parent Trap 2: Ally and Beth Reunite Two Old Ladies*."

"Right," Beth said. "And in a side plot, we'll set up our homeroom teacher with Mr. Martin from eighth-grade algebra, because they're just *so* perfect for each other."

"The *New York Times* calls it 'an insipid successor to the Lindsay Lohan remake!'"

They'd laughed together at the ridiculousness of the idea, but as her giggles subsided, Ally found herself surprised by how much she actually wanted to do it.

"I mean, we *could*—" she started to say, right as Beth began talking too.

"But what if we *tried*—" They had both stopped talking and stared at each other, then smiled.

"For Grandma Stella's sake . . ." Beth said. So they'd come up with a plan.

Now, from the other side of the door, a choked voice called out, "Oh . . . yes, come in."

Ally pushed the door open. Valerie sat behind a desk, frantically dabbing at her eyes with a tissue.

"Oh, I'm so sorry—should we come back?" Beth asked.

"No, no, please!" Valerie said, struggling to her feet and coming around to greet them. "Elizabeth, Allison, it's marvelous to see you." She gave them both kisses on the cheek, then sniffed loudly.

"Are you all right?" Ally asked, hyperaware of the wetness Valerie's kiss had left behind on her cheek.

"Oh yes, yes, I was just watching the most wonderful video," Valerie said, heading back to her desk chair and gesturing at her computer. "It's a—have you heard of—there are these things called flash mobs, and oh, they're so romantic. Have you ever seen one?"

Ally smirked and tried to catch Beth's eye, but Beth was watching Valerie with a pleasant smile and nodding.

"This one—" Valerie paused to blow her nose into the tissue. "It's a marriage proposal. The couple just met four months ago. He found her lost wallet. Isn't that just kismet? They knew right away that they wanted to be together for the rest of their lives. And he took her to their favorite spot—the loveliest park you've ever seen—and they were just sitting there on a bench, and"—here she started to tear up again, and her words got slower, incredulous—"she thought they were just *having—a—picnic*. I'm sorry." She stopped to wipe her eyes again. "Well, just watch. I'll start it over from the beginning."

So Ally and Beth walked behind her desk too, and bent down to watch the video over her shoulder. An ordinary-looking couple, Ally thought, sat on an ordinary-looking bench, and then a Nickelback song began playing. Other parkgoers got up and started to dance, surrounding the couple, and then the man got down on one knee. In her head, Ally thought of all the snarky comments she could make to Beth later, things about how she'd seen better dancing in an elementary school play, about how she felt sorry for anyone whose fiancé chose to mark an important life moment with Nickelback, about how the woman being proposed to was perhaps the definitive textbook case of an ugly crier. Again, she tried to catch Beth's eye, to make a sort of *Is Valerie serious?* face, but Beth was watching the video with total concentration for the whole, interminable five minutes it took to finish.

"Wow," Ally said when it finally faded to black.

"Beautiful," said Beth.

"I know. Let me just write a comment," Valerie said. She typed quickly, with a loud clacking, *A lifetime of joy to the both of you. I've never seen such a beautiful couple! You are destined for happiness, I just know it!! I hope someday I can find a love like the two of you share!!!*

She submitted it. "All right," she said, taking a deep breath and shaking her shoulders as she let it out. "Sit! Sit! Oh, wait, let me clear off—there's so much mess, just one second." She pulled over a flowered armchair so that it faced her own seat across the desk, then lifted a stack of romance novels off an ottoman. With the pile of books clutched to her chest, she used one foot to nudge the otto-man over next to the armchair, and then carefully placed the books down on the windowsill. Ally caught flashes of some of the covers— a man in pirate regalia, a woman in a gown fetchingly falling off her shoulders. She squinted at one with a bunch of cats pictured under the title *CAT-tastrophe in the Old Hotel* and wondered if that was a romance novel too, then tried to figure out if she could surreptitiously take a picture of it on her phone and send it to Gabby, since Beth still wasn't meeting her eyes.

"Go ahead, please, sit!" Valerie said, so she took the armchair.

Beth was already perched on the ottoman, leaning forward, her hands folded neatly in her lap. "What can I do for you two? I'm thrilled to see you."

"It's so nice to see you too," Beth said. "Actually, we're here to ask for your help."

"Of course!" Valerie said, her face overtaken by a smile. Her tears had smudged her mascara down underneath her eyes, which combined with her sharp little nose, made Ally feel like she was talking to a middle-aged raccoon. "Anything!"

"Well," Beth began. "As you know, my grandmother is leaving Britton Hills soon—"

"Oh, I *do* know! I can't believe it. It's hard to imagine this town without her. The going-away party sounds like it will be a bit of excitement, though."

"Good! We're glad you're coming," Ally said. She really wanted to reach over and wipe away Valerie's mascara puddles.

"I was thinking of bringing my deviled eggs. Do you think she might like them?" Valerie asked, looking worried. "I've been told they're very good."

"That would be wonderful, thank you," Beth said, and Valerie gave a relieved sigh. "So, the reason we're here is that we were going through her stuff to help her pack, and we found this letter. It looks like she was too afraid to send it to you." Here, Beth put a letter down on Valerie's desk. Valerie gasped, snatched it, and read it, silently mouthing some of the words as she did so. Ally had to stop herself from mouthing the words along with her. She nearly had it memorized after she and Beth had so carefully composed it.

Dear Valerie,

I'm worried that I'll never have a chance to reunite with my former best friend, and it's tearing me up inside. For a long time, we were incredibly special to each other. We always made time, no matter what, to meet up every Wednesday night at Monroe's for dinner. But then it all went wrong, and now we haven't spoken for years. One of us will be leaving Britton Hills very soon, and I fear that we won't ever see each other again. I want to reach out to her, to tell her how much I still care about her, though I may outwardly pretend otherwise. But I'm nervous that she doesn't feel the same way, and that she won't be able to forgive me for the long years of silence. The thought of showing up at her door to apologize terrifies me. What should I do, Valerie? I know she reads your advice column. Part of me hopes she sees this letter and lets me know that she still cares about me too, but just hoping for that feels like the coward's way out.

Sincerely,
Fearful Former Friend

"Oh dear," Valerie said, when she'd finishing reading. "How sad. How terribly sad to think of Stella, so afraid and so lonely. You never can tell about people. Of course I'll help. I'll write an answer now! Oh, I'm just bursting with ideas! 'FFF, Confront your fear head-on!' Maybe I'll encourage her to take out a full-page advertisement for an apology note. I could send over a photographer to take a picture of her looking really penitent, and I'm sure I could convince my brother to put it on the front page. Ooh, or what if she arranged for a hot-air balloon ride . . ." She reached out her hands and indicated that both girls should take them. They did, and she gave their palms a squeeze. "This is exciting," she said. "Don't worry about a thing, because I am going to fix it all up!"

"Valerie, that's so kind of you," Beth said, finally looking over at Ally.

Ally interjected quickly. "But actually, we were wondering if you'd print a response we'd written."

Valerie blinked, and withdrew her hands. "Oh. I—I'm sorry, what?"

"Well," Ally continued, "we came up with this idea that we think will really work, so we went ahead and wrote a letter, and thought it would be nice and easy for you to just print that. Here, I'll read it to you."

Dear FFF,

Oh, honey, I understand! It can be very scary to put yourself in a vulnerable emotional situation. But I'll think you'll be kicking yourself forever if you don't say anything to her. So speaking of kicking, I'm here to give you the kick in the pants you need. As I write this, I'm making a reservation for Monroe's tonight at 6 pm, two people, center front table, because, after all, it's Wednesday! Go, enjoy a bottle of Merlot on me, and talk it out with your friend. I'm sure she is just as fearful as you are. (FFF's friend—if you're

44444444444444

*reading this, which I assume you are, you'd better show
up!) Turn that Former Friendship into a Fixed Friendship!*

As always,
Valerie

When she finished reading the letter, she looked at Valerie expectantly. Valerie was focusing on the tissue in her hands, twisting it tightly, so Ally couldn't see her face. Nobody was saying anything.

"So," Ally said, "we hoped you could run it Wednesday morning. Thoughts?"

"That's a very sweet idea," Valerie said. Finally, she looked up and briefly met Ally's eye, blinking rapidly.

Ally's stomach dropped when she saw Valerie's face. All the hope and purpose of a few moments ago had drained away. Now Valerie only looked wounded. She'd understood perfectly why they'd written the letter themselves. Suddenly, Ally felt the terror of thinking that you'd made a life for yourself producing something of quality, only to have the world nonchalantly tell you that it was shit. She thought how heartbreaking it would be to try as fully and deeply as you could, and then to have nothing but fluff come out. She could so easily turn into Valerie, in another universe.

And then she wondered if maybe it wasn't only another universe, but this universe. Maybe none of the songs she had written were as laughable as Valerie's column. Maybe they didn't lend themselves as easily to derision. But were they actually any better? And then with the documentary—she hadn't even turned on the camera yet. At least Valerie tried, and followed through.

She wanted to rewind time to before she'd let Valerie know

- 162 -

what they really thought of her. Given that time manipulation was out of her wheelhouse, she thought about slinking out the door instead, running back to Grandma Stella's, and getting into bed.

Then she felt Beth's hand grab her own, squeezing gently. It anchored her.

"You know," Beth said. "Hearing what we wrote aloud—I think we got a little carried away. Don't you think so, Ally?"

"Yes," Ally said. "Totally carried away. I don't know what we were thinking."

"We wanted so much to help Grandma Stella, so we came up with the idea, and then just ran with it," Beth said. "But obviously we don't have your experience, so I think it lacks the spark of your real letters."

"You don't have to say that," Valerie said. "It's just as good as anything I could do. Better, even." She gave them a smile so weak it threatened to droop into a frown at any second. "Maybe the two of you should take over for me. Ha-ha."

"I'm sorry," Beth said. "But that's crazy. Do you seriously think this is as good as what you do?"

"Yes." She tossed the tissue toward the trash can, and missed.

"Well, try telling that to all the people you've helped, which must be about half of the Britton Hills population at this point." Beth was getting passionate now, speaking with an urgency that Ally couldn't look away from. "Try telling that to me, two summers ago, when I was feeling like total garbage, and I wrote in to you not really expecting anything, and then you helped me turn my whole month around. If you hadn't told me to get out there and, I quote, 'Make your own fun and you'll make a difference,' I probably would've just moped around the whole time I was up here."

"*Solitary Summer?*" Valerie asked. "That was you?"

Beth nodded. Ally wondered briefly what *Solitary Summer*'s problem had been, if it had been about her. Valerie's tremulous smile grew stronger and stronger, and she straightened back up, excitement returning to her face. "Oh," she said. "I'm so glad I was able to help."

For the first time in a while, Ally felt Beth's goodness as something not oppressive, but light and wonderful. She marveled at how effortlessly Beth could make people better and sensed her own self growing better in Beth's presence too.

"I'm sorry if we came off as insensitive," she said to Valerie. "You should write what you think is best. Beth's right. You really are the expert."

"No," Valerie said now. "Or rather, yes." She squared her shoulders. "I am the expert, but I love your letter. And there's something so romantic about the fact that the two of you wrote it, that you took matters into your own hands because you care about Stella so much. It's beautiful. I'm publishing it the way it is, Wednesday morning, journalistic integrity be damned!"

"You're sure?" Beth asked.

"One hundred percent positive."

"Well, thank you," Ally said. "That's wonderful. You're wonderful."

They stood up to leave, helping Valerie push her chairs back into place, and as they headed toward the door, Valerie called out, "Wait!" She opened a drawer in her desk and shuffled around in it, then came toward them shyly with two books, giving one to each of them.

"I self-published," she said. "Just a small printing. I haven't shown it to many people, but maybe you'll appreciate it." She kissed them again on the cheek, this time without all the excess moisture of the first kiss.

So they left with two copies of Valerie's own romance novel, *Big City, Strong Arms*. When they stepped back outside, onto the sidewalk, Ally turned to Beth.

"Thanks for saving that, after I nearly fucked it all up."

"No worries," Beth said, and Ally really felt like she meant it. "Now, let's get back to Grandma Stella's so that we can start reading this aloud to each other as soon as possible."

TWELVE

As Monday afternoon slipped into a gorgeous early evening, Beth stood in front of a mirror in the third bedroom, braiding her hair.

"No," Ally said. "You are not having dinner with Owen looking like this." She was sprawled on their bed, barefoot in yet another winsome sundress, her fingers picking at the tassels of a cerulean throw pillow.

"Yes, I am," Beth said. She gave her reflection the once-over, staring into her own green eyes. No makeup—she hardly ever wore it anyway. Her hair was pulled tightly back. She'd put on her usual denim shorts, which came to midthigh, and a loose, white cotton T-shirt with a slight V-neck. She'd gotten it in a pack of three extra-small men's undershirts from some big-box store while home in Wilmington. Her sneakers and a sweatshirt would complete the look.

"My God," Ally said. "Tell me that you're wearing sexy underwear. Please."

"Do fraying orange granny panties count?" She pulled the waistband up out of her shorts to demonstrate.

Ally groaned and threw the pillow at her. "You're hopeless." Beth caught the pillow and threw it back at Ally, who let out an "*Oof!*" when it hit her.

"No, I'm strategic. If I wear unsexy underwear, I'm less likely to let him see it."

"Fine," Ally said, pushing herself off the bed and joining Beth at the mirror. "Wear the granny panties. But at least let me do this." She tugged the elastic out of Beth's hair and, before Beth could protest, loosened the careful braid so that her hair fanned out across her shoulders and down her back. She combed it with her fingers, and Beth closed her eyes at the pleasant, gentle tug on her scalp. "Better."

"Okay," Beth replied. They smiled at each other in the mirror, their side-by-side reflections almost touching but not quite, Beth nearly half a head taller than Ally. "Will you be all right without me? I'll be home by nine, I'm sure."

"Don't worry, Mom," Ally said. She pursed her lips and played with her own hair, testing out a high ponytail. "I'm a big girl. I'll find some way to occupy myself." She gave up on the high ponytail, shot a last glance at herself, and then turned to Beth. "Now go!"

"Okay, okay," Beth said, walking down the hallway.

"I hope you two get *very* friendly," Ally called after her.

"We aren't going to!" Beth called back, and marched out the door.

OWEN was waiting for her outside Mulberry's, sitting on a bench, his muscled calves outstretched. He fiddled with a canvas bag at his side, moving things around within it. Like Beth, he wore sneakers, shorts, and a T-shirt. As Beth approached, she studied him for a second—his solidness, the easy unself-conscious way his body occupied space (in contrast to how she carried tension with her in her shoulders, her fists, clenching them sometimes without realizing it). In this moment, he had a slight nervous energy too, caused, she gathered, by the fact that he was waiting for her.

"Hey," she said.

"Hey!" he replied, jumping to his feet. He made a brief movement forward as if to hug her but seemed to think better of it.

The sky above them was a cloudless blue, smooth and unbroken. Beth thought fleetingly that she and Ally had won the weather jackpot for their trip. She could stand in this dry stillness for hours. Being outside felt as important to her as breathing.

"It's such an awesome night," Owen said, as if he'd read her thoughts. "Want to have a picnic?"

"I really do," she said.

"I was hoping you'd say that, 'cause I brought supplies." He held up the canvas bag. "Oh, I just realized—do you want beer or wine? I didn't pack anything like that, but we can stop off and grab some if you want."

"I'm all right," she said, shrugging her shoulders. "I'm not a big drinker."

"Yeah, me neither."

He led her past the harbor, over the rock beach and sand, and through the tall grass to his favorite picnicking spot.

"Are you going to give me the guided nature walk version of this?" she asked, so he did, picking up shells and rocks and handing them to her. He told her their names—scientific and not—sharing with her his wonder at the processes of nature that had shaped them into exactly what they were and nothing else. His glee for it all was contagious, and she found herself racing from object to object, picking up pinecones and kelp alike and saying, "Tell me about this!"

Eventually they reached their destination, a granite outcropping against which, lower down, the waves broke into foam. They sat down at the tree line, their backs against different trunks, and Owen pulled their dinner out of the canvas bag.

"We've got sandwich-making options," he said, laying out a loaf of sliced wheat bread, glistening fresh tomatoes, hummus, peanut butter, and jelly.

"Oh, Owen, this is too nice," she said, suddenly worried that picnics were synonymous with romance.

"Please, I pack amazing picnic dinners for all my friends. Owen 'Picnic King' Mulberry. That's me." He handed her the bread and she spread half of a slice with the hummus and tomatoes, and the other half with the PB&J. He did the same. "Besides," he said, "I'm not paying for your dinner. You owe me six dollars."

Owen passed his massive stainless-steel water bottle to her as they ate. He was, she thought, someone with whom she would very much like to be friends. He was intelligent and funny and considerate, with a warm, ready laugh and an ability to ask questions that made her think. He had just enough imperfections (the cookies he'd baked them for dessert had turned out rock-hard and bizarrely salty) to keep him from taking himself too seriously. The only problem was that as she watched his mouth move, saying thoughtful things, she couldn't stop wanting to press her own mouth against it.

The sky turned a rosy pink, reflecting in the ocean beneath them, as they asked each other getting-to-know-you questions. She divulged her love of all things science fiction, and that a major source of stress for her was finding the kindest way to tell people that they had food in their teeth. He confessed to tearing up during the occasional Pixar movie and that, once in college, when his friends had gone to a tattoo parlor, he'd tagged along and gotten a tattoo of a freckle on his leg, to see what it felt like.

"Let me see!" she said.

He stuck out his right leg. "I can't always find it," he said, "'cause I have so many actual freckles." He walked his fingers up and down his calf. "Oh! Okay, I think this is it. See?"

In the half light, she had to lean closer to make out the dark dot. "Oh yeah. Does it feel any different from an actual freckle?"

"Nah, not really," he said, rubbing his thumb over it. "It's not bumpy or anything. You can feel it if you want."

"Do you let all your friends touch your fake freckle?" she asked as she gently traced a tiny circle on his leg with her fingertip.

"Constantly," he said, his eyes on her face.

She drew her hand back and put it in her lap. "I think I'd be too scared to get a tattoo. Oh, that's a good getting-to-know-you question. What are you afraid of?"

He considered as the last of the light faded from the sky and pinpricks of stars arranged themselves in the dark. "I guess—the people I love dying, with no chance for us to say good-bye." He was silent a moment, and then he smiled. "That, or poisonous snakes. Hate them. Luckily, none of the species in Maine are venomous. What about you?"

She knew the answer to this one immediately. "That, in the moments that really matter, I won't be the person I want to be."

"I can't imagine any version of you not being good," he said. Somehow, they'd ended up only inches away from each other. Cicadas cheeped a quiet symphony in the trees. The waves whispered to the rocks below. The branches above them hung perfectly still, hushed in expectation.

"Do you sit this close to all of your friends?" she asked.

"No," he answered. "I can move away if you want me to."

"I don't."

His voice, when he spoke again, was lower, softer. "I promised I wouldn't try to kiss you," he said, "and I'm a man of my word."

So she leaned forward, bridging the distance between them, and kissed him.

THIRTEEN

S o what happened with the car?" Ally asked, poking her head into Grandma Stella's bedroom after the glint of Beth's hair disappeared down the driveway.

Grandma Stella sat in front of her dark wood vanity, brushing her short hair with halfhearted strokes. The far wall of her bedroom was lined with cardboard boxes. Earlier in the day, the girls had helped her fill them with winter clothes, shoes, and anything else she wouldn't be needing in her remaining week at home. Those boxes gave the room a strange, impermanent feeling, making it seem like it wasn't quite a place where somebody still lived.

"Oh, the car," Grandma Stella sighed. "That woman from the Internet is going to take it after all." Her voice sounded different than normal, more mumbly, and Ally realized, when she turned around from the vanity, that she didn't have her false teeth in.

She'd never seen Grandma Stella without her false teeth before.

Grandma Stella was very careful about them, and about her appearance in general. If she normally could've passed for seventy-five, with her dyed blond hair and her joyful energy, she now looked her full eighty-four years. Without her teeth, her soft face collapsed. Her mouth hung lower than normal. Ally felt that Grandma Stella, by allowing Ally to see her without her teeth, was letting her in on a secret. She wasn't sure that she wanted to be a keeper of this particular confidence.

"She'll be taking it away on Saturday," Grandma Stella said.

"Shit," Ally said.

"Yes, shit indeed. I hope Tim and Mary feel happy about that, because I certainly don't." Grandma Stella looked at Ally, defeated, for one more moment, and then she took her teeth from a case on the vanity and popped them into her mouth. She applied some red lipstick and picked up a book from the top of her dresser. Teddy Roosevelt's stern, mustachioed face peered out from the cover. Grandma Stella had gotten to pick the book for her last-ever Britton Hills book club, and she'd jumped at the chance to discuss the Bull Moose, who she always said had been the most attractive president.

She attempted to stuff the hardcover in her purse as she headed out the door. "Have a good night, dear," she said to Ally and then, to Teddy's unsmiling face, "Get into my purse, you testosterone-filled hunk of a man!"

ONCE Ally had the house to herself, she started her alone time by decimating the remaining chocolate chunk cookies, trying to stick to her new plan: intentional myopia. Since Beth had returned from the dump with Owen yesterday, practically vibrating with joy and confusion and a need for her friend, Ally had decided to simply toss away the worries of past and future, of what would happen when Beth went back to Haiti, of what had happened when she was there before. Instead she focused on having as much fun as possible for as long as possible. If she viewed herself and Beth through a soft-focus lens, she could believe that nothing had changed since high school, that they were still in those early years of college, before the splintering had begun. Everything they'd done that day—from printing and handing out flyers for the party to packing clothes into boxes—had felt good. Easy, fun.

Of course, her mother still expected an answer about whether she'd be taking that flight back to New York. She realized that she hadn't told Beth about Marsha's engagement. She had no idea what would happen when she saw Tom. She knew that Beth would be leaving her soon, and that Grandma Stella was miserable. All of these things cohabitated in a little room in the back of her mind, but she chose not to knock on their door. They could keep each other company, because she had other things to do.

She finished the last cookie and went to rifle through Grandma Stella's CD collection, which they had yet to box up. A whole lot of Barbra Streisand, with the occasional Aretha Franklin, Etta James, and Celine Dion—Grandma Stella clearly liked sassy divas with stratosphere-breaching voices. She put on Aretha's greatest hits, half walking and half dancing around the living room, her feet shuffling against the soft gray rug. As she listened to the singer wail her way through "Think," her hands started to itch. Stretching her fingers out into the air, she realized what she really wanted to do with her night.

She walked in the door of Hooked on Tonics at 6:56. Nick

had his feet on the counter, leaning back in his chair, his eyes shut. "We're closing in a minute," he said in the direction of the door, his voice laced with frustration.

"Is there enough time for me to buy a guitar?" she asked.

He opened his eyes and swung his feet to the ground. "Oh, hey. It's you."

"Take pity on me," she teased. "In NYC, things never close. I don't understand how small towns work."

"You don't have a guitar already?"

"It's broken," she said.

"All right, naif, here's how this is gonna go." He thumped his fist on the counter, making the coffee mug resting there rattle, then stood up and walked to the wall of guitars. Today, he wore a T-shirt with a picture of Stevie Wonder, even more threadbare and worn than the one he'd had on when she'd met him, with Jeff Buckley's face. "The wife wants me home for dinner at 7:30. But I will be generous, and keep the store open for another ten minutes, because I believe in encouraging talent."

"You're too kind," she said, already drawn to the Fender she'd used when they'd sung together the other day. "I think I'd like this one."

He took it off the wall for her. "You gotta test it out, right?"

"Is that okay?" she asked. He raised his eyebrow at her, like she was being incredibly stupid. He made her feel that she was taking an exam testing her own worthiness. "I mean, I know you have to go, and I played it the other day."

"I could've replaced it with a different Fender. You don't know. Don't ever buy a guitar without testing it out," he said, and handed it to her. She caught a whiff of his soap, or cologne, or something, as he got close to her—a clean, rainy smell, and then the scent of coffee. Quick as lightning, she flashed back to Sunday mornings with Tom, when, freshly showered, they'd sit side by side at her kitchen table, drinking cheap coffee. ("This coffee is terrible," he'd always say. "I need some water," and then he'd grab a chunk of her still-dripping hair and put it in his mouth, sucking out the moisture. She'd scream and call him a weirdo, and he'd pretend to be horribly affronted, and she'd very slowly unbutton his shirt while whispering apologies.)

"You should probably play it with another guitar," Nick said, nudging her. "I guess we could have a five-minute jam session. Just 'cause I'm so generous."

"I don't even know how to repay such benevolence," she said. They sat back on their stools from last time, and he asked her what her favorite song was.

"How is it even possible to answer that question," she asked, "when there are so many?"

"That's the correct answer," he said.

"Want to play 'Think'?" she asked. "It's stuck in my head." They fudged their way through it, and then he waxed rhapsodic about "Last Goodbye" ("It's just so fucking *lush*"), so they played that one too.

"What about Lou Reed?" he asked, fired up, color coming into his cheeks beneath the stubble. She looked at the clock ticking away above the counter.

"It's been over ten minutes," she said. "We've got to get you home."

"Oh yeah." He shrugged. "Fine." He led her over to the counter, where he put her new guitar into a padded black case. "So it doesn't get broken," he said, inadvertently reminding her of that night on the subway. Then he rang her up, poking at the cash register in a perfunctory fashion. She handed him her credit card, inwardly chastising herself. She was already getting close to her limit, and finances were tight this month what with her taking a week and a half off from all her babysitting jobs. Nick pushed a receipt over to her. As she bent to sign it, she paused.

"Wait—I think you made a mistake," she said. "The price on the wall for just the guitar said $275." She pointed to the $99.99 on the receipt.

He met her eyes and stared her down. She noticed that he had the undereye circles of an insomniac. "No mistake."

"Oh. But—" She looked at the guitar, then at him. "Are you sure?"

"It's my music store. I can give a customer a fucking discount if I want."

He seemed to be daring her to challenge him further, so she exhaled and then smiled. "Well, thank you."

"Come back earlier in the day next time, and we can record something in the studio."

"I'll try," she said. She slung the guitar in its case over her shoulders, its weight feeling as natural to her as a turtle's shell.

"Don't just try," he said. "Make it happen."

FOURTEEN

~~~~~~~~

Beth and Ally sat sprawled on a couple of sun-soaked rocks at the top of Breezeway Mountain, looking out over Britton Hills. "Mountain" was a slight misnomer for what they'd just climbed—it was more like a very large hill, but still, from their perch, downtown seemed so fragile. Beth could blot out the harbor with one hand. The ocean, though, that went on forever.

"Okay, I've got one," she said. She took a heaping handful of trail mix, then passed it on over to Ally. "Would you rather have the body of a Victoria's Secret model, but be so allergic to all types of clothing fabrics that you always had to walk around naked, *or* have the nicest, most flattering wardrobe imaginable with a normal body, but you also had a ten-pound bulldog permanently living on your head?"

Ally snorted. "Victoria's Secret model body, definitely. Obviously.

Come on." She tossed the trail mix back, and Beth caught it in one hand.

She had forgotten how wonderful it felt to have a best friend. The past few days, she and Ally had been nearly monogamous. They'd worked together with an old, familiar ease, checking off items on a *Helping Grandma Stella Move* list that Beth had written up with a ceremonial joy. They'd been more efficient than Beth had expected, planning the food for the party, finding a bartender, even deciding to combine the yard sale with the party itself so that they wouldn't have to worry about getting a large number of people to Grandma Stella's house twice.

With this unexpected efficiency, they had much more free time than anticipated. They couldn't do many of the items on their list until after the party. What would be the point of broom-cleaning the rooms if people were going to be tramping through them anyway? And Beth's parents would be coming up that Friday, arriving just in time for the celebration, so they'd provide two extra pairs of hands for the final days before the move. So that morning they'd sunscreened-up and decided to hike Breezeway Mountain one last time.

"Okay, but think about it for a minute," Beth said. "Constant nudity means you wouldn't be able to wear coats in the winter. You'd be freezing all the time."

"I could move to Hawaii," Ally said.

"Fair point," Beth said.

Ally laughed and got to her feet. "Shall we head back down? Stop by the grocery store to check in about the food for the party?"

"Yeah, perfect," Beth said. She sprung to her feet too and

stretched out her arms, looking down over the rocks one last time. "Good-bye, hilltop."

"May you prosper, and grow many trees," Ally intoned.

They hiked downhill in a companionable silence, listening to the birds chattering and to their own steady breathing. Underneath the shield of trees, everything was cool and peaceful. Beth placed her feet in careful patterns, navigating the steep slope, content.

"Okay, my turn," Ally said. "Would you rather know definitively that there is no God, nothing greater out there than randomness, or have God actually speak to you, but have him or her or it say, 'Hey, sorry about genocide and stuff, I've just been really distracted watching reality TV'?"

"Yeesh. That's a good one. What would you pick?"

"Oh, this one's easy for me," Ally said. "I'd rather no God for sure. That's no change from my current belief state. But this isn't a question for me. It's for you."

"I really don't know. The idea of a fallible God definitely scares me. Especially a God fallible enough to get addicted to reality TV."

"But here's what I don't get about believing in God. If God exists, he or she or it must be fallible, right?" Ally asked. "Because so much shit happens in the world that an infallible God would shut right down."

"Well, I don't think fallible versus infallible is the right way to describe it, necessarily."

"So what is?"

"Omnipotence versus non-omnipotence, I guess. I don't think God sits up there on a cloud taking requests and decreeing, 'I shall answer your prayer for a new car, but I'm going to look the other way as a dictator slaughters his own citizens.' In my mind,

God's more of this amazing creative force that started things. And now it's an energy, a source of comfort and hope rather than an active participant in shaping the world."

"I don't know," Ally said. "I have a really hard time comprehending the idea of a being who is powerful enough to create a world, then sticking around as a presence but nothing else. Did he or she or it just get tired and weak? It makes so much more sense to me to think about particles colliding and all that."

Beth pushed aside a couple of low-hanging branches in their way, and held them back as Ally walked past. "Yeah, I totally get that. Don't you ever feel really lonely, though, thinking that there's nothing greater out there?"

"Of course," Ally said. "But don't you feel lonely too, even thinking that there is?"

"Well, yes. But I like the idea that there's a point to things, a purpose to it all, a reason that we're all here."

"So you would choose the reality-TV God over no God."

"I guess I would."

"Interesting," Ally said. "Okay, moving on, would you rather bang Jesus or Martin Luther King, Jr.?"

Beth laughed. "You are insane. I'm not answering that." Jokingly, she pushed Ally, shoving her gently with one hand.

"Hey!" Ally said, and looked sideways at Beth, her mouth open in a big smile. Beth grinned back. Then Ally's mouth turned to a perfect little O of surprise. Her eyes clouded with a momentary confusion as she lost traction and fell. She hit the ground at an especially steep patch and kept on going, skidding down, making unnatural crunching noises amid the leaves and the sticks on the ground.

"Ally!" Beth screamed. For a few agonizing seconds, she didn't know how Ally would stop falling, or if she ever would. She might bump all the way down the mountain, or crack her head open against a rock. And as the nightmare scenarios threatened to paralyze her, she was right back in Haiti, overwhelmed by the same terror, with an identical feeling of things spinning out of control too quickly while she was powerless to stop them.

SITTING at that clunky Open Arms desk, Beth heard the screaming outside and didn't know what to do. *I should open the door,* she thought. But the door seemed to open on its own, pushing on its hinges to reveal a woman, thin, dragging a child by the hand. The screaming tore out of the woman's mouth, a wail mixed with Creole and some broken English, but the child stayed silent, bumping along in his mother's wake like a rag doll. He couldn't have been more than six years old, with his enormous eyes and his sticklike limbs. He had no shoes on his feet, and he wore a faded shirt that said *Cincinnati Bengals.* Beth noticed blood dribbling out of his mouth.

"*Doktè! Doktè!*" the woman was shouting, and all of a sudden Beth recognized her—the patient she'd seen Deirdre with on her first night at Open Arms. Nathaly? Yes, that was her name. Nathaly's sweet shyness was gone, replaced by desperation. "Didi!" she screamed.

"She's not here," Beth said. "They're not here—"

The boy's legs gave out from under him, and as he thumped onto the floor, his eyes registered a dazed surprise. Nathaly crouched down. She used her skirt to wipe the blood from his mouth and the sweat from his face, then let it drop. It swished back down around her ankles, and Beth noticed the way the threads unraveled from the hem. As long as she stared at the skirt, everything would be all right. She could solve the problem of the unraveling hem by re-sewing it, or by buying Nathaly something nice and new to wear. Then the ankles beneath the skirt moved toward her.

"You. Please. Help," Nathaly said, grabbing her arm so hard it stung. The little boy's eyes fixed themselves dizzily on her and his breaths came in shallow whines. His mother's face twisted itself into a hideous contortion of grief and desperation.

Beth clearly needed to do something. She was good under pressure. Levelheaded. Calm. She knew these things to be true about herself. Just a few months ago, back in college, as her friends chugged coffee and collapsed over their desks in tears, overwhelmed by exams and papers, she'd sat and methodically done her work until she'd finished it all. How ridiculous to think about college now, as if it had any relevance to what was unfolding around her. The words—*levelheaded, calm*—ran through her mind on a revolving ticker. But they were describing a different Beth, an effective Beth, not the current, neutered version of herself who was paralyzed with indecision.

There had been screaming at Open Arms before, crying too. It didn't happen often. Deirdre and Peter tried to spread the word that emergency cases should go to the hospital, that this little clinic was best equipped to deal with patients who could wait. Early signs of malaria, checkups and consultations, cuts and breaks that caused no immediate threat to one's life, that was what Open Arms did best. But still, occasionally, desperately ill people came anyway, the hospital too far away for them to travel on foot or by donkey, hoping for miracles. A couple of times before, Beth had seen these types of people, in their terrifying need. Always, though, Deirdre and Peter had been there, knowing just what to do, how to help.

Now, she was the only one. Deirdre had told her when they'd left that morning that she and Peter wouldn't be back for hours.

The boy let out a little wheeze of a breath, and she moved toward him, finally, finally able to unfreeze her body. But her mind still stuttered. She tried to make mental lists. *Boy's Symptoms. Possible Diseases. Course of Action to Take.* She could see these headers in her mind, nice and neat, underlined, but underneath them, blank white paper expanded without end.

Somehow, she got down onto the floor with the boy and pulled him onto her lap. He flopped there, dead weight, but kept his gaze glued to her face, scared and hurting, trusting her to make it better. Her stomach curdled to see the redness in his eyes, the patches of bruising on his skin, and she tried not to flare her nose at his smell of fish and feces. Crusted vomit had dried on his shirt, over the tiger's ears. A dribble of blood from his gums painted a little dipper on her thigh.

As Nathaly watched her, too near, her tiny body closing in on her, Beth put her hand on the boy's forehead. The first step of some sort of medical exam, she told herself. But she didn't know what she was doing. She was failing him. This little boy was dying in front of her, and she was doing nothing to stop it. Minutes ticked by.

Maybe if she just wished hard enough, she could return to the moment she'd gotten out of bed and everything in the alternate version of this day would be better, normal. She could start from the beginning; she could go back to this morning and . . .

Then, as if Beth had wished it into reality, the door creaked open and Deirdre walked in.

"Beth," she said. "Peter forgot—" Her face, set in a mask of annoyance, changed as she registered the scene—keening woman, dying boy, useless Beth. Beth watched her one moment of stupefaction, so brief she wondered afterward if it had even really happened at all, and then Deirdre snapped into action.

"What's wrong with him?" she demanded. As Beth gaped, stammering, trying to figure out what to say—did she even know?—Deirdre turned to Nathaly and started speaking in Creole. Relieved at finally being understood, Nathaly poured out a stream of words, and Deirdre nodded. She grabbed a pair of gloves from a box on the desk and put them on, a simple gesture of competence and precaution that Beth hadn't even thought of. Then she lifted the boy from Beth's lap, murmuring to him quietly as she cradled him in her arms, and started to carry him down the hallway to the room with the hospital cots and the medical supplies.

"Come on," she said, and Nathaly followed her anxiously, hopping from one foot to the other. Beth stayed on the floor, her body shaking like she was having a never-ending cold spasm, which made no sense because it was so hot out, so hot that the air wrapped around her and smothered her. The concrete floor beneath her seemed to be pulling itself apart, ready to swallow her up and drag her into the ground, and she had to get out of there, get away from the horror and the stink of sickness and the flies lazily buzzing inches from her face. So even though Deirdre had said, "Come on," and the boy had continued to stare at her as Deirdre carried him away, his eyes asking her to stay with him, Beth ran. She opened the main door, stepped out into the dust, and ran away.

FIFTEEN

Ally had never been able to do a somersault. She wasn't great at yoga, or even Zumba. But, forward-rolling down Breezeway Mountain, her body contorted into all sorts of gymnastic positions previously unknown to her. She flipped over herself. She banged one outstretched knee on a rock. And then she came to a stop at the base of an oak tree. She lay on her back, next to the gnarled root that had finally halted her fall, and looked up at the light shining through the green leaves above her head. Everything hurt.

Distantly, she heard Beth scrambling down the fifteen feet or so after her, pebbles skittering under her feet. She felt the impact as Beth dropped to her knees, slamming onto the forest floor beside her. And then Beth's hands grabbed her shoulders, shaking some sort of clarity back into her.

"Ally. Are you okay?"

"Ow," Ally said. "Fuck." The *fuck* came out of her in a low, long tone.

"I am so sorry for pushing you," Beth said, her voice strangled. "Oh God. Are you all right? Is anything broken?"

Ally analyzed the pain and shook her head. Slowly, she began the process of sitting up. "I don't think so," she said. "But you're the one who's going to be the doctor. Examine me."

"Um," Beth said, "wiggle your fingers and toes. Can you move everything?"

Ally stretched out her fingers and waved them around, then repeated the process with her toes. Her knee ached where she'd gashed it on the rock, and an occasional black spot clouded her vision, but otherwise, things seemed to be returning to normal. "Yeah. I don't think there's permanent damage," she said. Beth held out her hand to help Ally up, and Ally grabbed it. "Whoa, your palm is really sweaty."

"Oh," Beth said, and took back her hand as soon as Ally was upright. She wiped it on her shorts, then curled it into a fist. Her face was red, almost violently so, like someone had slapped her hard on the cheeks, and her eyes were clouded. "I am so, so, so, so sorry. I feel like such an idiot. I don't know what I was thinking, to push you like that."

"Hey, you didn't push me," Ally said. "At least, that's not why I fell. I'm just a clumsy oaf, and wasn't watching where I was going." She looked at Beth's face again, unsettled by what she saw there. "Are you okay? You're all red."

"Hah. Yeah. Sorry. I'm just— Sorry. I got really worried for a second there. I'm sorry."

"It's fine, seriously." Ally started brushing leaves off her butt and wiping the dirt from her arms, wincing occasionally. Beth looked down at the ground. Ally could hear her breathing fast and then swallowing.

"I can call Grandma Stella," Beth said, "and ask her to pick us up at the base of the hill so you don't have to walk all the way home. Or—or we could go get ice cream. My treat. I really am sor—"

"Stop apologizing!" Ally snapped. She closed her eyes and took a breath, then opened them. "It's okay," she said. "Let's just get off this mountain."

They walked the rest of the way down the hill without saying much, but the type of silence had changed from before. Beth led, mapping out a path. She kept looking back, a bizarre combination of worried mother and wounded animal. Her concern was palpable—it vibrated in the air around her.

"I'm fine," Ally said, unable to keep the annoyance out of her voice. She focused pointedly on her feet. She watched her sneakers navigate the hill, trudge after trudge after trudge. They made a sort of drumbeat and then, slowly, a melody to go along with it came into her head. At first she thought it was a preexisting song, it made so much sense to her. But as it repeated itself, she knew she'd never heard it before. The melody settled in and walked with her all the way to the base of Breezeway Mountain, past the long blocks to the town center, where they stopped in front of the big windows of the grocery store.

"Shall we?" Beth asked at the door.

"You go ahead," Ally said. "There's something else I have to do."

WHEN she walked back into Hooked on Tonics, Nick didn't look up from his book. "Can I help you?" he asked in a monotone. She couldn't believe that the store hadn't gone out of business by now, given how blatantly annoyed he was by the prospect of customers.

"Want to make some music in your semicrap recording studio?" she asked.

The grin started to spread across his face even before he caught her eye. "Hell yes," he said, pushing *Infinite Jest* away—*of course he was reading* Infinite Jest, she thought—and unfolding his long limbs as he stood. He flipped the sign on the front door from *Open* to *Closed* and motioned for her to follow him.

He'd been right in his description of the recording studio. Amateur soundproofing was peeling from the walls like neglected wallpaper. The carpet looked like it hadn't been cleaned in years. But he had microphones, solid and full like promises, and a couple of straight-backed chairs. A keyboard and a drum set occupied two corners of the room, and she marveled anew at how much space you could get when you didn't live in New York City.

She climbed into one of the chairs. "Shit. What happened to your leg?" he asked. "It's bleeding."

"Oh." Ally looked down. Little droplets of blood leaked from the gash on her kneecap. "My friend Beth pushed me down a mountain." She stood up from the chair. "Sorry, I don't want to get it everywhere."

"Nah, sit back down. I'll be right back," he said, and disappeared. He returned a minute later with a wet paper towel and a tube of Neosporin.

"Look at you, all prepared," she said.

He shrugged. "My wife made up a first-aid kit for the store. I thought it was useless, but I guess not." She held out her hand for the paper towel, but instead of giving it to her, he knelt down in front of her on the dirty carpet.

"Oh, hey, that's fine—"

"Nah, I got it," he said. "You're wounded. Relax." He grasped the back of her calf and pulled it toward him. Without meaning to, she flexed her leg. Concentrating, he dabbed the blood away with the wet part of the paper towel, then folded it over and pressed the dry part to her cut. Neither one of them said anything. His hand was cold, and holding her calf harder than she thought necessary. She was glad she'd shaved recently, although, of course, it hadn't been thoroughly.

"So," he said after a minute, "down a mountain, huh? That's shitty." He took the paper towel away, balled it up, and tossed it into a wire trash can in the corner. "How's your new guitar working out?" He applied the Neosporin, rubbing it in slowly. It tickled and stung at the same time. She bit down on her lip. As soon as he paused in the rubbing, she pulled her leg away.

"Thanks. Um, I haven't had a chance to play it yet. I would've brought it, but I wasn't planning on coming."

"Okay, hold on. Let me wash my hands and grab us some guitars."

When he came back this time, he handed her a Martin—way more expensive than her Fender. It rested naturally in her lap as he checked her sound levels. She sang tentatively into the mic at first, her nerves making her breath catch in her throat.

"Oh, come on," he said, and something in the way he smiled

at her calmed her down. She sang louder, a couple of *la la la*s, and as they left her mouth, she decided that she was proud to have put them out into the world. Satisfied, he plopped down into a chair opposite her.

"So whatcha thinking?" he asked, as he idly plucked on his own guitar, showing off. "We can just play, or if you have anything particular in mind . . ."

"Well, I had this in my head." She played her melody (she already thought of it as *hers*, something precious) and hummed along. When she was done, he nodded his head.

"Yeah. Yeah, yeah, yeah, that's good." She leaned in, glad that she hadn't been crazy, thankful that someone else had validated that what she'd made was worthwhile. She played it again, and he joined in this time, their guitars getting closer and closer. "Funny, I didn't expect that from you," he said, when they had finished.

"What did you expect?"

"I don't know, I thought it would be . . . cuter."

She sat back a bit. "Golly gee, thanks."

He held up his hands as if to placate her. "No, no, hey, don't get offended. The song we made up the first time you were here, it was very . . . sweet-sounding, and I thought that was your gimmick."

"My gimmick?" She didn't know how annoyed to be with him. Her cuteness was a fact, something people automatically decided fit her because of her petite stature, her round face, her quickness with a smile. For the most part she enjoyed the benefits of "cute," but something about how he'd said it rankled her.

"Yeah, everyone has a gimmick, right? Even Dylan, with the folksy political stuff. I just thought you did sweet, you know, major chords, everything resolving neatly, all that, which is fun, but this is better. More interesting."

"Why did you want to jam if you thought it was just going to be boring and sweet?"

"I never said sweet is boring," he said. "Besides, I've got nothing else to do and you're talented. And it's a moot point, anyway, 'cause I already said I think this is really good."

"Well, then, thank you." He was right in a way, she thought to herself. Most of what she wrote *was* cutesy, happy, maybe a little bit gimmicky. With this new melody, it was like her mind had been working overtime without letting her know. She wasn't sure where it had come from, but she wanted to follow it.

"You got lyrics?" he asked, and when she shook her head, he continued, "I'm no good at them. I can put together words that scan and all, but if I tried to write lyrics for this, they'd probably come out like emo kid journal poetry. I'm just gonna figure out some stuff on the keys." He put his guitar down and went over to the keyboard, and she tried to find words to complement the sound.

She knew she didn't like her first try. The levity of the words clashed with the tune, creating an uncomfortable dissonance.

"Whatcha got?" he asked her, and she sang a bit, dubiously.

Rest your head upon my shoulder, kick those shoes off of your feet.
And we'll stay like that forever, 'cause I think you're pretty sweet.

Nick's face reflected her own dissatisfaction.

"Too cute," she said. "I know."

"Yeah. You know, it's okay for you to write about real feelings."

"Ouch," she said, laughing to cover the sting.

"Just saying. Music's supposed to be messy, not sanitized. Not to be a didactic old asshole or anything. Clearly, I am a huge success story," he said, gesturing at the peeling soundproofing.

"Hey, I like your crappy studio," she said, and he smiled. Then she tucked her feet up on her chair and closed her eyes as he played her song through again on the keyboard, filling it out. As the music ballooned around her, she seemed to start buzzing from the inside, and she concentrated on that hum, the way that for a second she was aware of all her body's organs doing their work. She went up to that little room in her mind where all of the things she'd successfully been ignoring lived together. She knocked on the door, and it swung open.

When she opened her eyes again, Nick was looking at her like he wanted to know what she'd been seeing. "Okay," she said. "What do you think of this?"

SIXTEEN

⟡

On the day of the grand Grandma Stella and Penny Joan Reunion, Beth knocked on Grandma Stella's door, then pushed it open.

"Hey, need any help in here?" she asked.

Grandma Stella looked up from her jewelry box, bracelets and rings filling her hands as she sorted through what she wanted to keep. Two large piles of jewelry lay in front of her on the bed.

"Oh darling, I'm all right. Take a little break, why don't you? Watch some TV or something. You've been working so hard to help me out."

"Are you sure? I don't really like TV. It rots your brain, and all that."

Grandma Stella patted the bed next to her. "Well, I certainly won't say no to company, then. And you can tell me what jewelry in here I should save for you." Beth climbed up next to her grandmother, trying not to wrinkle the downy bedspread. She put her head on Grandma Stella's shoulder, breathing in her comforting lavender scent and watching her little fingers detangle a heavy red necklace from the other chains in the box.

"So much to sort through," Grandma Stella said, sighing. "There's a whole other drawer, and I'd like to be able to fit all the jewelry I'm taking with me in this box. I don't even know where I got all of this." She held up the necklace, then dropped it in the yard sale pile. "Why did I buy this and when was I planning on wearing it? Lord knows."

Beth reached out and picked through the reject pile, making her way through rhinestone flower pins and a large owl on a leather cord. "I want to hear about the jewelry you do remember getting."

"Well, that's mostly this stuff over here," Grandma Stella said, patting the pile she'd be taking with her. "This ring, for example, oh, I remember your grandfather buying this for me at the Grand Bazaar in Turkey. We saved up for years to go there. Did I ever tell you about that? They have the sweetest tea there in Istanbul, and your grandfather and I, we must've drunk gallons of it—when I came home and went to the dentist, he said the backs of my teeth were all stained from the way I'd swish the tea in my mouth."

"I love hearing about the traveling you and Grandpa did," Beth said.

"He loved you so much, you know? When you were born, he said to me, 'Stella, that is the best damn baby in the entire world.' I thought you were wonderful too, of course, but he wouldn't stand for anyone saying that you were anything less than the tops. Once, he almost got into a fistfight with our friend Louis, who was insisting that his grandson was better. A joke, of course—they wouldn't have actually fought. Or maybe they would've, just a punch or two, but we—Louis's wife and I—we wouldn't have let them."

"I wish I'd known him better."

"I know, darling, me too. He was a special man, a once-in-a-lifetime kind of man. The only one for me, just like your dad is for your mom. I hope you find a man like that someday too." Grandma Stella kissed her on the top of her head, and then went through the other pieces in her jewelry pile, telling a story for each.

"This necklace I bought for myself. I think it's so important to have something that always makes you feel beautiful whenever you put it on, no matter what else is going on in your life. When I saw this in the store, I just said to myself, 'Stella Abbott, get out your pocketbook because that's it!'" She held up a thin gold necklace, with little clear stones woven into the chain like dew. Beth *ooh*ed in appreciation. It was an everything necklace, she thought, lovely and delicate enough to wear with a dress but also simple enough that you could wear it on your drabbest days and not feel too fancy. She didn't consider herself a jewelry person— jewelry got in the way, it was an unnecessary expense—but she would've worn this necklace in a heartbeat.

"I love it," she said, reaching out to touch it. "I've seen you wear it before. I remember."

"Do you want it? You should have it. It's yours."

"But you want to bring it with you! It's in the Sunny Acres pile."

"Pssh," Grandma Stella flapped her hands. "That's all right."

"Grandma, don't be ridiculous. I'm not going to take your beautiful-day necklace away from you."

"Well then, I'm not going to be at Sunny Acres forever. I want you to have it after I'm gone. I'd like to leave something for Ally too. What do you think she'd like?"

Beth picked a bracelet from the Sunny Acres pile, one with fake emeralds for Ally's birthstone, that Beth's dad had given Grandma Stella for Mother's Day when he was off at college. "She'd like this."

"Wonderful. You two really can have them now, if you'd like. I don't think I'll have much of a reason to get gussied up at Sunny Acres."

"Grandma," Beth chided, "come on. It's going to be nice there. You'll have people to impress, reasons to look pretty."

"Mmm," Grandma Stella said, but Beth could tell she didn't really agree. "Well, I'll put it in the will, then." Beth didn't like the way she brought up her will so mildly, as though she weren't afraid of dying. She squeezed her grandma's hand tighter.

"Thank you," she said. "But I hope I don't get it for a long, long time."

"Anything else you see around the house that you might want, let me know and I'll put it in the will, or you can just take it home with you. Use it to furnish your apartment, when you get one. Maybe you want that lovely glass-topped table, or some of the paintings."

"Maybe. We'll see," Beth said. A big glass coffee table wasn't going to make the move to Haiti with her. But she wasn't going to tell Grandma Stella that, at least not yet. There'd be plenty of time to tell her, and her parents, and everyone else, after Grandma Stella had gotten settled in at Sunny Acres.

"My beautiful darling," Grandma Stella said, "I think I'm going to take a little nap."

"Okay," Beth said. She got up to leave the room and then added, "Anything interesting in the paper today?"

"Oh, just more bad news about the world. It can really get a person down, huh?"

"I know. But hey, at least you've always got Valerie's advice column to cheer you up, right?" Grandma Stella gave her a strange smile in response, like she wanted to say something but wasn't going to, and Beth marveled at her lack of a poker face. "Okay, well, I guess I'll try to read a little bit. Let me know if you need anything."

Beth settled down on the couch and tried to concentrate on the book Deirdre had lent her, about the seemingly superhuman activist doctor Paul Farmer. Farmer treated the poor in Haiti, made a difference all over the world, and saw his wife and child once every couple of months. "This is what we're attempting to do," Deirdre had said, pressing it into Beth's hand as she left for the airport. "I hope it inspires you like it inspired me." Deirdre's notes cluttered the margins of each page. She'd underlined passage after passage. The book did inspire Beth. It troubled her too, and made her feel like she wasn't doing enough. She found herself fascinated by Farmer, but also by Ophelia Dahl, Farmer's former lover, who now ran the foundation in Boston that funded his work, who hadn't been able to quite keep up with his selflessness.

Beth had read the book once already on the plane home, flipping pages without really thinking about it. But as she sat with it now in her lap, she kept flashing back to Owen, interrupting what she was trying to learn about Dr. Farmer's attempts to treat multidrug-resistant tuberculosis.

They'd kissed for half an hour straight the other night, the grass soft against them. Breathing heavily, the scent of pines heady around her, she'd pushed his hand away when he'd moved it to her shorts, and said, "No. Too complicated." In the day and a half since, she'd been kicking herself repeatedly, half-furious that she hadn't just had sex with him anyway, when she'd so badly wanted to, and half-furious that she'd even kissed him at all.

"Okay, so I guess we can't just be friends," she'd said, when she'd finally pulled away, and then she hadn't given him a straight answer when he'd asked when he could see her again.

She shut her book and put it on the glass-topped coffee table. She needed to move. Yes, that was what she needed—motion, a walk maybe. The sun sparkled outside, and she hadn't yet fully taken advantage of its light today. Maybe she'd check in with the grocery store about when they were going to deliver the snacks for the party, or she could find an anniversary present for her parents (twenty-five years, a big one), and then enough time would've elapsed that she could just go straight to Monroe's to meet Ally who, ever since yesterday's fall on the mountain, had been a little distant, offering to do errands around town on her own.

She shut the front door quietly and half walked, half ran, going over her Creole flash cards in her head again, until she got into town. But she didn't end up at the grocery store, or at any place where she could buy a suitable gift. She paused in front of Mulberry's, looking at the big *GOING OUT OF BUSINESS— FINAL SALE* sign and wanting so badly to go in.

She could see Owen ringing up a customer at the cash register. He turned his head as the customer dug through his wallet for change, and noticed her through the window. She put her hand up in a dumb wave and he waved back at her, an expectant half

smile starting to spread across his face. He held up his index
finger in that time-honored gesture. *I'll be right out*, it said.

Elizabeth Abbott, you look like a creeper, she told herself.
Her phone vibrated, startling her. Open Arms. She walked away
toward the water as she answered.

"Hello?"

"Beth?" Even a fuzzy connection couldn't dull Deirdre's voice.
"Hello."

"Hi. How are you? How's Peter?"

"We were happy to get your message."

"Good. Yeah, I'm happy about it too—about working with
you more, I mean. How's everything going there?"

"Same as always. Too many problems, not enough money or
manpower to fix them all. When will you come back?"

"Um, I need to look at flights and all that. Maybe around the
middle of July?"

"Okay, send us an e-mail or leave us another message when
you figure it out. The sooner you get back the better, obviously.
The literacy program has really been suffering without you."

"Right," Beth said, nodding even though Deirdre couldn't
see her.

"It's going to be very helpful to have you. I'm proud of you,
for choosing to come back. You're doing the right thing."

"Thanks," Beth said. She bit her lip and pressed her phone
harder against her cheek.

"Okay, I should hang up. Patients waiting. We'll talk more
soon."

At the beep signifying the end of the call, Beth felt dizzy. She
finished walking to the harbor and sat on the ground, staring out

at the never-ending water in front of her. *You're doing the right thing*, Deirdre had said. But the memories of that morning in Haiti grew stronger, pushing themselves up past the barriers Beth had erected to stop them.

BETH ran away from the little boy's eyes on her, from Nathaly's look of surprise at her uselessness. She blew past Peter idling in the truck outside, ignoring him as he called after her. She ran until her breathing sounded like the wheezes and whines the boy had been making. She put feet, then miles, between her and him, but still she saw his face and felt his blood, now dried on her leg. She clawed through the heat and the thick air, and then she tripped on a root and hit the ground with a thud. The impact knocked the pain of everything that had just happened into her, and she began to cry. She sobbed into the dirt, balling it up in her fists. Her tears and sweat salted the ground beneath her.

She didn't want to go back. She was so afraid. As long as she stayed out here, she didn't have to know whether he'd died. She'd come to Haiti to help, but she'd wanted to offer halfway help, the kind that made the helper feel good, not the kind with endless potential for disaster, real people dying on her. But you couldn't go in halfway forever. And now Beth wanted out completely. If she could have run all the way across the ocean, back home, she would have.

Eventually, though, she had to return to Open Arms. She couldn't stay in a heap on the side of the road forever. Her throat burned, and her head pounded. Dread slowly propelled her back to the clinic.

Peter's truck was gone. The courtyard was empty, like a ghost town. When Beth pushed open the front door, she saw Deirdre sitting at the desk, her arms folded, her eyes dark, staring at a pile of papers spread out in front of her.

"Is . . . is he okay?" Beth asked. Her voice came out raspy, like it was barely there at all.

Deirdre looked up then. "I don't know," she said. "It started out as cholera but became some sort of secondary infection. Peter took him to the hospital. I stayed here to wait for you."

"Oh God," Beth said.

Deirdre shuffled the papers around in front of her, staring at them as if they held solutions. "If we could raise the money for that damn water purification system, maybe nice young women like Nathaly wouldn't let their kids drink stagnant water out of old bleach containers, and then they wouldn't get fucking cholera."

"I'm sorry," Beth said. "I'm sorry, I didn't know how to handle it. I just froze. He was so helpless and I was so useless—" She started crying again. She couldn't seem to stop shaking, and she wanted to force the tears back behind her eyelids, but they kept coming. The distance between her and Deirdre felt endless, so she closed the gap, longing for a hug. There she stood, in front of Deirdre, every inch of her body yearning for comfort.

Deirdre looked up at her, her eyes cold. "You know, Beth, in a situation in which a child might be dying, the last thing I need to do is waste valuable time worrying about where you've gone."

Beth stepped back. "I know. I'm sorry. I wish I hadn't—"

"If you want to be one of those people who come here for a year, do some good work, and then go home, that's fine. But don't expect me to coddle you when shit gets real. Don't think that throwing a pity party for yourself will fix anything. These things happen, and they are going to happen again. You have to pull yourself together and work harder. This isn't about what you did or didn't do this time, it's about what you're going to do next time. And if you don't think you can handle that . . ." Deirdre shook her head.

The front door creaked open then, so slowly it seemed that it had gotten fifty pounds heavier. Peter walked in, his eyes red, his shoulders slumped. He looked at them, and he didn't have to say anything for them both to realize what had happened. Deirdre slammed her palm down on the desk. The hollow thud rang through the room.

"Oh, no," Beth said.

"It was too late," Peter said. "By the point we got him to the hospital, they couldn't do anything for him." His voice cracked. Deirdre stood up and walked over to him, and the two of them held on to each other, wrapped tightly in one another's arms.

Beth turned and walked out of the room to the phone to call Ally. She needed her best friend.

It rang to voice mail. She punched the number again. Again, voice mail. She kept calling. She would keep calling, she thought, until she could talk to Ally. This time, on the third ring, Ally picked up.

"Hello?"

"Allygator?" All the crying had corroded her voice, leaving it rusted and dry.

On the other end of the line, hesitation. Then, "Beth? What's up?"

"Oh, Ally," Beth said, the simple act of saying her friend's name filling her with the first measure of hope she'd had since she'd first heard Nathaly screaming. "I really need to talk to you—"

"Look, love, I'm so sorry but this isn't a good time. I kinda have to go."

"Wait." Beth hadn't expected this. Everything was going to be okay again once she got Ally on the phone. "Don't go. Please. I did something terrible, and a little boy died—"

In the background on Ally's end, Beth heard someone else talking. A guy. Tom. Ally couldn't talk because she was hanging out with Tom.

"I'm gonna go, but call me back tomorrow, maybe," Ally said, speaking in a rush.

"Ally, no, wait. Please don't hang up. I need you. Please—"

But Ally had already gone. Beth pressed the dead phone against her ear until her ear turned red and throbbed. Then she drank some water, retched it all back up, and went to bed.

She spent all the next day tangled in her sheets. Deirdre and Peter checked in on her, and she smiled at them when they came into her narrow room and told them that she wasn't feeling well but she'd be better soon. When they shut the door, she busied her mind with thoughts of going home. She thought about her English degree, and how maybe, if she was really efficient about it, she could apply to grad schools for next year. She could read Virginia Woolf all day long in quiet, cool libraries.

The second morning after it happened, she woke up to beautiful sunlight streaming in through the window and, for a good ten seconds, felt peaceful and happy. Then she remembered the little boy, and her panic, and she cried again. But she splashed some water on her face from the jug by her bed, walked out to where Deirdre was eating breakfast, and said she was better. She did the tasks assigned to her, the ones she was good at like book-keeping and writing letters, and organized the clinic's files with a smile glued to her face.

The day after was Internet café day, so she biked over there as usual. She hadn't told Deirdre and Peter, but this time, she planned on buying a plane ticket home. As she rode, she only felt the bump of the bike seat, smelled the truck exhaust ahead of her, saw in her mind the boy's face as he lay on her lap. She chained up her bike outside and sat down at the computer, deciding to briefly check her e-mail before looking for flights. There were five new e-mails from Ally. She clicked on the first one.

Shit. Shit. Phone chat? Call me?

It had been sent the day she'd called her. So Ally did care. She'd made a mistake in hanging up, and regretted it, and had been trying to get in touch with Beth ever since. Beth couldn't wait to get home to her. Then things would be better. She clicked over to the next e-mail, sent a few hours later.

Beth,

I'm so sad. Tom and I broke up. I don't know what to do. He's going to Portland and I'm staying here, alone. This e-mail might not be coherent. This sucks this sucks this sucks I hate everything except him (and you). Right now I feel like I'm never going to be happy again. Why does life have to be so awful and unfair???

Another e-mail. And another. But no mention of Beth's phone call. Ally had sent this one the next day:

Beth,

I know you probably haven't gone to the Internet café yet, and I don't know how to call you, but when you get these e-mails can you pleaaaaaaaaaaase e-mail me back? Or call me? Or fly home? (Kidding on that last one. Unless you want to.) I need to talk to you. I'm just a mess. I haven't stopped crying for longer than an hour since Tom left except to sleep, not that I've slept well. My heart feels numb except when I can actually physically sense it breaking into a billion little pieces. All I want to do is lie in bed, or run to his door and beg him to let me come to Portland with him. I can find things to do there. I'd play guitar on street corners, or work at a feminist bookstore, or bake gluten-free cupcakes at a vegan bakery. Really, I'd find something to do. It wouldn't matter what it was, as long as I could come home at night to an apartment we share and just love him. That would be enough for me. Why isn't it enough for him?

And the next day:

Beth,

Today, I woke up, ate three bowls of oatmeal, and fell asleep on the couch for two hours. Then I walked all the way to the subway in the rain before realizing that I'd forgotten my umbrella. I'm watching *Shakespeare in Love* on repeat. I need to talk to you. What if he's already hooked up with someone new? It's possible. He's so cute, he could go out and find another girl who's prettier than me. This is awful. I feel like shitty shitty shit.

Ally had just sent the last one an hour ago.

Beth,

Please, as soon as you get this, can we talk?? I need you and your wise words and the fact that you love me. I don't really like emoticons, but this is how I feel :(:(:(:(:(:(:(I'm an ugly failure and no guy will ever love me ever again and I'll never love any guy as much as I love Tom and I'm just going to be alone forever, or have some totally loveless marriage with some guy I'll barely even want to have sex with because I get so desperate. Please help me feel a little bit :), if that's possible right now. I'd even settle for :/

Beth closed out of the window with a quick click and stared at the screen, her vision clouded by fury. She realized her hands were shaking, so she sat on them. Ally's e-mails were so oblivious to everything except her own problems. She had abandoned Beth when Beth had needed her more than anything, had hung up on her when Beth had told her that something terrible was happening, just like Beth had slipped out the door, too overwhelmed to stay with that boy and help in any way she could, making the situation about her instead of about the person who really mattered. She didn't even know the little boy's name. She didn't know anything about him. She'd failed him by not knowing how to fix him, and then she'd failed him again by running away from him.

Deirdre was right. Sitting around pitying yourself accomplished nothing. It blinded you. She wasn't going to coddle Ally, and she wasn't going to coddle herself.

She'd finish out Haiti, but for real this time. She'd redeem herself in the months she had left. And then, maybe, she'd go to med school, so that instead of staring uselessly at a collection of symptoms, too scared to function, she could snap into action like Deirdre had. She wasn't better than Haiti, she realized now. But she wanted badly to be better than she was.

And she was so mad at Ally. She left the Internet café without writing any e-mails, without buying a plane ticket home, and went back to Open Arms. She walked straight up to Peter and Deirdre and said, "What was the little boy's name?"

"Michel," Peter answered.

"Michel," Beth repeated. Then she turned to Deirdre and said, "I'm ready to work harder." After that, she didn't talk to Ally, or to anyone, about the boy again.

BETH stared out at the boats rocking in the harbor until her phone buzzed. I'm at Monroe's! came a text from Ally. You close? She power-walked over, trying to concentrate on Grandma Stella's reunion plan. Again, her palms had gone all sweaty. She wiped them on her shorts and paused outside Monroe's, taking deep breaths to calm herself down. Through the window, she could see Ally hovering at a table, placing a bottle of wine in the center and saying something excitedly to the waiter, a spindly boy in his late teens who was staring at her in awe. The waiter nodded so hard that Beth worried he'd hurt his neck, then ran off into the kitchen.

"Hey," Beth said, walking through Monroe's front door.

"Hi!" Ally said. "Perfect timing. Ready to be the coolest spies ever?" Beth nodded. "Okay, great. I told the waiter about our plan, and he said we could sit in this booth over here. It's the private, romantic booth, apparently, so you can look out and watch other people in the restaurant, but they can't really see you." Ally led Beth over to a dark red booth in the corner, separated from view of the main restaurant by a row of fake potted plants.

Together, they scooted onto the red leather seats, and then Ally reached into a yellow tote bag she'd slung over her shoulder. "I know nobody will be able to see us, but I bought little Groucho Marx glasses to wear anyway, because I thought we'd look smoking hot in them." She handed a pair to Beth and put hers on, waggling her own eyebrows underneath the fake tufts of hair. "So I just paid for the bottle of Merlot, and the waiter is bringing a basket of bread to the table now."

Beth felt all confused inside. This helpful Ally seemed completely different from the one who'd written those slap-in-the-face e-mails half a year ago. This was Ally Without Tom—a different creature from Ally With Tom. "Thanks so much for setting this up," she said now, and put her glasses on too.

By 6:05, the center front table was still empty. The bottle of wine, the beige tablecloth, the basket of crusty bread, all took on a pathetic loneliness. The waiter swung by their booth, handing them their own basket of bread through the trees. "Um, is everything okay?" he asked, his voice cracking a bit on the last word.

He seemed to be trying to cultivate facial hair, but so far all he had was a neck beard and part of a mustache. He looked back and forth between his two customers, attempting to be suave but coming off terrified. "Are they coming?"

"I don't know," Beth said.

"Valerie put it in the paper just like we asked her to," Ally said. Then the door opened and Penny Joan Munson walked in. She sat down at the table, her spine rigid, staring at the wall. The waiter let out a squeak, then cleared his throat and nodded very formally at Beth and Ally. He headed over to Penny Joan, taking his order pad out of his pocket. Beth and Ally squeezed their hands together tightly. Penny Joan waved off the waiter as he approached. He shot a glance back at the booth and then went behind the bar, where he stacked glasses in despair.

Penny Joan continued to stare at the wall, her lips pursed tightly, avoiding the window. She didn't touch the bread or the wine. Beth watched her zip and unzip the pocketbook in her lap, over and over again, even as her upper body stayed completely still.

"Come on, Grandma Stella," Ally whispered in Beth's ear. Each time the door opened, the two of them started, but the people who came in were inevitably strangers. With each new customer, Penny Joan's posture got straighter and straighter, but she kept her back to the door. At every door jangle, she seemed to stop breathing until it became clear that the new visitor wasn't who she was expecting, and then she swallowed a big swallow and drew in a sharp breath.

Fifteen minutes went by like this, and then, swiftly, Penny Joan stood up and left the restaurant.

"Shit," Ally said. "Where is Grandma Stella?"

"Oh no," Beth said, taking off the Groucho glasses. "Why isn't she here?" Suddenly she felt panicky and rummaged for her phone.

"Oh my God, do you think—" Ally started to ask, then trailed off. She took her glasses off too, and folded them in her lap nervously. "I should've . . ." she said, as she picked at the eyebrow tufts.

Beth punched in Grandma Stella's home phone number, certain no one would pick up. She remembered the way Grandma Stella had talked about her will that afternoon. She looked into Ally's brown eyes as the phone rang, seeing her own worry reflected there. She couldn't look away from Ally or something bad would happen, so the two of them just faced each other as Beth held her phone to her head. And then, finally, Grandma Stella picked up.

"Hello?"

Beth exhaled in relief and nodded her head vigorously at Ally, who let out a big breath too, and dropped her face into her hands. So she wasn't dead, at least.

"Hey, Grandma, it's me. Um, Ally and I are out in town and we just wanted to know if . . ." Beth couldn't think of anything and made a *help me* face at Ally.

"Uh . . . uh . . . flowers? For the party?" Ally whispered.

"We wanted to know if you wanted us to pick up some flowers for the party."

"Oh, darling, it's only Wednesday. Shouldn't we wait till Friday morning so they're fresh?"

"You're right. You're so right. What were we thinking? By the way, is everything okay? How are you doing? How are you feeling?"

"I'm just fine, except the Sox are down two runs and I don't know if there's any coming back from this."

"Okay. Well, we'll be back soon. I love you."

When Beth hung up the phone, she and Ally stayed silent for a second longer. Beth tried to turn Grandma Stella's absence into an explanation that made sense.

"So I guess she just didn't want to come," Beth said.

"Are you sure she saw the paper?"

"I asked her if she'd read it today, and she said yes. And I even referenced *Dear Valerie*, and she looked all weird and guilty."

Ally tapped on her lips with her fingers. "I guess you're right, then. She didn't want to come."

"Yeah."

"Well. I didn't expect that of her."

"I know, me neither. I feel so bad for Penny Joan."

"Yeah." Ally was quiet, and Beth imagined that, like her, she was thinking of the embarrassment and disappointment Penny Joan must have felt as she sat alone at the table. Then Ally said, "We should drink."

"Huh?"

"The bottle of wine, I mean. We paid for it. I want to drink it, so this isn't a total waste."

"Um . . ."

"Oh, come on," Ally said. "We're here. We tried, and our experiment failed, so we should at least get something out of it. Let's have dinner and get drunk. It's been almost a week since I've had something to drink, and my body's confused."

Beth certainly could stand to forget about things for a little while too. The phone conversation with Deirdre had unnerved her. And her momentary fear that something terrible had happened to Grandma Stella had given her the jitters. A bit of oblivion could be nice. So she stood up, grabbed the bottle of wine from the front table, and waved the waiter over.

After the waiter had opened the bottle (fumblingly) and poured out two generous glasses of rich maroon for them, lingering at their table until his manager called sharply, "Ricky! Stop bothering them!" Ally held hers up. "Cheers," she said. "To Britton Hills and Grandma Stella, even though she didn't show up."

For their second glass, Beth gave the toast. "To you," she said, "for coming up here with me. I'm so thankful to have your help on this. I didn't realize how much harder it would be to pack up and get everything together for this party without you." Her face felt warm from the wine, and she couldn't quite remember why she'd been mad at Ally for so long.

"Aw," Ally said, her eyes dark and unreadable in the candlelight. "I'm really glad I came up too."

Tenderness for her friend overrode all the past weirdness and made Beth ashamed of how snippy she'd been with Ally. She was glad that at least they still had another half a week together. She took a gigantic sip of her second glass. "I love you such much."

Ally laughed. "Did you say 'such much'? Are you tipsy already?"

"No . . ."

"You are such a lightweight! I love you such much too, you drunkard."

"*You're* a lightweight."

"Not me. I have the tolerance of an overweight frat boy." Ally's phone dinged, and she checked it. Her face broke out into a smile and when she caught Beth looking, she closed her lips back over her teeth.

"Who is it?" Beth asked.

"It's Nick. From the music store."

"He has your number?"

"Yeah, I gave it to him so he could let me know about this song we recorded yesterday. He says he's done mixing it, and that I should stop by the store and get it. Can we go on our way home?"

So they finished their Americanized Italian food at Monroe's and drank the wine down to its dregs. Or rather, Ally drank the dregs—after finishing her second glass, Beth let Ally do the heavy lifting for the rest of the bottle. Then, leaving the waiter a big tip, they walked arm in arm to Hooked on Tonics. Nick was watching out the window, and when they appeared, he opened the door with what seemed to Beth like studied nonchalance.

He introduced himself to her with a nod, but his eyes stayed on Ally, who wove back and forth a bit as she walked into the store, her boast about alcohol tolerance apparently unfounded. She looked really pretty, Beth thought, flushed and wide-eyed but not sloppy, her lips dark from the wine. Had she been wearing makeup this whole time, or had she put it on in the bathroom at Monroe's before they left?

"So I hear you pushed her down a mountain," Nick said to Beth. At first, Beth didn't know who he was talking to, because he was still looking at Ally.

"What?" she said. "I—no, I didn't mean—"

"I was *joking*," Ally said. "You jerk."

"Anyway, here's the track. I think it's really solid," Nick said, and held up a CD.

"Yeah? Yes!" Ally smiled really wide, and walked closer to grab it from his fingers. Nick smiled wide in response.

"A CD," she said, taking it from his hand more slowly than Beth thought she had to. "How nineties of you."

"Unfortunately I already used up all my records and cassette tapes. Sorry." Ally guffawed, and Nick smirked, pleased with himself.

"So you wrote a song together?" Beth asked, propping herself up against the counter and feeling like a forgotten third wheel.

"She wrote it, mostly," Nick said. "I just recorded it."

"Oh, come on," Ally said, and swatted at his arm. "Team effort!"

"Yeah, team effort. She wrote the music and lyrics."

"He figured out awesome piano stuff for it, and saved me from myself when my original lyrics were terrible."

"Don't forget the drums," Nick said.

Ally gasped. "And drums! Oh no! I forgot the drums." She leaned toward Beth like she was going to tell her a secret and said, "He also played the drums."

"I take it you girls had a good time tonight," Nick said. It rankled Beth that he called them girls.

"Yes. We drank a lot of wine," Ally said.

"No shit. Drunk at eight P.M. That sounds about right for Britton Hills."

"I can't believe you got it all finished so fast. You are a musical recording genius." Ally was giving Nick the superhero look, and Beth could see him enjoying how his cape fluttered in the wind.

"Should we listen?" Nick asked. "I can put it on."

Ally hesitated, pulled back, looked reflexively at Beth. "Um. Maybe not now. We should probably get back and check on Grandma Stella, right?"

Beth couldn't tell if Ally was being sensitive to her increasing awkwardness or overly shy about the song for some other, strange reason. Regardless, she figured it was best to get out of the store as soon as possible, to get Ally away from Nick's hungry gaze, so she gave Ally the nod she was asking for.

"Cool," Nick said. "Okay. Cool. Yeah, well, let me know when you want to jam more."

"Definitely. Thank you, sir," Ally said, and held her hand out for a mock-serious handshake. He grasped it in his own, and they laughed as they moved their hands up and down.

"Okay, bye," Beth said, and pulled Ally out the door.

Grandma Stella was just heading to bed as they got back, acting much more normally, Beth thought, than someone should after standing up her former best friend. She didn't like what this night had made her think of her grandmother. So after Grandma Stella shut her door and the two of them had sat at the kitchen table in silence for a moment, she turned to Ally and said, "Let's have more to drink."

"Yup," Ally replied immediately. They took inventory of Grandma Stella's alcohol collection. Beer and wine in the fridge, tequila and scotch under the sink.

"It's like the rebellious high school experience you and I never had," Ally whispered, holding up the various bottles, "rifling through the adults' liquor cabinet."

"I haven't ever tried scotch before," Beth said.

"Shut up, really? Oh my God, let's have some of that, then. Scotch is the best because you can pretend you're an old man at a classy gentlemen's club."

She filled up two glasses generously and squinted at them. "That's roughly a couple shots each. Shall we?"

"We shall!" Beth took a big sip and grimaced. She shuddered a bit as it went down her throat, but then the tingling in her body amplified, and she decided she liked it enough to keep going. As she continued to sip, she could feel herself loosening even more.

She realized that she wanted to talk to Ally about Haiti. She was tired of keeping it locked inside her. Ally hadn't cared before. But she had a feeling she'd listen now.

As Beth tried to figure out how to formulate the words, Ally's phone, which she'd set on the table, started to vibrate. It whirred against the wood, as distracting as the amplified buzz of a fly.

"I'm very popular," Ally said in a silly voice, then glanced at the screen. Then she pressed ignore. Beth geared herself up to talk, to ask Ally if she could tell her something important, and then the vibration recommenced.

"Someone really wants to talk to you," she said.

"It's just my mom," Ally said, rolling her eyes and hitting ignore again. "I can call her back later."

Then Beth's own phone began to ring.

"Weird. Your mom's calling me now. What if it's an emergency? I should probably pick up."

"Just ignore it. Ignore it—" Ally started to say, but Beth had already picked up the phone.

"Hi, Marsha!" she said. She hadn't spoken to Ally's mom in years. But Marsha's voice was the same as it had always been.

"Beth! Radiant, intelligent young woman, I simply cannot believe it has been so long! How *are* you?"

"I'm fine—"

"Is my daughter there with you?"

"Yes, she is. I'm sitting right across the table from her." Ally was making frantic, hand-me-the-phone gestures, but Marsha was talking a mile a minute. Beth held up one finger and mouthed, *One second*. She smiled at Ally. Then she actually tuned in to what Marsha was saying.

"I'm so *terribly* sorry to be stealing her away from you, but my fiancé and I just arrived in New York and we're wondering what time we can expect to see her tomorrow. I know her flight gets in around eleven. Oh! And aren't you going to congratulate me on my engagement?"

SEVENTEEN

A cross the table, Ally watched Beth's face change. She had just been thinking that Drunk Beth had an agreeable looseness to her. But now something hard stole in and replaced the glow. Ally gave up on trying to steal the phone away before Marsha could ruin everything, realizing that she already had.

"Congratulations," Beth said into the phone, her voice suddenly sounding very hollow. "Tomorrow?" She paused, then said, "Here she is," and handed the phone to Ally.

"Mom, I'm going to call you right back," Ally said, and hung up, not bothering to listen to her mother's protestations. She had been floating pleasantly in a sea of alcohol, and now she tried to tread water as the tide changed. Without her mother's voice on the phone, silence permeated the kitchen.

"So when were you planning on telling me that you were leaving tomorrow? As you were walking out the door?" Beth asked.

Her voice was quiet, and her eyes were downcast, staring down at the table.

"Beth, Beth, no," Ally said.

"No what? No, you weren't planning on telling me at all? You were just going to disappear?"

"I probably wasn't going to go."

"Probably?" Beth looked up, her eyes boring straight into Ally's, and the anger Ally saw there startled her. "Right. Of course. You had a plane ticket, but you were *probably* just going to let it go to waste."

"I didn't buy it! They just bought it for me, without asking me."

"Oh yeah, *they*. Some fiancé you didn't bother to tell me about." Suddenly, Beth gasped. "Oh. Oh! And when you said Tom was coming back to New York soon, and that you were going to see him . . . That's why you're going back too, isn't it?"

Ally had no good explanation, no way to deny it.

"Well . . ." she said instead, "well, I don't see how you can be that mad at me for leaving when you're the one who is going away forever. You're choosing to leave me permanently. Sure, I was going to leave a couple days early, but you're the one who's really jumping ship on this friendship."

"Oh, I'm jumping ship on the friendship? You want to talk abandonment? You abandoned me first!"

Ally had no idea what Beth was saying. "What are you talking about? I'm not going a million miles away. I didn't ignore all your e-mails."

"First of all, Haiti is less than two thousand miles away from New York, not a million."

"Oh my God."

"But you're the one who made it very clear that I wasn't your person anymore."

"My person?" Ally said.

"The person who's most important to you. The person you'll be there for, no matter what. The person you love most. Don't worry, I got the message. You did a great job of letting me know that Tom had kicked me out of that spot."

"You mean when I didn't come to Britton Hills that summer? Beth, I asked you if that was okay, and you said yes."

"Yeah, because it was obvious what you really wanted to do, and I didn't want to force you into hanging out with me when you'd rather be elsewhere. 'Oh, Beth, you know how much I love you and Britton Hills, but this is the only time that works for both me and Tom. I totally won't go if you don't want me to, though.' What is that? How is anyone supposed to say no to that?"

Ally bristled. "You aren't supposed to say no to that. You're supposed to realize that a best friend doesn't necessarily stay *your* person forever. She stays *a* person, an important person, but she also gets boyfriends and spends time with them. It's not that big a deal, it happens. It could just as easily have been you. It's not my fault that you didn't have a serious boyfriend and I did."

"I know that."

"Then why didn't you tell me you were angry, instead of going off to Haiti?"

"I didn't go off to Haiti because of you."

"So why the fuck did you go? And why didn't you answer any of my e-mails? I needed you. I was such a sad mess. I literally begged you to write me back, and heard nothing from you until suddenly you asked me to come up here with you. I thought maybe you were dead, until I realized that if you had died, at least I would have heard about it. And you know what? I'm mad at you. I'm really mad at you about that." *Hah!* Ally thought. *So there, Beth. You are the one who's at fault here.* She had staked the moral high ground. Game, set, and match.

"I stopped answering your e-mails because I couldn't help a little boy, a sick little boy, and he died, and you hung up on me when I called you about it so you could be with Tom."

The floor disappeared from underneath Ally. "What?"

"Yeah. That's right. You hung up on me, and I had to deal with the fact that I just ran away from trying to help that boy all by myself. And then you never even apologized! You never even asked me about it, you just had to keep talking about Tom and oh no, how life was so terrible for you."

All of a sudden, Ally remembered: picking up the phone because it had kept ringing, and wanting, needing to hang up once she'd realized it was only Beth on the other end.

"Hey," Ally said, trying to reach for Beth's hand across the table. But Beth got up and went to the window. "Hey, I had no idea."

"But I *told* you!" Beth said. "I said it on the phone!"

"No, you didn't."

"Yes, I did." She turned her back to Ally, putting up her wall again.

"Then I didn't hear you. I was really distracted. I'm sorry." Beth was silent, so Ally went up to her and put her hand on her back. She could feel Beth flinching under her touch. Her back had hardened into steel beneath Ally's hand. "Tell me what happened, please."

"I don't want to talk about it with you now."

"Is that why you feel like you have to go back? I'm so sorry, if I had known—"

Beth whipped around. "But you didn't know, because you didn't listen and you didn't ask, and that's because you're selfish. You're selfish, Ally."

Ally recoiled. "I don't think that's fair. It wasn't like Tom and I were just hanging out when you called; we were about to break up, and then that kind of took precedence in my mind over everything else for a while." Tears started to prick at her eyes, and she silently pleaded with them to go away. She hated being the one who had to cry, while Beth got to stand there, composed and unmoving. "And I'm not really that selfish, am I? I mean, I'm here helping Grandma Stella."

"Right, and going off and flirting with a married man for hours."

"What? You mean Nick?"

"Yes, I mean Nick. Ugh, the sexual tension between the two of you is so thick I almost choked on it."

"That's not true."

"He looked like he wanted to rip your clothes off the entire time we were there, and you were doing everything you could to encourage him."

A little part of her kindled with the pleasure of being wanted, even as she launched into her protest. "Like what? What was I doing?"

"Everything! Shaking your butt when you walked, touching him, smiling up at him like he was Superman."

"I was not." She took a big gulp of her whiskey, then wiped her mouth with the back of her hand. "You're jealous. You were jealous about Tom. And now that you won't let yourself just do what you want to do with Owen, you're so sexually repressed that you're pushing all your frustration onto me."

Beth laughed, a mean laugh. "Go ahead and tell yourself that if it makes you feel better. Just like it makes you feel better to tell me that the reason you're going back to New York is because your mom bought you a ticket, when really it's that you want to go throw yourself at Tom as soon as possible even though he doesn't want to be with you. The plane ticket excuse is just bull."

And that was when Ally snapped. She banged her glass down on the table so hard that Beth jumped. "Say *bullshit*, Beth. Can you just fucking say the word *bullshit*? Refusing to swear like you're some holy angel actually just makes you sound like a little girl."

"Fine. Fine. You want me to swear?" Beth paused, then said quietly, "You're a fucking bitch."

"Maybe I am a fucking bitch. Boo-hoo. How sad. I wish I could be as good and pure and kind as you. Perfect you, Saint Beth, the savior of the world. Give me a break. You're such a sanctimonious asshole. Telling me that I'm a bad person doesn't make you a better person. I'm sorry not all of us want to give up everything that makes us happy. I'm sorry some of us want to be normal. You cut me out of your life for a mistake I didn't even know I'd made. That's not exactly perfect-person behavior. You're overpunishing me, just like you're overpunishing yourself right now with this ridiculous idea that you have to go live in Haiti forever. That's not going to change whatever happened with that little boy. You're just wallowing in your guilt, and some weird twisted part of you likes it."

Beth's pale face whitened more than Ally had thought possible. Maybe it wasn't too late to turn things around, but Ally couldn't stop. "If I met you now," she insisted, "I'd never become friends with you."

"I feel the same way," Beth whispered.

"Fine. Then why don't we stop pretending?"

"Fine. Go back to New York and go hook up with Tom. That's probably what you've been wanting the whole time you've been up here anyway."

"I will. And you can go save the world and neglect all the people who actually care about you."

"I'm getting out of here." Beth downed the rest of her scotch and walked toward the front door. "I'm going for a walk."

"I'm going to be gone when you get back," Ally said.

They stared at each other for a second. Ally knew she was memorizing Beth for the future, and she wished it were some other version of Beth she was looking at, not this hateful, blotched, drunk girl.

As Beth walked out the door, Ally ran to the bedroom and threw her clothes into her suitcase, then grabbed her toiletries from the bathroom. She crammed everything into her bag, not bothering to fold her sundresses or separate her shoes or even to fully zip the suitcase's multiple pockets. Then she said good-bye to the house, furtively, quietly. She went through each room, except for Grandma Stella's bedroom, and tried to take mental snapshots. Everything felt discolored, overexposed. But it didn't matter. She knew these images wouldn't last her long. She was no good at paying attention to details.

It wasn't the house that really mattered, anyway, but the fact that Grandma Stella had made a place for her in it. But the prospect of waking her up and explaining everything felt insurmountably difficult. Ally sat on the edge of the bed she and Beth had shared and tore a page out of her notebook.

Dear Grandma Stella,

I'm so sorry I didn't get a chance to say good-bye, but I had to go back to New York unexpectedly. I love you so much. Thank you for everything. You are the best surrogate grandmother I could ever ask for. I know your party is going to be the highlight of the year for everyone in town. Good luck with the move. Please let's talk soon?

Love,
Ally

She walked quietly to Grandma Stella's bedroom door and slid the note beneath it. Then she pulled out her phone. It had gotten late, but the person she was calling picked up anyway.

"I have to go back to New York now. Can you take me to the airport?" she asked.

"I'll be right there," Nick said.

EIGHTEEN

B eth crunched down the road on foot, barreling through the dark, heading away from Ally more than toward anything else. She couldn't quite believe what had just happened—the venomous things she'd said, and what Ally had said back to her. Some thoughts were meant to hide away in a part of your mind, acknowledged by you but no one else. Some thoughts just shouldn't be spoken aloud, because once they were, they changed everything.

And then, as that last shot of whiskey she'd downed kicked in, she decided on her destination. Her body knew it more than her mind did.

SHE stood outside the house where Owen lived and tried to figure out if it was too late to ring the doorbell. She didn't have his cell phone number: ridiculous, she knew, when she spent so much time thinking about him. A light was on in one of the front rooms, so she decided to chance waking his parents up and knocked on the door quietly. The harder she stared at the crisp, painted wood of the door, the more it wobbled.

After a minute, Owen appeared at the door. He was wearing glasses, and she liked what they did to him, how they made him a little nerdier, a little more vulnerable. His face when he saw her took on a beautiful mixture of befuddlement and happiness.

"Beth? What are you doing here?"

"Heeeeyyy," she said, the word slurring itself out longer than she'd intended. "I have a proposition for you." She wasn't sure if that was right. "No, I want to proposition you. No, the first one. I have a proposition for you."

He closed the door behind him and stepped out onto the porch. She liked the way he closed the door too, decisively but gently. She liked pretty much everything about him. She threw herself at him, into a kiss. She wanted him to blot out everything that had just happened with Ally. He was warm and that was nice, but this kiss had nothing on their previous ones. It felt fuzzy, like static on a television screen. He kissed her back for few seconds, then removed her hand from his butt.

"Whoa there. Hello." He shook his head a little bit and breathed out. "So, uh, what's your proposition?"

"Oh. Right. I propose that you have sex with me now. So I guess it's both actually, noun and verb."

"Um, right now?"

She sat down on the wooden slats of the porch and started to take her shoes off. Removing them was a necessary first step. She would take off her shoes, and then they would have sex, and then the rest of this night wouldn't matter anymore. "Yes. Nobody else is around."

"Beth, no."

"Come on," she said, and grabbed his hand, pulling him down onto the floor with her. "I want you to have sex with me." Half of her brain screamed *THIS IS MOMENTOUS AND RIGHT* and the other half yelled *WHOOOA WHAT IS HAPPENING?* She kissed his neck, and he let out a little moan, leaning into her. Then he pulled away.

"You're really drunk right now. I think this is a bad idea."

"Schmad idea." She started to unbutton her shorts. She saw him look at her, then very deliberately look away.

"Come back tomorrow, sober, and I will be very, very happy to have sex with you, but this, right now? No."

"Fine, then." He was ruining everything. She didn't want him tomorrow. Or rather, she did, but she wouldn't be able to have him without the excuse of drunkenness. She stood up and held on to the wall for balance as she crammed her foot back into her sneaker. "You've lost your chance, then. One-time offer." She nearly fell down the steps as she walked away, and Owen ran after her.

"Hey. Beth. Stop. Let me give you a ride back to your grandma's."

"No, thank you."

"Come on. I want to make sure you get home safe."

"I'll be safe. I'm an excellent walker. I don't need your help." She didn't need anyone's help, not his, not Ally's. People needed *her* help. This role reversal did not fit her comfortably. She kept walking. He grabbed her hand and pulled her back.

"Let go of me!"

"What is going on with you? Why are you drunkenly wandering the streets of Britton Hills at ten P.M.? Where's Ally?"

"Ally's gone! Back to New York."

"Why? Is she okay?"

"Yes, she's fine. She's dandy. Hunky-dory. Although if you ask her, probably the whole world is falling apart and everything is terrible and she'll never be okay again. Because did you know that's what happened when her boyfriend broke up with her? The whole world ended. She didn't run away from a dying kid like I did, but her life was the worst ever."

When she finished her speech, all that was left was bone-deep exhaustion. Owen watched her, looking really sad. "Please," he said. "As a favor to me, let me give you a ride home."

He looked so sincere and serious that, grudgingly, she let him lead her to his car. Her stomach wobbled as they drove, and she put her head in her hands, trying to make things stay still. Eventually she rolled down the window and let the wind wash over her. Owen pulled up to Grandma Stella's house and parked the car in the driveway. She put her hand on the car door handle but let it rest there without opening it. She could feel him watching her like he was trying to decide whether to say something.

"Did you know I had a sister?" he finally said. She shook her head. "Yeah, I didn't think you did. I don't know if you would've ever met her. She was older, and she didn't spend much time at the store because she hated it."

"Why would she hate Mulberry's?"

"I don't know. Because she was a cool teenage girl and cool teenage girls don't hang out with their parents in hardware stores, probably. But I thought she was incredible. I was just starting to get into that awkward middle school phase, and she was already in high school and had friends and a driver's license. She didn't really want to spend time with her younger brother, but sometimes, if I was lucky, she'd drive me home from soccer practice and we'd listen to show tunes in the car, which she made me swear never to tell anyone. Because, she said, the musical theater kids were nerds and she wasn't one of them, she just wanted to listen to really happy songs with dance breaks sometimes. She knew all the words, though, and could sing all the high notes. And then one night, when I'd just started sixth grade and she was a junior in high school, she drove home drunk from a party, crashed into a tree, and died."

Suddenly, she felt more sober. A lot of things made sense to her now. Why Owen had spent every day after school at the store with his parents. Why his father went six months without smiling. "Oh no," she said. "I'm so sorry. I didn't know."

"Yeah, my parents don't ever really talk about it. No one does. But for a long time after that, whenever any of my friends complained about something, it made me mad, you know? Like, oh no, your dog died. Big deal, your dog's not a person. My sister died. That's worse."

"Well, it *is* worse. You were right."

"Yeah, but you can't live your life like that. Everyone has their own crap to deal with, and you can't get wrapped up in judging other people's and saying that yours is crappier, even though maybe it is. 'Cause then you're just staring at crap all the time, and there are lots of better things to look at. It's like . . . like forcing yourself to stay at the dump instead of going to swim in the pond."

She could have told him that he was right, that she was tired of looking at everything that was bad, but instead she said, "I didn't realize you knew everything," and walked out of the car into Grandma Stella's house without looking back. She vomited in the toilet and passed out, curled up tightly, in one corner of her otherwise-empty bed.

NINETEEN

A lly sat in the passenger seat of Nick's car as they headed toward the highway that would take her away from Britton Hills.

"Thanks for coming to pick me up," she said.

He shrugged. "Wasn't doing anything else, so . . ." His car was nicer than she'd expected. She'd pictured something beat-up, with crumpled take-out wrappers strewn about, and CD cases all over the floor. But this car smelled like someone had recently vacuumed it. It looked like a family car, once the kids had grown past the car-seat phase. She wondered if his wife cleaned the car, and then she wondered what his wife was like.

And then she felt weird being in the car at all, so she pulled out her phone. She planned to send Tom an e-mail, to tell him that she was coming home early, but a message from him already waited in her inbox.

Hey Al,

So, short version of a long story: I mentioned to my boss here that I had a final-round interview elsewhere, and he offered me a raise I couldn't turn down. Looks like I'll be staying in Portland after all for the time being. Rain check on the coffee? I'll let you know next time I make it out to NYC, and I hope you know that you'll always have a place to stay if you ever want to explore Oregon's hipster wonderland.

Best,
Tom

Ally shoved her phone back into her bag and put her hand over her mouth. She was such an idiot. "Coffee" really had just meant coffee, not "We're going to get back together and live a romantic dream life." She slumped down in her seat and tried not to cry. She'd get to the airport. She'd find a chair and sleep on it for a few hours, and then she'd fly away from all this.

When she finally looked over at Nick, he was looking back at her.

"You look a lot less happy than when I saw you earlier tonight," he said. "You okay?"

"I don't know."

"You still drunk?"

"Yeah. Whiskey after wine is not the best idea."

"So, why you leaving?"

She sighed. "Beth is being such a bitch. I can't stay with her anymore, and she doesn't want me to stay, anyway."

"What's she doing?"

"She's just being so holier-than-thou. Nothing I do is good enough for her."

"Yeah, she seemed a little uptight. When you guys came to the store tonight, I mean. I could see how that would get really fucking annoying."

Ally fought off a weird urge to defend Beth from this person who barely even knew her. "Besides, my mom and her fiancé are in New York right now, and they really want me to come back. I have family responsibilities too. So it makes sense that I should go. And I've been up here for almost a week. That's a long time."

"Yeah, especially for Britton Hills."

"Yeah." She nodded, and then reconsidered. "Well, no," she said. "I love it here, actually. I'm going to miss it."

"You'll probably come back sometime, right?"

"Probably not. My friend's grandmother won't be here anymore. Plus, this is a me-and-Beth place, and I don't think there is a me-and-Beth anymore. Not after tonight." She could see the entrance ramp for the highway up ahead, getting closer and closer. Suddenly she felt like she couldn't get on it, not yet. "Wait a minute," she said. "Can we—can we stop?"

"Shit, what?" He hit the brakes and they both bounced forward against their seat belts.

"Sorry! Sorry, sorry, sorry. I just—I know this is silly, but could we drive through the center of town before we get on the highway? I know I'm already inconveniencing you, but I'd really like to look at it one more time. Say good-bye, and all that. It's ridiculous, I know."

He looked at her in disbelief. "Really?"

"Never mind. Forget it. It's stupid. Let's just go."

"No, it's okay, sure, we can," he said.

"Are you sure?"

"Yeah," he said, and turned the car at the next intersection. He put on an old Smiths CD and drove slowly down the town's main street, and she pressed her nose to the window, looking at all the shops. When he reached the harbor, she got out and stood, looking at the water, pulling her sweater tightly around her. She picked up a stone and tried to skip it, but it sank after one little jump.

"Okay, I'm ready," she said.

They pulled into the airport's parking lot a little under an hour later, no traffic to contend with. Nick turned off the ignition. Without the hum of the motor, everything felt eerie and deserted. The terminal glowed faintly.

"Thank you again," she said.

"No problem."

"For everything, I mean. It was really nice of you to drive me here, but also for all the music stuff. I'd sort of given up on it. I thought I was terrible, and had basically resolved to never, ever do it again."

"You're not terrible."

"Thank you." She gave a little laugh. A modest, dismissive laugh.

"I mean it," Nick said. "You laughed that off, but you shouldn't. Your voice is really pretty, and the stuff you write has a lot of potential. It's a little Joni Mitchell–ish."

"Thank you," Ally said. She didn't laugh this time, just looked at him straight on and accepted his compliment.

He looked away first. "I'm sorry we won't get to jam anymore."

"I know," she said. It felt so good, after this night, to have someone say nice things to her, nice things about her. She wanted more. The hole Beth had blasted in her self-esteem stretched way down toward the core of the Earth. "Let me know if you're ever in New York, or anything."

"Will do."

Neither one of them said anything, but she didn't get out of the car. She heard Beth's voice in her ear. *Ally!* it said. *Remove yourself from this situation right now! Walk out of this car and don't look back.* But she ignored it. She'd spent the entirety of the last week trying to do what Beth wanted, and that hadn't worked out for her. Nick clenched and unclenched the steering wheel, then drummed on it a little bit. She twisted her hair into a coil and brushed it against her cheek, and tried to think of something else to say. She felt an urge to babble, to stave off the loaded silence, but nothing came to mind.

Finally, after a minute of them neither speaking nor looking at each other, she reached down to gather her shoulder bag from where she'd tossed it at her feet. "All right. Good-bye," she said as she pulled the bag up to her lap. She turned to give him one more smile.

"Wait," he said, and launched himself over the emergency brake that separated them. His lips met hers urgently, and his stubble scratched at her cheek. He pulled her into him like he wanted to forget, and she wanted to forget too, so she let him. The emergency brake pressed awkwardly against her stomach, so she climbed over it and onto his lap, straddling him. Her sundress rode up around her legs, and he slid his hands beneath it to run up her thighs. She ran her fingers through his hair. It was messy like Tom's had always been, and for a brief second, she imagined that he actually was Tom, that she and Tom were doing what they'd done hundreds of times before and what she'd thought they'd be able to do again soon, and that everything was all right.

Whenever thoughts of Beth came to her mind, she kissed Nick harder. She banished Beth's disapproving face by licking his ear and seeing how loudly she could make him breathe. (The answer— very loudly, in a slow-motion gasp.) He pushed the straps of her dress down over her shoulders roughly until the dress bunched around her waist. She could feel him, hard, underneath her.

"God, you're beautiful," he whispered, and so she undid the buckle on his belt. She lifted herself up, sitting back against the steering wheel, and he pulled his pants to his knees, then pulled her back into him. They rubbed against each other, separated only by underwear, and she thought how nice it would feel to have him inside her, filling her up, concentrating everything she thought and felt into the act of sex itself. He wanted her, and she wanted him. It would be so simple to give in to that. His hand crept inside her underwear and played with the wetness he found there.

"I brought a condom," he said.

And something in the fact that he'd come into the night prepared for her to say yes to this selfish thing they were doing broke her heart. Because if he'd expected this of her, that she'd have sex with him despite his vows, despite his wife, just because she wanted to, then maybe Beth's accusations weren't just paranoia and prudishness. If he'd expected this of her, maybe he'd seen the same selfishness Beth had.

"I—I have to go," she said, jutting back against the steering wheel again and accidentally honking the horn.

"What?" The look of disbelief on his face might have been

comical in another circumstance. She yanked her dress back up over her breasts and climbed back to the passenger side of the car.

"I have to catch my plane."

"I thought you said it didn't take off until nine A.M.," he said, reaching for her. She evaded his grasp and started to gather up her things.

"We shouldn't. And I'm drunk. And—"

"Fuck those excuses. Come on."

"I'm sorry," she said, stumbling out of the car, and opening up the door to the backseat to grab her suitcase and guitar.

"Ally, what are you doing?" he called out after her. "Come back. You shouldn't be here all by yourself."

"And you shouldn't be here at all. Go home to your wife," she said, and his face changed from annoyance to anger. She couldn't tell how much of it was directed at her, and how much he had reserved for himself.

"Fine," he said. He started the car up again and sped out onto the main road. She watched him recede from view, her stomach curdling as she realized what she'd done. She'd crossed a barrier she had never expected to cross. Ally Morris, seducer of married men. Shit. Shit. She wasn't even that drunk anymore. The wine and whiskey had mostly worn off on the ride to the airport, and now that desire had faded, she was left with just a numb disgust. It made her want to crawl inside her suitcase and zip the zipper all the way up, so that she could just stay in that tiny dark space forever.

But, no, she hadn't seduced him. He was just as much to blame as she was. Not just as much, more so. She hadn't taken any vows.

She wheeled her suitcase through the automatic doors of the

terminal. The only person around was a wizened, half-asleep security guard, and he nodded a silent assent when she said, "I didn't want to miss my flight. Morning traffic. Can I sleep here?"

She curled up into the fetal position on a hard metal chair and closed her eyes, but sleep eluded her. Sleep said, *You don't deserve me right now.* She felt like she'd just chugged a cup of coffee dangerously fast, before it had gotten a chance to cool down. So she walked back and forth from one end of the terminal to the other, her guitar nestled on her back, wheeling her suitcase behind her, her energy jostling uncomfortably with her fatigue. The old man watched her silently, disapproving, and she frowned at him. Then she pulled out her phone to see if anyone had sent her a message or an e-mail. Maybe Nick had texted her. *(FYI, my wife and I just got divorced! So what you did wasn't bad.)* But he hadn't. She stared at the screen, empty except for the time (3:04 A.M.). She'd changed the background wallpaper just yesterday to a picture of her and Beth trying on the gigantic hats at Eloise's. They were laughing, half looking at the camera and half convulsing in giggles, their decorated heads leaning toward each other till they almost touched.

She deleted the picture, leaving the background blank. She didn't want to think about Beth ever again. She texted Gabby—Coming home early.—and her mom—Should be back at my apartment by noon. Excited to see you! She typed out a text to Tom too—I miss you—and stared at it for a little while before erasing it. Then she went back to her metal chair, sat down, and waited for sleep.

TWENTY

The sun pounced repeatedly on Beth's face, and she cracked open her eyes. Oh, her mouth tasted bad. Stretching it open to yawn took real effort, as did turning to look at the empty pillow where Ally's head had lain every other morning.

She didn't think she'd ever been this hungover. She cringed as memories of last night swam into her mind—yelling at Ally, throwing herself at Owen, treating him so unkindly when he'd told her a private, meaningful thing. She'd thought that too much alcohol was supposed to rub away details, but these memories were crystal-clear in their brutality.

She'd been drunk, she told herself, as she pressed her hands into her forehead and tried in vain to massage away her headache. That was a valid excuse. Even as she said that, though, she knew it wasn't true. Being drunk didn't turn you into someone you weren't. It just ripped away the checks and balances you normally imposed on yourself in order to act the way you were supposed to act.

She needed to eat a big helping of something greasy. She also needed to take about five Advil, unscrew her head and replace it with one that didn't hurt so much, and go back to last night so that she could do it all over again. But she'd start with the food. Her walk to the kitchen felt like a hike in the Everglades. She waded through the swamps of leftover alcohol in her body and reached the table, triumphant. The wood beckoned to her, so she put her head down on it and rested there. After a couple of minutes, she heard someone clomp urgently into the kitchen.

"Sweetheart, what's going—"

Beth lifted up her head blearily, and Grandma Stella gasped, her already worried face contorting itself into full-blown panic. She rushed over to the table, her flowered dressing gown swishing through the air, her hands fluttering with good intentions.

"Are you all right? What's the matter? Do you have the flu?"

Beth shook her head, and then groaned. Too much movement. "I'm fine," she murmured. "I just drank too much last night."

"Oh, that's all? Phew. Happens to the best of us. Coffee? Tea?" When Beth nodded silently, she bustled over to the stove and put on a teapot. "Now what's wrong with Ally?" Beth snorted, and Grandma Stella turned around. "I've been worried sick ever since I woke up and got her note this morning."

"Her note? What did she say?"

"Just that she had to go back to New York and that she was sorry."

Typical, Beth thought. Of course she'd fly away and leave Grandma Stella to worry, rather than explaining. Of course she wouldn't accept the blame. Suddenly, incredulous that she hadn't thought about it before, she wondered how Ally had gotten to the airport, and worried that maybe she'd done something dangerous. She thought, *I should check on her, just to make sure that she's all right*, but she pushed that impulse away.

"Is she okay? Is it a health thing? Oh my goodness, someone in her family died. Oh no. Oh, poor Ally. That's it, isn't it? Is that what happened?" Grandma Stella was pressing on, staring at Beth intently. Beth had the opportunity here for a total ally, but somehow she couldn't tell Grandma Stella the whole story.

So instead, she said simply, "Her mom came up to NYC unexpectedly—you know how Marsha is—and she really wanted Ally to come back and see her."

Of course Grandma Stella was no fool. She possessed one of the finest BS-meters around. Her eyebrow began to make its well-traveled journey up her forehead. "And so she left in the middle of the night? Without saying good-bye to me?"

"Um, yeah. Her mom bought her a plane ticket, sort of impulsively, I think, and she didn't want to miss her flight." She could see on Grandma Stella's face how lame her excuses sounded. Grandma Stella sat down next to her at the table.

"Darling," she said, and reached for Beth's hand. "You can talk to me. What's really going on? Are you and Ally all right?"

Beth shook her head.

"What happened?"

"We got in a fight. A massive one."

"Oh, darling. About what?"

"It doesn't matter. I don't really want to talk about it, if that's okay. I'm sorry."

LAURA HANKIN

"Well, you'll patch it up. I know you will. The two of you mean too much to each other to let a little thing come between you."

Beth was so tired of people thinking that they knew more about her and Ally than they actually did. Why was it that everyone who talked to her about this assumed friendship existed in a frozen state? If you once mattered to a person, it didn't mean you'd matter forever. She and Ally hadn't been trapped in ice at age seventeen. No one had shut them up and cocooned them together from the influence of the outside world. "I don't think it is a little thing!" she said, more harshly than she'd meant to. "And I don't know if I do want to patch it up."

"Of course you do," Grandma Stella said.

"No! I honestly don't know if it's worth it for me and Ally to be friends anymore."

"Darling, you're just feeling that way now, but soon you'll realize that what you and Ally have is stronger than whatever fight you had last night. She's too important to you. I mean, just look at how you've been going around this week, two peas in a—"

Beth stared at her grandmother. "Are you seriously lecturing me about friendship right now?"

"Yes, I suppose I am," Grandma Stella said. She chuckled a bit, missing the warning tone in Beth's voice.

"I don't think you should be giving advice on this subject."

Grandma Stella stopped laughing. "Excuse me?"

"You have all the answers about friendship? Then why did you and Penny Joan Munson fall apart? I don't want to take advice about saving my friendship from someone who ruined hers. Stop telling me to do things you won't do yourself."

Grandma Stella gaped at her. Beth felt as though she'd reached over and torn off the Grandma Glasses her grandmother normally wore, the lenses through which Beth appeared to be perfect. *Surprise!* she felt like saying. *I've actually been a rotten person all along.* The teapot began to whistle. Louder and louder, its birdcall punctuated the silence until Grandma Stella went to the stove and turned it off. Without saying anything, she poured the hot water into a cup for Beth, who sat motionless at the table, trying to figure out how to apologize. Then, her body shrinking into itself, Grandma Stella shuffled back into her bedroom and shut the door.

Beth prickled. The brambles grew out of her skin and poked anyone who tried to get too close to her. She felt dangerous, hurtful. She spent so much time trying to make people feel better, and now she'd hurt three people she cared about in the span of twelve hours. And she couldn't seem to stop. She wanted to warn people to stay away from her, to steer clear, because who knew how they'd be wounded if they tried to love her? Somehow, she'd been transformed into a kind of Frankenstein's monster, leaving destruction wherever she went, and it hadn't just started twelve hours ago. It had started in Haiti.

The only way to make it stop, she decided, was to work harder. She had to go back to the source and try more fully. Be better. She would go away again, back to Haiti. But in the meantime, she would clean. She would make sure Grandma Stella had the best going-away party she could give her.

So she made a list. She got out the bleach and the Windex. She organized everything that the party guests would see if they came in from the lawn and into the house, and the stuff that they wouldn't see too. She scrubbed the toilet in the guest bathroom and vacuumed up strands of Ally's fine brown hair from the floor.

She even rearranged the fruit in the fruit bowl into the most aesthetically pleasing arrangement she could manage—bananas on the bottom, peaches in the middle, kiwis on the top.

She went into town and checked with the caterers. She walked from store to store with reminders about the party. She gave Mulberry's a wide berth, still worried the entire time she was in town that she'd run into Owen. Thinking about the way she'd left him the night before actually physically caused her body to hurt.

And then she came back and went into her bedroom.

It was a disaster zone. Ally, in her hasty, drunken exit last night, had left stuff scattered about. And Beth, uncharacteristically, had just tossed her own crap on the floor when she'd gotten in after the debacle with Owen. She picked up all her clothes and folded them, putting them back into the bureau. Then she picked up Ally's remnants, the stuff that must have fallen out of her bag. A couple of dirty socks, mismatched, clearly from different pairs. Ally wasn't going to come back and get them, so she threw them out. Tossing them in the trash can gave her a strange satisfaction, so she did the same with some crumpled receipts. If she could remove all evidence that Ally had been here, maybe it would be like none of this had happened at all.

She tucked the sheets on the bed tightly and smoothed out the comforter, then surveyed the results of her work. Pretty good. And the rest of the house sparkled. The smell of cleaning solution pervaded the air. She'd done everything on her list for the party, at least everything that she could take care of today. There was nothing left for her to do, so she stood, feeling useless, uneasiness still running through her.

Then she left the bedroom and looked at Grandma Stella's closed door, which had stayed shut, to the best of her knowledge, since she'd yelled at her this morning. She thought, *No. I haven't done everything I can do today.*

She knocked on the door, and when she heard the soft "Come in," from the other side, she opened it. She walked straight to her grandmother, who was still in bed, sitting propped up, looking defeated, her eyes red. Her heart ached to see Grandma Stella like that. She climbed onto the bed and curled into her.

"I'm sorry," she said. "I was so mean to you. I don't know what happened with you and Penny Joan, and you don't have to tell me because it's none of my business. I made stupid judgments about you and that was unfair of me." She held on to her grandmother, her heart rattling around in her chest. "And I love you so much, and feel terrible that I hurt you."

"Oh, darling," Grandma Stella said, returning the hug, her arms trembling with how tightly she was trying to squeeze Beth, "I know."

"Sometimes I'm not a good person, but that's all I want to be. I try so hard, but badness leaks out."

"It leaks out of me too. It does with all of us. And that's why I haven't told you about Penny Joan, because when it comes to her, I let enough badness out of me to fill up the whole Atlantic Ocean. I don't want you to think of me differently, to think that I'm a bad person, and I've been scared that if I tell you about it, that's exactly what will happen."

"Do you think that I'm a bad person, after how I treated you this morning?"

"No, I think that you're just a person who has her faults and her snippy moods like we all do. But darling, this is much more than being mean to someone once at breakfast and then apologizing a few hours later." Grandma Stella twisted her hands together, fiddling with her ring.

"It's okay," Beth said. "You don't have to tell me."

"No," Grandma Stella said. She sighed. "I do."

TWENTY-ONE

⁓

Ally lugged her suitcase up the last of four flights of stairs and bent over in front of her apartment doorway, panting. The hard metal chair at the airport had not been conducive to sleep. On the plane, she'd meant to nap, but instead she'd taken out Valerie's romance novel, about a small-town girl on vacation in Boston for the week and her unexpectedly magnetic tour guide. She'd read it straight through until the plane descended at LaGuardia. It distracted her, like she wanted, and left her strangely titillated. All in all, she'd gotten about three hours of sleep, and her body shook a little bit whenever she moved.

But now she was home, about to walk into an apartment where Beth had never been, and she could start the process of forgetting all about her week in Maine. In her bedroom, resting on top of her bedside table, her computer would still be sitting there, with all the Netflix she could watch until the problems of Robin and Ted or

Liz and Jack felt more real to her than her own. That had gotten her through the immediate aftermath of Tom (well, that and copious amounts of drinking). It could definitely get her through Beth.

It felt fitting to think of this as a breakup. Someone who had been very important to her was not going to be important to her anymore. Beth would no longer exist in Ally's world, because she'd turned up her nose and said that Ally's world wasn't good enough for her. Ally didn't want Beth in her world anyway. It might sting for a little while, but ultimately she'd be fine. There were plenty of other fish in the friendship sea.

She unlocked the apartment's front door and pushed it open. Gabby jumped up from the couch and greeted her with a hug, and she thought, *Ah, here it is. Here is the easy love I've been looking for.*

"Oh my God oh my God, how are you?" Gabby was saying. "I missed you so much! I saw a cockroach the other day, and I was like, 'Ah! I liked my old roommate so much better! You can't live here with me, bug!' So I killed it! Aren't you proud of me?" As Gabby jabbered on, Ally smiled to herself and felt the warm glow of being loved.

Then she went into her bedroom and took a long, disorienting nap.

WHEN Ally woke up, she immediately checked her phone, certain that something would be there. Nothing from either Nick or Beth. Nothing from her mom either, so she called her.

"Sweetheart!" her mother yelled into the phone when she picked up. "We're in Chelsea. We made friends with gay men!

They told us about the best restaurant, that we just *have* to go to, as soon as we can. Come join us."

"Um, okay. I can do that. Or do you want to come see my apartment?"

"Oh but you're in *Queens*. Isn't that far? It's much easier if you just meet us in the city. We'll get dinner."

So she got on the 7 train. The subway jerked her like a roller coaster. She rattled in her seat as a man walked down the aisle of the train, barefoot, asking for change. He kept his balance improbably, not holding on to anything as the train lurched from side to side, and then he lay down on the train's dirty floor, which was speckled like an egg with discarded gum and other shit. He rested at Ally's feet. Everyone ignored him. The woman across from Ally pursed her lips and gave her a sympathetic look, as if to say, *Too bad he didn't choose a different car.* Ally pulled out her phone and reread old text messages until he left, a couple of stops later.

She didn't want to be selfish, but sometimes she couldn't help feeling that shutting out the world was the only possible way to keep your wits about you. If you kept giving and giving, eventually there'd be nothing of you left. Beth always chose to give, to the point where she'd handed away every recognizable bit of herself to strangers.

Blasts of hot summer air roasted Ally as she walked from the train to the restaurant. She was glad to be back in the hustle and bustle of New York, the city crowds jostling her as she walked, so that she couldn't just think her own thoughts. She had to pay attention to where she put her feet. In New York, people didn't love her the way that people did in Britton Hills. She couldn't pick a shop at random and be reasonably sure that the storeowner not only knew her name but would want to give her a hug. But that was okay, because when people loved you, really loved you, they expected certain things from you. They expected you to act in certain ways, and do things for them when it was inconvenient for you, and sometimes that was exhausting. Better to be anonymous, to be able to have a conversation with a stranger on a train that made you feel good, get a compliment from a man in a bar, have sex with a guy you wouldn't have to worry about running into on the street. So maybe being temporary to people was a good thing. Here she had friends like Gabby, friends who knew the way things worked. They both understood in an unspoken way that although they spent lots of time together and had a lot of fun in each other's presence, they wouldn't stay that way forever. Other things would come up. They wouldn't be roommates for the rest of their lives. One or the other would move away at some point. They'd likely both get married and then drift apart, and that was fine. They'd still be able to meet up for lunch and have a great time, without all the weird tension and bitterness she'd felt with Beth.

She pushed open the door to the restaurant, a trendy, loud Japanese place, and scanned the interior. In the center of the room, on a raised platform, a smattering of tables skimmed low to the ground, chairs replaced by pillows. On one of those pillows she saw a woman with her back to her, wearing chunky earrings and a pashmina, her hair held in a messy bun by way of two decorative chopsticks, gesticulating wildly at a waiter while the man across the table stared at her in awe. Yes, that was Marsha. Ally walked toward her mother, climbing the platform stairs and feeling like a giant among all these customers sitting so low to the ground.

"And *that's* the problem with our healthcare system, I think, when artists are limited in their self-expression because they have to commercialize themselves to make money so they can afford insurance, well you know, I'm sure, you're an actor—"

She tapped her mom on the shoulder twice before Marsha looked up, clearly annoyed at being interrupted when she was about to solve the healthcare crisis.

"Oh, it's you! Horatio," she said to the waiter, reaching out to hold his hand familiarly, "here she is, my long-lost daughter!"

The waiter, reed-thin with poofed-up hair, smiled and said, "Daughter? You look like sisters."

"Oh, Horatio, stop it! Or keep going, I don't mind. I *was* only in my early twenties when I had her—bit of a surprise, you know. Another round of sake for us all, please, darling." Marsha extended her arm and gave Ally a side hug that landed somewhere around her butt. "Sit," she said. "You look tired."

"Thank you," Ally said, sitting down next to her.

"Ally, this is Glen!" She pointed to the man across the table.

"Hello!" he said, struggling up from his floor pillow to give her an awkward hug. She stood back up too, and they reached over the table. He stiffly patted her back, then released her, and they both sat back down. He must have been at least ten years older than her mother. Delicate beads of sweat dotted his face, and he picked up a napkin to blot his forehead, then his jowly chin.

"Nice to meet you," she said.

"Glen has been just so excited for this, haven't you, Glen?"

"Yup!"

"I've told him all about you, how he's getting the most amazing new daughter. Your beautiful voice, how pretty you are, how intelligent, and now he can see it all for himself. Right, Glen?"

"Yup!"

"Aw, thanks," Ally said, accepting a cup of steaming sake from Horatio as he flitted back to the table. She took a tentative sip and let her mom put her arm around her, drawing her close, into her steady patter.

"Oh, we have had the *most* exciting day so far. New York just has this incredible pulsing energy. Don't you agree? As though everywhere you go people are really living, having the real extremes of all human experience, lovers quarreling and uniting, people dying tragically and living wildly, great art being made, great money being made. Not like in Delaware, or I'm sure in Britton Hills, right? Oh, and there's so much to do, and I know you are just taking advantage of it all, you are a resident of this city and therefore you will always be interesting . . ."

As Marsha talked, Glen nodded. They made an odd pair, Glen so quiet and deferential, Marsha pouring words out of her mouth in a steady rush, Glen so ordinary-looking, so clearly starting the descent into old age, Marsha all boho-chic glamorous. But as Ally drank her sake and felt her mother building a castle of approval and warmth around the three of them at their little table, a fondness for Glen was kindled inside her. She liked the narrative Marsha spun out about her and about this new family unit they were making together, and the night slipped away as they ate soft raw fish and filled up their bellies with hot liquid.

When Glen went to the bathroom, Marsha turned to Ally and clasped her hand. So many tendrils of her hair had fallen from her bun that the chopsticks in her hair were listing dangerously, close to clattering on the floor. "I know you cut your vacation short," she said, her eyes squinty from drinking. "And I'm so grateful you did. I don't want to be like your father about these sorts of things and just disappear from your life. I want you to be my maid of honor."

Ally's father hadn't invited her to his second wedding. He and his new wife had gone to their local courthouse, and he'd only told her when they'd talked at Christmas that year, three months after the fact. She couldn't believe that her father had been walking around married for three entire months without her knowledge. She'd thought about how, perhaps at a barbecue in the California sunshine, he'd introduced Carol as his wife to some stranger he'd just met, and that *stranger* had learned this essential fact about him before his own daughter did. Realizing that, she'd slid down to the cool tan tiles of the kitchen floor and sobbed. When Marsha had walked into the kitchen, she'd silently gotten down on the floor with her, stretching out alongside Ally even though the floor was dirty and she had been wearing a nice new dress. They'd stayed there for half an hour while Christmas carols played on the radio in the background. Marsha had rubbed Ally's back, for once not saying anything, knowing exactly what Ally had needed.

Now, in the Japanese restaurant, Marsha tucked a hair tendril behind her ear, then did the same for Ally. "Your father," she said quietly, "doesn't know what he's missing."

When Glen came back, Horatio and his waiter friends were with him, bearing a round of free green tea ice cream to celebrate the engagement. Everyone nearby cheered as Marsha climbed unsteadily to her feet and proclaimed, "We're getting married! I love this man, and I love my daughter, and life is just a beautiful and crazy thing, isn't it?" and Glen stood up and said, "Yup!" Then Marsha turned to Ally and put her hands on either side of her face.

"Aren't you glad you came back to the city?" she shrieked, above the din of loud, happy diners.

"Yes!" Ally said, and meant it.

ALLY woke up the next morning even before her alarm rang. She was meeting her mother for breakfast in the city at ten ("Just you and me," Marsha had promised the night before, when they were saying good-bye, "for some girl chat!"), but had time to kill, so she hung over the edge of her bed and reached for her old guitar. She pulled it out, squinting against the dust it stirred up, and brushed it off. She looked at it—the broken neck, the sprung nylon strings, the little scratches its deep red body had accrued over the years she'd carried it with her everywhere.

Then she carried it down the stairs, out the main door of her building, into the alleyway with the trash cans, and threw it out.

When she came back up, she pulled her new guitar out of its case and tuned it, twisting the knobs until the sound was right. She arranged her fingers in a C chord and, when she strummed, it reverberated against her body, beautiful and whole.

She started to play the song she'd written with Nick, but something about it took away the brightness of the day and allowed complicated feelings to creep in. She stopped and played through some of her older stuff instead. The familiarity of it cooled her down, so she stuck with that until it was time for her to leave.

She was late to breakfast, but so was Marsha, so neither one of them cared. They settled into a booth at a tiny French café and ordered matching lattes with pretty patterns drawn on them in foam.

"Don't you just adore Glen?" Marsha asked.

"He seems nice."

"He is, a total sweetheart."

"He really seems to love you," Ally said, taking a sip of her still-too-hot latte.

"Oh, he does," Marsha said, and chortled. "It's so exquisite to be worshipped like that. And he loved you too. He just raved about you all the way back to our hotel."

Ally liked imagining monosyllabic Glen raving, her greatness enough to move him beyond his usual limit of talking. She and her mother chatted about nothing and nibbled on croissants, until her phone, sitting on the table, lit up with a text. Her heart started to pound, as she wondered if it was from Beth.

Hey, it said, under *Nick Music Store*. Ally had no idea how she was supposed to respond to it, but everything that had happened in the airport parking lot came rushing back to her. A sharp stab of lust ran through her body, followed immediately by the guilt and immense sadness. She rested her forehead on her fist and took in a deep breath.

"What just happened to you?" Marsha asked.

"Nothing."

"Liar. Your face just fell faster than someone jumping out of a plane."

Ally considered. She hadn't told anyone about Nick yet, although she rarely allowed herself to digest the fact that she'd hooked up with someone new before texting at least three of her friends about it. The untold story of what had happened between them pounded on her from the inside, demanding to be let out. She looked at her mother, who was gazing at her firmly, and decided, *Screw it.*

"I did something bad."

"Oh, honey, what?"

"I . . . um . . . I kissed someone I shouldn't have. In Britton Hills."

Marsha looked steadily at her daughter. "Who? Oh, was it Beth? I always thought maybe—"

"What? No, no, not that. I'll tell you, but please don't judge me. I feel terrible about it. It was a huge mistake."

"All right. So tell me."

"His name is Nick. He's married."

"Oh," Marsha said solemnly. She looked down into her latte. "Only a kiss?"

"Well, no. More than that. We had almost-sex." Marsha continued staring into her drink and, terrified by her silence, Ally started to prattle. "It was bad, but really was it *that* bad? I mean, he's the one who's married, not me. So he's the one with responsibilities. I didn't initiate anything, he did. And I'm not the head of the morality brigade!"

Marsha looked up. "Morality brigade, that's a good one."

"Huh?"

"It's a clever turn of phrase."

"Wait, so you don't hate me for what I did. What I almost did?"

"Oh, absolutely not. Why would I hate you?"

"I thought—well, you weren't even looking at me just now—I thought you were really disappointed in me or something."

"Oh no, I agree with you one hundred percent—his responsibility, not yours. I thought you were about to get all defeated about it. You were building it up like you'd killed someone or something."

"Well, it's still not *good*. I feel a little like a . . . like a home-wrecker."

"You can't beat yourself up about it forever. Don't be *masochistic*, sweetheart. There's no need to become some kind of self-flagellator. And you know, this sort of thing happens all the time."

"Yeah, I guess it does."

Marsha leaned closer then, confidentially, and said, "And sometimes, good comes of it. After all, Glen was married when I met him."

"Wait, what?"

"Yes, yes, it's actually a little funny, I never would have met him if it hadn't been for his wife. Rather, his ex-wife. She adores supporting artists, not that I think she actually appreciates *art*, mind you, but she likes to be out and about, feeling like she's important. Anyway, she dragged Glen to a pottery exhibition one night, and some of my bowls were on display. And Glen wandered over to my section, and he told me later that one of my bowls just *spoke* to him, that he'd never seen a piece of pottery so full of meaning. It unlocked the artistic soul inside him, and made him realize what he wanted his life to be. He just offered to buy it from me for some ridiculous amount of money, and that's when I decided I'd like to get to know him better."

"Know him better how? Like as friends, since he was married?"

"Oh, you know. Know him better intellectually and spiritually and artistically. And in a biblical sense too." She smiled at her own wit.

"And what about his wife?"

"Well, sweetheart, it was *clear* that he was unhappy with her, and that he and I were much better suited for each other. My bowl spoke to him! Did she ever make anything that unlocked his artistic soul? No. All she ever made were casseroles."

"Is she okay?"

Marsha nodded. "She'll get over it. People do. We're a remarkably resilient species. And this opens her up to opportunities that are better for her! So you see, punishing yourself for this sort of thing is pointless."

Ally imagined herself sitting at a table in a café twenty-five years from now, blithe and chatty, pushing away the responsibility for all her mistakes, convincing herself that all she had done was right and good. She watched herself excusing the hurt she caused others because her actions served her own personal narrative so well, not allowing herself to feel the pain and guilt that came along with tricky decisions and mistakes. This future self of hers went for the easy love every time, pushing away everything when it became too much of an effort. And then she wasn't looking into the future, but into the past, the night before last, watching herself tell Beth that punishing herself for something had no purpose, and then packing her bag and flying away.

She looked back at her mother, who evidently considered the subject closed. "So Glen and I are thinking an April wedding, with the flowers just starting to bloom. Or maybe a destination-type of thing, in which case we could get married earlier because it's always warm in the tropics."

She pushed back her chair from the table and stood up. "I'm sorry," she said, "but I have to go."

TWENTY-TWO

Grandma Stella heaved out a large breath, then began to talk.

"Well, as you've gathered," she said to Beth, "Penny Joan was my best friend and I was hers—except for our husbands, of course. We met when she and Louis—that was her husband's name, he died about ten years ago—moved to Britton Hills as newlyweds. Almost from the instant we first met, at a town hall meeting, we just couldn't get enough of each other. I remember seeing her from across the room and thinking she was just so stylish—she'd grown up in Boston, you see, and had gone to Radcliffe and all sorts of fancy schools before that, and she had the right clothes and the right hair and the right lipstick, and for little old me, who had barely ever traveled outside Maine at that point and hadn't even attended college, it was thrilling to meet someone like her. But more than that, she was so friendly, not stuck-up like you might think a city gal plunked down in Britton Hills would be, and we made each other laugh like none other, and I just thought nothing would ever change that.

"And for a very long time, nothing did. We had children, and our children grew up and moved away, and your grandfather and Penny Joan's husband were close too although they always said that they'd never be as friendly with each other as we were. But then your grandfather died. He had that heart attack out of nowhere, and I came undone. I was . . . I was just devastated. He was the electricity in my life, and without him, I felt completely alone and in the dark.

"And because Penny Joan was my best friend, I expected a lot of her. Too much, I think. I wanted her to fill up the emptiness that Grandpa had left. I thought she should drop everything she was doing if I was sad, and run over to comfort me, and for a couple of weeks she did. She was very good, but of course she had her own life, and she couldn't be with me all the time. I didn't know that back then, obviously, or else I wouldn't have acted the way I did. Right now I'm feeling very wise, probably because I'm so ancient and wrinkled, but at the time I was absolutely certain that she wasn't doing enough, and as she began pulling away more and more, trying to get back into the swing of her normal life, less able to come running every time I called, I started to get resentful. I was scared of being alone, and I was jealous that she still had Louis, and that her children lived in Boston while your dad and your mom and you lived all the way down in Delaware.

"So I grew more and more insistent, calling her in tears at eleven o'clock at night, asking her to come over and stay with me when she had other things to do. And one of those evenings when she was here, I was crying, telling her the same things I'm sure I'd told her a hundred times before about how sad and alone I felt, not listening to any of her suggestions about how to maybe feel a little bit better. I just had to get all of my grief out, I thought, or else I would die. I remember that on that night, my missing your grandpa all felt particularly sharp and painful. Penny Joan kept checking her watch. She was trying to be sneaky about it, but I noticed. And then she asked if she could use my phone. She went into the kitchen to make a call, and I put my ear to the other side of the wall, where she couldn't see me, to listen in. She was talking to Louis, telling him that she'd be home soon, that she was just trying to 'extricate' herself. That's the word she used, 'extricate.' She said something like, 'Oh, just another situation to handle here, same as yesterday and the day before' in this exhausted, somewhat sarcastic tone of voice. Like my pain meant nothing to her. Like I was being ridiculous. Which I wasn't and was at the same time."

"Then what happened?" Beth asked.

"Oh, I confronted her, of course. I yelled at her about how she was making a mockery of my feelings, and how she had better just wait until something horrendous happened in her life because now I wasn't so sure I would be there for her one hundred percent. At first she tried to apologize, but then she told me that I was overreacting, and she understood that I was grieving but that I was also being a real pain in the you-know-what. We said a lot of horrible things to each other that night. I told her I didn't need her anymore, that I would take my grief to someone who wouldn't treat it like it was rotten. She left, and told me to call her when I had cooled down. But I never did."

"And she just gave up? She didn't reach out to you?"

"No, she did. She called me the next day, and the next, but I just didn't return her calls. I ignored her when I saw her in town too, and finally she stopped trying."

"Well, that's not *that* bad, Grandma. You were grieving. People do crazy things when they're sad."

Grandma Stella nodded, her lips pursed tightly together. "But that's not the worst of it, darling." She paused, and looked away from Beth's eyes. "The worst thing is that, when Louis died, I didn't do anything. I didn't call her. I didn't go visit, or send flowers. I never even went to the funeral. After everything she'd done for me. And that was years later. I should have cooled down by then, but I just had this grudge and it blocked my front door every time I thought about reaching out to her to see if she was okay. I knew that she'd be sad, that she'd need a friend, but I didn't try to help her. I was punishing her because she wasn't a perfect friend to me. No one is a perfect friend all the time. I certainly wasn't. So now you know. Your grandma is a mean, prideful, ungenerous old lady."

Beth looked at her grandmother. "You're not all of those things," she said. "You're a wonderful old lady, who has her mean, prideful, ungenerous moments."

Grandma Stella cracked a smile. "Ah, so you admit I'm old. And that's the one I was most worried about!"

"Besides, it's not too late. You can still make things better."

Then Grandma Stella started to cry. "I tried. She doesn't want to speak to me. I called her this afternoon after what you said to me. I thought I might try to apologize, finally, or at the very least ask her to come to the party. And as soon as she heard my voice, she said, 'Trying to make a fool of me again? I have nothing to say to you,' and hung up the phone. I don't know why she thinks I've made a fool of her."

Beth looked at her, surprised. "Well, probably because you didn't go to Monroe's on Wednesday."

"What do you mean? Why would I do that?"

"Um," Beth said. "Because of *Dear Valerie*. Didn't you read it yesterday?"

"Darling, I haven't been reading the *Bugle* at all over the past few days."

"But you always read it. You love the *Bugle*."

"I know. I love that silly little paper even more than I love the *Times*. But it's a self-preservation thing. I've been trying to wean myself from Britton Hills a little bit at a time, so I won't miss it so much when I'm not here anymore."

"Oh," Beth said, realizing how careless she and Ally had been. "Oh no."

"What in the world does *Dear Valerie* have to do with me and Penny Joan? And what is this about going to Monroe's?"

"WELL, darling," Grandma Stella said after Beth had finished explaining how she and Ally had meddled, "I appreciate how much the two of you care about my happiness, but this has put me in a real pickle, hasn't it?"

"I know. We really didn't intend to screw everything up for you."

"You know what?" Grandma Stella asked, throwing off the covers and stepping out of bed with more vigor than Beth had seen since she and Ally had arrived. "Get the car keys. Make yourself presentable, and I'll do the same. We're going over to visit Penny Joan."

"Really?"

"Yes! I know what I want to do, and I'm going to do it. But you're going to have to drive because I'm so nervous I'd probably steer the car into a ditch."

Twenty minutes later, Beth pulled up outside Penny Joan's house, a pink gingerbread Victorian, its front yard bursting with azaleas. Next to her, Grandma Stella trembled. She'd overcompensated in the makeup department, and with her obscenely red lips and overly rouged cheeks, she resembled a clown with stage fright.

"All right, here I go," she said, but she didn't move. "I look ridiculous. What am I doing? Let's go back home."

"Absolutely not," Beth said.

"Absolutely yes, let's go."

"I'm not driving you away until you do what you came here to do."

"Well then, give me the keys and I'll drive."

"Nope," Beth said, and threw them out the window. They landed with a swish in one of the azalea bushes, disappearing completely between blossoms. "Sorry."

Grandma Stella stared hard at Beth for a long moment, then broke into a nervous laugh. She kissed her, leaving a thick lipstick print on her cheek. "Have I told you enough times how much I love you, darling?"

She squared her shoulders, marched up the flagstone walkway to Penny Joan's door, and knocked. Beth leaned up against the side of the car and watched. For a long moment, nothing happened. Grandma Stella knocked again. Then Beth noticed a face peeking out the window. Grandma Stella saw it too. But when she turned from the door to look again, Penny Joan ducked back behind the curtain.

"Penny Joan Munson, I know you're in there!" Grandma Stella chucked her polite knocking in favor of an insistent pounding. "Open up this door right now, you stubborn coward!"

"*I have nothing to say to you,*" came the retort through the walls.

"Well, I have things that I need to say to you, things that I should have said years ago, and I'll say them to your face or I'll say them to your door, but you're going to hear them!"

No response. Then, a moment later, classical music began blaring inside the house. Horns and violins commenced an auditory assault, and Grandma Stella turned around, shaking her head. "Darling," she said to Beth, "get the keys."

"Are you sure? Maybe if we just wait a little bit—"

"Get the keys."

So Beth ducked into the azalea bush, trying to push aside the sweet flowers as gently as possible as she searched for the key ring. She crouched and stuck her hand out, feeling through the dirt and the branches. Right as she'd finally grasped them, the classical music got louder. When she stuck her head out of the bush, she saw Penny Joan Munson standing in her open doorway, her face pinched and furious, her arms waving wildly in the air.

"Shame on you, getting your granddaughter to root around in my azaleas! They are a *delicate* flower and you have no right to ruin them," Penny Joan roared.

All in a rush, Grandma Stella began to talk. "I'm sorry I have been a terrible friend. I'm sorry that Louis died and I wasn't there for you. I'm sorry that I stood you up on Wednesday night—I didn't even know about meeting you at Monroe's, I didn't read the paper that day, and so I missed the letter in Valerie's column, which I didn't even write, and . . ." Grandma Stella seemed to realize she was rambling. She stopped for a moment to compose herself. "I'm sorry. I'm sorry for all of it. I'm sorry because"—tears started to cloud her voice, so she cleared her throat—"because I have missed you every day since we stopped speaking."

The song inside Penny Joan's house came to an abrupt end, and the two women faced each other in silence.

"You're a crazy old mule, Stella," Penny Joan said. And then her face crumpled and her eyes got wet. "And I've missed you too."

Simultaneously, they wrapped their arms around each other. Another piece of music came blasting out of Penny Joan's house. Some greatest classical hits CD compilation, Beth figured. Timpani and strings bellowed in a great fanfare, startling the two women apart, and they both wiped their eyes.

"Can you turn off that infernal music?" Grandma Stella asked.

"If you'll get your granddaughter out of my flowers."

"Meet you back here in a minute."

Beth stepped out of the azaleas as Grandma Stella came toward her. Her face was still streaming tears, but her walk was definitely a little lighter. She even did a little hop as she approached, an old-fashioned dance move.

"Thank you, my darling," she said, wiping leaves and dirt off Beth's face and giving her that completely focused Grandma Stella look that promised nothing but love. "Now, I'm not going to push and pry about what happened with you and Ally, but I am going to say that I wish I'd done this twenty years earlier."

Beth considered the way Grandma Stella radiated relief, and how nice it would be to join her in that lovely state. But still, the mention of Ally made her chest feel tight. It might have been hatred, or anger, or something else that she couldn't quite identify, but she knew she didn't like the feeling. She wasn't sure if she could forget everything that Ally had laid on her, or forgive her as easily as Penny Joan Munson seemed to have forgiven Grandma Stella. All that Ally had said and done the night she left stuck in her throat.

Beth hugged Grandma Stella silently. "Get back to Penny Joan!" she said.

THE next day, Beth stood amid all the party preparation as the hours ticked away. Her parents bustled around her, setting up folding chairs and tables under a huge white tent on the lawn. They'd gotten in early that morning, with their long hugs and their go-getter determination to give Grandma Stella a good time. "Oh," her mom had sighed when she'd gotten out of the car and breathed in the fresh Maine air, "it feels so good to have all of us here, back together again. But where's Ally?"

They'd been more easily deflected by Beth's excuses than Grandma Stella. After years of dealing with Marsha while scheduling trips and playdates for the girls, Beth's parents were all too familiar with her scattershot planning and last-minute ideas, so they carried on, helping with the party setup and oblivious to the secrets rebounding inside their daughter, oblivious that they were about to lose her to Haiti again, oblivious that she'd sworn off contact with the girl they considered practically a second daughter.

Beth was racing to finish tagging all the furniture and knick-knacks they'd dragged outside for the yard sale when a car pulled into the driveway. She looked up, wondering which hyperpunctual guest had arrived so early. But the guy getting out of the car didn't look like he'd come for the party.

"Hey," Nick said. "Beth, right?"

"Um. Yes. Hi."

He stood awkwardly, his scruffiness out of place in Grandma Stella's yard. She felt herself standing awkwardly too, folding her arms reflexively around her waist in a self-protective gesture. "Ally's not here," she said. "She had to go back to New York."

"Yeah, I know," he said, and something in the way he said it raised the hairs on the back of Beth's neck. "I drove her to the airport." He looked smug saying this, but also deeply uncomfortable, and that was when she knew that something had happened between them. She didn't want to picture it, but she couldn't stop herself from seeing a brief flash of the two of them, pressed together. *Ally, how could you?* she thought. And then she remembered lying in bed with Ally years ago, at the first of their many sleepovers, and summoning up the courage to ask her why her parents had gotten divorced.

"I don't really know," Ally had said in a small voice. "A lot of reasons. I'm not sure, but I think maybe my dad cheated on my mom."

"Really?" Beth had been shocked. "Why do you think that?"

"She's said some stuff about how you can't trust men. So I think that's what she means."

"That sucks, though. And it can't be true! There are lots of good men in the world! I bet James Van Der Beek would never cheat on the woman he married, or Carson Daly."

"Yeah," Ally had agreed solemnly, absolutely certain, like Beth, about the infallibility of their celebrity crushes. "I just don't understand," Ally had said then, turning over and squeezing her pillow. "Like, why would you ever do that to another person? My husband is never going to cheat on me. I'd never marry a man who would do that." They'd agreed then, righteous and pure, that there was a certain way that the world should work, and that they weren't going to have anything to do with people who spoiled that.

"What do you want?" Beth asked Nick now. The anger she felt at him and at Ally made her words come out abruptly.

"She left this in my car," he said, holding up a CD. "I think it fell out of her bag. I wanted to send it to her, but I don't have her address."

"Don't you have her phone number?"

"Yeah." Now the smugness disappeared. "She's . . . uh, not really answering my texts. Can you just send it to her?"

"Sure. Fine," Beth said, and held out her hand for the CD.

"Cool," Nick said. As soon as the CD left his hands, he turned around and headed back to his car. He opened the door, then stopped, turning back to look at her like he didn't want to say what he was going to say. "You might want to listen to it before you send it to her." Then he got in and drove away.

Beth walked inside, headed straight to the trash can. She pressed down on the pedal, flipping the lid up. But her hand hesitated. It wouldn't let go of the CD. She didn't really want to hear Ally's voice right now. She didn't know if she could stand a cutesy song, all the *doo doo doo*s and Ally's honeyed tone in light of what she knew. But she couldn't throw it out. She remembered Ally pulling back at the record store when Nick had asked if they should play the song, and how she'd looked at Beth almost fearfully.

She took the CD to the living room, to the old player Grandma Stella had next to the television. She turned the volume way down low, not wanting her parents to see or hear what she was doing. She lifted the CD out of its case and into the player, sat down on the floor, and put her ear against the speaker. Then she pressed play.

Beth heard nothing for a couple of seconds, then, softly, the first notes from a guitar. They started spare, then built into melancholy chords. Finally, Ally started to sing.

Won't you come to the battlefield? We'll lay there in the grass
We can stay in the battlefield and somehow time will pass
'Cause the moss and the willow trees, they grow to cover bone
Won't you come to the battlefield? I can't go there alone.

Now the guitar got louder, and piano notes cascaded. The gentle but insistent thump of drums anchored the background. Beth tried to stay unmoved. *This isn't that great*, she told herself. *These lyrics aren't even grammatically correct. It's* lie, *not* lay. But already a lump had started to rise in her throat.

I can throw away my horns there. Break your halo into two
And then we'll attempt to share it. I'll take half of it from you
'Cause it's hard to see the battlefield when light surrounds
*   your head*
Please come to the battlefield, don't leave me here for dead.

Ally's voice no longer sounded to Beth like a little pot of honey. Now it was a honeycomb lifted straight from the hive—still sweet, but messier, with hidden channels, and the possibility of a sting.

We'll be safe in the battlefield till we've had time to heal
Oh yes, safe in the battlefield, just tell me how you feel
'Cause we've run from the battlefield too many times before
Oh come to the battlefield
Come to the battlefield
Come to the battlefield
We'll settle up the score

Beth didn't want the song to end, but it did. The last notes trembled in the air as they faded. She lay down on the floor, her face against the rug, and wept. As her nose ran and her body heaved, she felt as if she'd unleashed more than a great torrent of tears and snot. The sadness that had been pushing against a dam inside her was all rushing out with a *swoosh*, faster than she could release it. These tears felt different than the ones she'd been crying in Haiti. Yes, they were wretched and painful but they were also hopeful. And grateful.

Because now she could admit to herself something that she'd been trying to ignore for months. She didn't want to live in Haiti. She didn't want to leave her family, to leave the possibility of a life with some modicum of normalcy. She wanted to help people, and then she wanted to be able to come home. And she wanted, maybe someday, to share that home with someone, with a guy who cared about helping and doing good too, but who also cared about splashing in ponds and kissing her hard in the sunlight.

Somehow Ally's song had revealed her need for all of this. Now that Beth's longings were laid bare and she was facing them full-on, they squirmed a bit under her scrutiny. Still, they stood their ground.

Ally was right. Beth's halo had gotten too heavy. She didn't think she could wear it anymore. But that was okay.

She'd thought that running away from Haiti was the only kind of running away there was. But that wasn't true. Going back was a form of running away too, of running away from the people she loved and who loved her. And half a halo wasn't bad at all.

Ally had changed from the girl Beth had fallen in love with back when they'd met in fifth grade. Sometimes she looked at her and didn't recognize her, but then again, sometimes she didn't recognize herself. She thought about that day when they'd gone to the battlefield together a few years into their friendship, when Ally had told her things and she'd told Ally things right back, things she hadn't thought she could tell anyone. Ally had flaws, sure, but she had told herself that she could love her anyway. Grandma Stella's words from yesterday rang in her head. *She wasn't a perfect friend to me. No one is a perfect friend all the time. I certainly wasn't.* Somehow she'd forgotten what eighth-grade Beth had known with such certainty.

She'd spent parts of the last two weeks, and all of the last two days, telling herself that a friendship with Ally made no sense anymore. They'd grown too far apart, stood on opposite sides of an ocean and tried in vain to translate each other's shouting. But they hadn't needed to shout. Ally could write a song and understand something so fundamental about Beth, about who Beth had been and who Beth was now and who Beth might be in the future. And that was something worth fighting for. Even if the fighting was messy and painful, there would be time for both of them to heal.

"Pumpkin," her father called, pulling her back to the here and now. "The guests are starting to arrive! Come outside!"

Beth cleared her throat of the mess her tears had made. "I'll be right there!" she said. She ran to the bathroom and splashed water on her face, then pulled her phone out of the pocket of her shorts. Shakily, she dialed Ally's number, trying to rehearse what she was going to say when she picked up. She found it difficult to make the words form logical sentences, and hoped blindly that they would arrange themselves into something that made sense once she heard Ally's voice. The phone rang once.

"Hey—" Ally said.

"Ally! Listen, I—"

"Apparently I can't come to the phone right now. Nooooo! But leave me a message and I'll get back to you as soon as humanly possible. Thanks!"

Voice mail. Panicked, Beth hung up and stared at the phone, uncertain how to cope with this roadblock. She tried calling back. Still no Ally, just her chirpy message.

"Ally," she said. "I need to talk to you. Please call me back." Her voice sounded much calmer than she'd expected it to. "Thank you for your time," she added, and then hung up.

She thought about how Ally had sent her e-mail upon e-mail, begging for her response, and she'd ignored them all. Twenty minutes earlier, if Ally had called her, she probably wouldn't even have picked up. In fact, she might have deleted any messages Ally left for her without listening to them, her anger stronger than any attempts at apology.

Maybe she could take the car and drive down to New York. She even started toward the bathroom door, ready to toss some supplies in a bag and go. But as she opened it, she heard the murmur of guests on the lawn outside. She had to stay for the party. Grandma Stella needed her. She could go tomorrow. She'd get through tonight, and then if Ally still hadn't called her back, she'd go stand in front of her door until something changed.

Still, alternate scenarios kept running through her head. What if, somehow, between now and tomorrow, Ally had hardened herself beyond a breaking point?

No, she decided. She'd go tonight. Grandma Stella would understand.

She walked out to the lawn, unable to concentrate on anything but finding Grandma Stella. Already, dusk had darkened the sky. The lanterns had been turned on. They hung in trees and nestled in flower beds, turning the entire yard into a glowing wonderland. The scent of roses from the garden blew along on the breeze. People milled around, chatting and laughing. Some of them poked through the belongings lying out on the lawn, deciding what piece of the house they wanted for their own. Beth walked right by Valerie, squaring off with a bespectacled, pleasant-looking man over Grandma Stella's love seat, just in time to hear him say, "Fine, I'll let you have it if I can take you to dinner." Then she passed Mr. and Mrs. Murney, who called out to her excitedly about how, even though they'd closed the arcade, they'd been getting together the funds to open a new business, this time with more video games. "I really think the youth will enjoy it!" Mr. Murney said, and Beth nodded absently, her mind somewhere else completely.

It seemed like the entire town had turned up for the party. Beth knew how much this must have meant to her grandmother, seeing everyone who loved her gathered in one place. *But dammit, this makes it really hard to find anyone.*

She walked past Owen's parents, doing a double take as she registered who they were. She tried, furtively, to look around for Owen as they walked toward her. "Beth!" Mr. Mulberry said. "We haven't seen you all summer! Owen mentioned that you came into the store last week. I hope he offered you a lollipop."

"Oh yes, he was very generous." She did her best to sound casual as she asked, "Is he here tonight?"

"No," Mrs. Mulberry said. "He couldn't make it, unfortunately. Said he was feeling too tired. I don't know why he'd pass up a party like this, but I suppose we've been working him hard at the store."

"Only because we know he can handle it," Mr. Mulberry said. "And because we need to get as much of him as we can before he leaves us for the big city in the fall."

"That boy," Mrs. Mulberry said, sounding like she was about to cry. "We're so lucky to have him. He's a treasure."

"He is," Beth said. "And you both are too." Spontaneously, she hugged them both, quick and hard, then pulled back. "Excuse me, I have to go find my grandmother."

Finally, she pushed through a group of men silently drinking beer and saw Grandma Stella standing by the bowls of chips, surveying the party. From her perch at the snack table, Grandma Stella beamed and kissed people as they walked past. Then Penny Joan came up and slipped her arm into the crook of her elbow. Calmly, they stood together, in the eye of some beautiful party-storm. Beth

hated to interrupt them. But she had made her decision. She needed to leave.

As she took a step forward, she felt a tap on her shoulder. *I'm never going to get out of here*, she thought. She turned around, ready to shake off another neighbor with a brief, professional smile. "I'm sorry, but I can't talk right now—"

"Hey," Ally said.

TWENTY-THREE

Ally watched the smile slide off Beth's face and worried that this was going to be even harder than she'd anticipated.

"What are you doing here?" Beth asked in a stunned voice.

Ally figured the best strategy was just to get it all out, no matter how much it scared her. "You were right—sometimes I am selfish. I've done some bad things, things I feel terrible about, but I feel worst about not being there when you needed me, and saying that you were overpunishing yourself about that boy, because, again, I wasn't there, so I don't know what you need to do to get over it. If you want to go back to Haiti, you should go back, and know that I will support you and try to stay in your life as much as possible, if you'll have me. I could come and visit you there. Maybe I could help you."

"No," Beth said, and Ally's heart sank.

"Oh," she said.

"No, no, no," Beth said. "I mean, I'm not going back."

"What?"

"You were right too—I don't want to go back. I never did. I thought I had to, thought I needed to, but then I listened to your song, and it made me realize that going back there is just another form of running away. And I don't want to run away from you."

Beth reached her hand out to Ally's, and Ally grabbed it like a life raft.

"Oh, thank God. I'm so glad," Ally said. "But how did you hear my song?"

"Nick brought it over. He said you'd left it in his car."

"Ah. Did he tell you what we did?"

"No, but I sort of figured it out anyway."

"Yup. As I've said, I've done a bunch of things I feel terrible about."

Beth squeezed Ally's hands tighter. Then suddenly, she shook her head. "Wait," she asked. "How did you get here?"

"I drove. I rented a car in the city and drove up."

Beth paused, incredulous. "You drove? In New York?"

"I did."

"Like *through* New York? In the actual city?"

Ally had left her mom at the café and power-walked to the nearest rental car company. Then she'd lurched, in abject panic, the thirty city blocks to the highway, narrowly avoiding at least five accidents. People had honked at her, a lot. She nodded.

"How was it?"

"Oh, terrifying. It was absolutely terrifying." They both laughed, and then Ally stopped laughing. "Somehow, though, it wasn't as terrifying as not being your friend anymore."

Beth started to cry then. Ally hadn't seen her cry in years. She'd forgotten how the tears welled up in Beth's eyes slowly and then exploded down her cheeks. "I love you," Beth said. "Even if sometimes I can't stand you and you can't stand me, I hate not having you in my life. And I'm sorry I've been punishing you so much."

Suddenly, the crowd around them parted for the woman of the hour. "Ally! You came back!" Grandma Stella said, and descended upon her with a tsunami of kisses.

"Yes, of course," Ally said, as soon as she caught her breath back again. "I can't believe I ever left." Then she noticed the woman next to Grandma Stella, who stood beaming at her side.

"Hello, Ally," Penny Joan said. There was that familiar smile, the crooked tooth. The two of them together looked as radiant as they'd looked on the beach that day, in the old photo.

Ally turned to look at Beth, the question on her lips, but before she could even ask it, Beth nodded, the tears still running down her face. And then Ally burst into tears too.

"Oh goodness," Grandma Stella said. "What's wrong?"

"Nothing," Ally wailed.

"We're just so happy!" Beth sobbed, choking the words out.

"You and Penny Joan are friends again." Ally let out a tearful hiccup. "And the party is so beautiful."

"Yes, it is!" Beth's voice had reached a higher pitch than Ally had thought possible. She fully expected dogs to start howling at any moment. People were starting to stare. Beth soldiered on. "And we're really glad we get to be here and support you."

"My darlings," Grandma Stella said, putting an arm around each of them, "I appreciate your dedication. But for crying out loud, get out of here. You're causing a scene, and *I'm* supposed to be the center of attention at my party."

So they sneaked off into the house, went upstairs, and climbed into their bed together. They curled up toward each other and pulled the covers up to their chins. As the party hummed outside their window, Beth told Ally everything that had happened in Haiti. For half an hour straight, Ally listened. She imagined Beth going through all of that on her own, and her heart ached.

"Have you told Deirdre and Peter yet that you're not going back?" she asked.

"No," Beth said. "I'm scared."

"Why are you scared?"

"I don't know—I'm afraid she'll make me change my mind, maybe. I should just get it over with, though. Stay here with me and be my moral support?"

"Of course."

So Beth put the phone on speaker and dialed. As it rang on the bed between them, Ally wondered if Beth had somehow found a way to pump nerves from one person to another via some empathic pipeline, because all of a sudden she was terrified.

"Hello?" Deirdre's voice was brisker than Ally had expected.

"Deirdre?"

"Oh, Beth. Hello. What is it? Did you decide on a flight yet?"

"No. No, I didn't." Beth paused and looked at Ally. "I've decided not to come back."

The ensuing silence on the other end of the phone was so profound, the air seemed almost to buzz with it.

"Hello?" Beth asked. "You still there?"

"Yes. Well. I'm disappointed, I must say. And a little confused. You told me you wanted to come back just a few days ago. From my end, this all feels like it's come a little out of nowhere."

"I understand why you might feel blindsided. I'm sorry that you're disappointed in me." Beth was scrunching her eyes shut, and Ally watched her, worried.

"I think you really had the potential to do some excellent work here. I don't want you to waste your talents."

"I know. I don't want that either."

"Are you sure about this?"

"Yes, I am," Beth said. "I need to stay here."

Ally let out an audible sigh of relief, then clamped her hand over her mouth.

"I don't think I'm meant to be a Paul Farmer like you, but I'd like to try to be an Ophelia Dahl. I still want to work with you, and help you if I can. If you'll have me. You need someone here in the U.S. to talk to donors and organize outreach, reach out to sister organizations, do all of the stuff we've been trying and failing to do at the clinic. It would be so much more efficient taking care of all of that from here."

"Hmm," Deirdre said. "Tell me more."

"You've been trying to raise that money for the water purification system, and it's taking forever because you have no one really working on it, no one who is able to dedicate herself to actually go talk to people with the money. They just get a letter in the mail from Haiti once every couple of months, and that's not enough. And I like coordinating things and getting people excited about causes. I could set up an office in Philly or New York, or someplace like that, and be based there but come back to Haiti for a few weeks each year. I'd like to make that water purification system happen. For Michel, and everyone else."

"Let me think about it," Deirdre said.

"Okay, please do."

"I'll talk to you soon. And Beth?"

"Yes?"

"When I said I was disappointed, I meant disappointed you wouldn't be coming back. I'm not disappointed in you."

"Thanks," Beth said. "We'll talk soon." She hung up, then let her body go limp on the bed. "Whew."

"I'm so proud of you for doing that," Ally said. "And way to be amazingly badass and competent. Did you *just* come up with that idea about working on the fund-raising end of things?"

Beth smiled. "Sort of. I guess I'd thought about it a little bit in the past, but never as a serious option. And then, just now, on the phone, everything sort of clicked." She sat up, resting her head on her hand, and looked at Ally. "I want things to click for you too. I know you've been talking about documentaries and production companies and all of that stuff. But your song—I meant it when I said it was really beautiful. I mean, I liked your stuff before, but this was a whole different level of good."

Ally didn't need Beth's approval this time to be proud of what she'd done with her music. For one of the first times since she'd been writing songs, she felt confident about what she'd created. She liked the feeling and wanted more of it. She'd want more of it even if some people listened to her music and said *Meh*. But still, it felt completely lovely to have Beth's decidedly non-*meh* response. "Thank you. You sort of ended up being my muse on this one."

"Well, thanks. Being a muse suits me beautifully, and I don't think you should give up on doing music. It just lights you up like nothing else does."

"I'm not going to give it up," Ally said. "But I was thinking about what you said, about me being selfish."

"I didn't mean—"

"No, no, it's okay. So I obviously had a lot of time to think in the car on the way up here. And after I spent an hour worrying that I was going to die in a fiery wreck on the highway, and then another hour worrying that you were going to tell me to go fuck myself, I decided to actually think about what to do with myself that put some good in the world but also made me happy. You know, something besides babysitting that I can do in addition to my music, or alongside my music."

"Ally, that's awesome. So what *are* you going to do?"

"Oh," Ally said. "I have no idea. I reached zero conclusions. But it's only the first day of thinking about it. I'll figure something out."

And then Beth said, "Tell me about you and Tom. I want to listen."

Ally reached inside herself for that box that always overflowed with her heartbreak and longing for him, and found that it wasn't there anymore. Or rather, it was there, and would always be there, she suspected, marked *Tom—First Love*. But now, the lid actually fit. She could open the box any time she wanted, she supposed, but she could also close it back up again when she was done. And for the moment, she liked the lid on.

"You know what? I actually don't feel like talking about him now. But don't worry. Someday, you are going to get so many details that you'll pass out from the overwhelming boredom. More importantly, are you going to tell Owen how much you want his bod, and that you're maybe a little bit in love with him?"

"Oh no, I made such a mess of that," Beth said, pulling the sheet over her face. With her voice muffled by it, she told Ally what she'd done after their fight.

"Oof. That's bad," Ally said. She pulled the sheet from Beth's head. "But I don't think the situation is unsalvageable. The question is whether you want to salvage it. Because if you do, you just need a really good plan."

"Yeah," Beth said. Then, suddenly, she sat straight up. "Wait. I think I have one."

TWENTY-FOUR

Saturday morning came in chilly and drizzly, and Beth shivered in her hoodie. She had been doing so much apologizing lately that she'd hoped by now to be an old pro at it. But still, her shoulders tightened up with nerves as Ally waved her off, calling out "Good luck!" as she left the driveway and headed toward Owen's house.

Ally and Grandma Stella had forgiven her, but they also knew her better than Owen did. She and Owen, she had to keep reminding herself, had only really hung out a few times, at least recently. She kept forgetting that, because she'd felt so familiar with him from the start. So her first knock on his door landed weakly, as her hand trembled. She breathed out, shook herself, and tried again. An infinity later, the door opened.

"Hey," Owen said. She thought of the last time he'd opened

his front door for her, how his face had kindled with delight when he saw her standing on his porch. Now he only looked wary.

"I have something for you," she said, and handed him a big plastic bag.

"Um," he said. "A bag of trash?"

"Nope. A bag of recycling."

He smiled weakly. "Oh. Ha. Thanks."

"I have more," she said. "From the party last night. People drank a lot of beer and used a lot of plastic cups. The car is almost completely filled with bags of recyclables. There's just enough room for a few more bags, and a passenger. I thought maybe you could come along and show me the best way to get to the recycling center."

"It's right up Route 182," he said. "Pretty easy to find. I'd give you more detailed directions, but you made it pretty clear last time I saw you that you weren't a fan of me trying to help you." He handed the bag of recycling back to her and turned around to go back inside.

"Owen, please. Wait," she said.

He whirled back to face her. "You said that you didn't realize I knew everything. Well, guess what? I don't. I don't know you at all. I thought I did, but after Wednesday night, I'm starting to think that I was wrong." He turned again, so she spoke desperately, quickly, to his back.

"You weren't wrong," she said. "The me on Wednesday night wasn't who I really am. I was trying to talk myself into doing something I didn't want to do. But I can't do that anymore. You're right. I don't want to look at crap. I want to look at you."

He faced her again, uncertain. "What are you saying?"

"I'm not going back to Haiti. So if the offer still stands, I'd really love to go on a nonfriend date with you."

He hesitated, his eyes locked on hers, and she felt herself falling into those gray eyes. She wasn't going to run away this time. She was going to run forward.

"Okay," he said.

"Wait—really?"

"Yes. Okay."

A slow smile began to spread on her face, and he smiled back at her. They both stood there, awkwardly frozen, grinning goofily at each other, but she still felt like the wall between them had yet to fall completely. Then she remembered what else she'd brought with her.

"Oh," she said, "I almost forgot. I have something else for you too." She pulled three folded-up sheets of paper out of her back pocket, smoothed them out, and handed them over to him.

He studied them, uncomprehending, each sheet nearly completely covered in hundreds of different handwritings. "You brought me a . . . list of names?"

"Yup. A list of the Britton Hills citizens who strongly endorse a recycling program for the town. There are two hundred thirty-seven signatures on there, all gathered in one night." She smiled. "There were a *lot* of people at Grandma Stella's party."

He looked up from the paper, dumbfounded. "You did all this?"

"Well, me and Ally."

"Ah," he said. "Ally's back?"

"Yes," Beth said. "Thank goodness. Anyway, the town council will have to take a recycling proposal seriously now. In fact, if you look at names number forty-three and one hundred twenty-six, you might recognize them."

"Stuart Hodgkins and Sarah Bolton." He laughed. "Town council members."

"They just needed a little sweet-talking. And I convinced August Neiderbacher of the program's merits, and he's going to write an editorial for the *Bugle* about it."

"Beth, you amaze me," he said, pulling her into him. He kissed her gently, then hard, in his doorway, and the drizzle disappeared.

Eventually, Owen was the one to pull away. In a husky voice, he said, "Well, should we go take care of this recycling?"

"We could," she said, looking at the trash bag very seriously. "Or, we could do that later, and instead, right now, we could go upstairs to your bedroom."

"That's a much better idea," he said.

TWENTY-FIVE

A lly woke up at dawn the day they said good-bye to the house. She slipped out of bed and softly made her way to the window seat. There she sat, in a pair of Beth's pajamas (in her unexpected dash to get back to Britton Hills, she hadn't brought any of her own with her), and watched the sun come up. One last chance, she thought, to pinpoint that moment the walls changed from pale to sunny yellow. One last chance to watch the trees emerge from the darkness.

The sky began to lighten, and she savored the way it became something new right in front of her. In the bed, she heard Beth stirring, the little stretching sighs she made as she woke up.

"Mmm. Morning," Beth said, her voice muffled in the sheets. "It's early."

"Come and watch," Ally said, and so Beth joined her on the window seat, leaning up opposite from her, entwining her feet with

Ally's. Ally looked down at the tangle of their toes and legs, and then, by the time she looked back up at the walls, they'd turned sunflower yellow again.

"I can't believe this is our last morning here," Beth said.

LATER that afternoon, Ally wedged a final box into the trunk of Beth's parents' car and stood back, surveying the way an entire life could be crammed into a minivan.

"Thank you, darling," Grandma Stella said, and gave her a big lipsticky kiss on the cheek. Then she turned around and gave one to Beth too. Ally caught Beth wincing slightly at the pressure on her cheek, and she smiled to herself. Beth had come back from Owen's the day before, flushed and happy, late in the afternoon. And that morning, she'd woken up with a serious case of stubble burn.

"Okay," Beth's dad said now, slamming the trunk shut. "Looks like we're good to go."

"Well, wait just a second," Grandma Stella said. She faced the house and stretched out her arms wide. "I've got to give it a hug good-bye." Then she shouted, "You hear that, house? This is your farewell hug, so you better enjoy it. And here's a little smooch to remember me by." She blew it a kiss. Beth and Ally exchanged smiles.

"Ready, Mom?" Beth's dad said.

"All right, all right, hold your horses, Mr. Go-Go-Go. I'm coming. I reckon I can say good-bye to my own house." She grabbed one of Beth's hands and one of Ally's hands. "You two beauties will lock up, and then meet us over there?"

"Absolutely," Beth said. "See you soon." Grandma Stella nodded, hesitant to leave. Her hand flew to the necklace around her neck, a lovely, thin gold thread with little clear stones, and she fiddled with it.

"You look wonderful," Ally said.

"Well, of course. I've got to make a snappy first impression on the Sunny Acres gentlemen," Grandma Stella said. "You know how it is. All right. Off I go." She waved good-bye to them, bent to get into the car, and drove off with Beth's parents.

Ally turned back to the house. From the outside, it looked the same as it always had, except that the curtains were gone, so the windows seemed larger than normal. And when she looked closely at them, beyond the glass into the inside, she only saw emptiness.

Someone else would have to inhabit the house again, someone she didn't know and probably wouldn't ever meet. This place wasn't hers anymore, or Beth's. The two of them would come back to Britton Hills—they'd already decided that. Penny Joan had offered at the party to let them stay at her house whenever they wanted to visit. They'd swing through Bangor and pick up Grandma Stella on their way, and all four of them would have wild long weekends together. Still, it would never be the same again.

She wanted so badly to capture all that the house represented— to distill Grandma Stella's particular warmth as she ran to meet them in the driveway, to bottle up the smell of the flowers in the planters lining the streets downtown, to paint the way the sky and the ocean met one another in an infinity of blue. And she would. She would write it, and sing it. She would sing the people too, the ones from Britton Hills and the ones elsewhere— Grandma Stella, Tom, Nick, Marsha, and most of all, Beth.

"Should we lock it up?" Beth asked. They walked to the front door together. Beth put the key in the lock and turned it. They headed back down the driveway.

"Want to drive?" Beth asked, proffering the keys.

"Absolutely not," Ally said. "But thank you for asking." They smiled at each other. They didn't say anything about it, but somehow they both knew, simultaneously, to pivot back around to the house again.

Like Grandma Stella, they each blew it a kiss. Then, together, they got into the car and drove away.

READERS GUIDE

THE
SUMMERTIME
GIRLS

DISCUSSION QUESTIONS

1. *The Summertime Girls* is told in alternating viewpoints by Beth and Ally. Did you relate to one character more than the other as you were reading—and did you change your mind at any point? Why?

2. While the girls seem to fit into opposite personality stereotypes at first (Ally is the loose cannon, Beth is the uptight perfectionist), why do they not, in fact, fit these stereotypes at all? What actions give them away?

3. When they first meet as children, Ally decides Beth is like the kind and quiet Beth March from *Little Women*, while Beth silently thinks that Beth March was "kind of boring. Jo got to be the one with adventures, with the fire inside her." How is this significant, and does the sentiment fit in with Beth's actions as an adult? By the end of the novel, do you think she's lived up to her real March sister hero, Jo, or is she still catering to the expectations of others?

4. Ally worries about Beth going back to Haiti because "she didn't want to be temporary to another person." How have the

important people in her life made her feel temporary, and specifically what impact have her parents had on enforcing this feeling?

5. Toward the beginning of the novel, Beth philosophizes on life: "You *had* to be good, because if you weren't, where did you put all the guilt? How could you ignore it, as it piled itself higher and higher?" What is "guilt" to Beth? By the end of the novel, what other ways has she found to face this guilt?

6. From Grandma Stella to Penny Joan, from the hardware store to the *Britton Hills Bugle*, the town of Britton Hills is its own lovable character in *The Summertime Girls*. What purpose does the town serve to Ally, Beth, Owen, and Grandma Stella?

7. When Ally and Beth fight, Ally says, "a best friend doesn't necessarily stay *your* person forever. She stays *a* person, an important person, but she also gets boyfriends and spends time with them. It's not that big a deal, it happens." To what extent is she right or wrong about their relationship's falling out?

8. Beth's experience in Haiti is truly unimaginable. How does her reliance on Ally for comfort mirror Grandma Stella's dependence on Penny Joan after her husband's death? Is Beth right to blame Ally? Is Ally right in her anger?

9. How did you react to Owen's family's story? How much do you think his experience is a factor in Beth's decision to forgive Ally—and what other factors influence her?

10. What about Nick attracts Ally to him? Do you think they have a real connection, or is he simply a rebound affair for her?